Dec 2018

PRAISE FOR
NATALIE D. RICHARDS

"A haunted love story about a couple who bring out the best—and worst—in each other."

—Mindy McGinnis, author of *The Female of the Species* on *We All Fall Down*

"Full of drama and suspicion."

—*Kirkus Reviews* on *One Was Lost*

"An intriguing story line… Readers will be drawn in to the mystery of what happened to Chloe and will never guess the ending."

—*VOYA* on *Six Months Later*

"This romantic thriller will leave readers on the edge of their seats until the very last page."

—*School Library Journal* on *Six Months Later*

"An intense psychological mystery. [This] novel has the feel of a high-stakes poker game in which every player has something to hide, and the cards are held until the very end."

—*Publishers Weekly* on *Six Months Later*

D0050164

"A smart, edgy thriller."

—*Kirkus Reviews* on *Gone Too Far*

"A gripping whodunit with a challenging ethical dilemma at its center. Richards maintains a quick pace and creates enough red herrings to keep readers guessing."

—*Publishers Weekly* on *Gone Too Far*

"Brimming with suspense and intrigue, *My Secret to Tell* hooked me from the very first page and refused to let go. A thrilling, romantic, all-around captivating read!"

—Megan Miranda, author of *Fragments of the Lost* on *My Secret to Tell*

"*My Secret to Tell* is as addictive as it is unpredictable… Will keep you second-guessing until the nail-biting end."

—Natasha Preston, #1 *New York Times* bestselling author of *The Cellar* and *Awake* on *My Secret to Tell*

WHAT YOU HIDE

ALSO BY NATALIE D. RICHARDS

Six Months Later

Gone Too Far

My Secret to Tell

One Was Lost

We All Fall Down

WHAT YOU HIDE

NATALIE D. RICHARDS

Copyright © 2019 by Natalie D. Richards
Cover and internal design © 2019 by Sourcebooks, Inc.
Cover design by Kerri Resnick
Cover images © Marcin Klepacki/Arcangel

Sourcebooks and the colophon are registered trademarks of Sourcebooks, Inc.

All rights reserved. No part of this book may be reproduced in any form or by any electronic or mechanical means including information storage and retrieval systems—except in the case of brief quotations embodied in critical articles or reviews—without permission in writing from its publisher, Sourcebooks, Inc.

The characters and events portrayed in this book are fictitious or are used fictitiously. Any similarity to real persons, living or dead, is purely coincidental and not intended by the author.

All brand names and product names used in this book are trademarks, registered trademarks, or trade names of their respective holders. Sourcebooks, Inc., is not associated with any product or vendor in this book.

Published by Sourcebooks Fire, an imprint of Sourcebooks, Inc.
P.O. Box 4410, Naperville, Illinois 60567-4410
(630) 961-3900
Fax: (630) 961-2168
sourcebooks.com

Library of Congress Cataloging-in-Publication Data

Names: Richards, Natalie D., author.
Title: What you hide / Natalie D. Richards.
Description: Naperville, Illinois : Sourcebooks Fire, [2018] | Summary: After a tragic death at Fairview Public Library, frequent patron Mallory and community service volunteer Spencer discover they are not as safe as they thought.
Identifiers: LCCN 2018032222 | (pbk. : alk. paper)
Subjects: | CYAC: Haunted places--Fiction. | Libraries--Fiction. | Family problems--Fiction. | Community service (Punishment)--Fiction.
Classification: LCC PZ7.R3927 Wh 2018 | DDC [Fic]--dc23
LC record available at https://lccn.loc.gov/2018032222

Printed and bound in the United States of America.
VP 10 9 8 7 6 5 4 3 2 1

For the best library staff in the world. You know who you are.

WHAT YOU HIDE

SPENCER

Thursday, October 19, 1:13 a.m.

Fairview Public Library

I've broken curfew for plenty of stupid reasons, but climbing the public library? I can't *really* be thinking about doing this.

I am, though.

Not that I could tell you why. Why would a perfectly rational guy decide to take a jog at one o'clock in the morning? And why did that jog turn into a dead-panic sprint, until I stopped in this alley, sweaty and alone on the narrow strip of pavement between the parking lot and the book drop?

I can't figure out *most* of tonight, but I know this: I want to climb to the top of the Fairview Public Library.

It's not a good idea. Climbing that wall has *Terrible Choice* written all over it.

But it'd be easy. Thirty, maybe thirty-five feet tall, which I could scale in my sleep. Especially with all those chunky slabs of stone creating perfect crevices for my fingers and toes. I can't believe I've never noticed them. Back in fourth grade, I walked here every other Tuesday for class visits. It was a building full of books then. Now it's an unexplored vertical trail, my ticket to a view I've never seen.

I do this a lot: scan buildings for ascent routes. That's what happens when you love climbing. I want to climb rocks and trees and the football stadium and the water tower. And apparently the library.

Seriously, I could do it in five minutes. Maybe less.

Which is still plenty of time to get arrested in this town.

Here, tucked close to the side of the building in the alley, I'm not easy to see from Main Street. Halfway up the wall, though, I'd be exposed.

So, don't be stupid.

I wipe my sweaty hands down the front of my pants and move closer, dragging two fingers down the stone. Rough. Grippy.

A memorial plaque sits on the ground near a weeping cherry tree: HIGHER KNOWLEDGE FOR OUR BEST FUTURE.

I flinch, images flipping through my mind like flash cards. Dad at his spreadsheet, Mom at her leather journal, and me typing as fast as my fingers will let me, stacking up rows of words that paint a pleasing story about who I am and what I want.

I don't know that I decide to start climbing. I just kick off my shoes and socks, and it happens. I test the edge of a curved brick with one hand, and my toes find a natural perch on another. It's a strong position. A good hold. One upward glance and the path reveals itself—a push with my foot, and my left hand will go to the slightly darker stone. My right will reach the slab below the first-floor windows. Then the edge above it. I see one smooth white stone that might give me trouble, but I can always go for the ledge of the second-floor window if I need to.

I start my ascent, slow and steady. The world slips quietly away. I can't hear my mom listing college hockey stats, and I can't see my dad's postgraduation salary predictions. None of the things I should do and be matter up here.

Eyes open. Core engaged. Grip strong. There is only the steady hunt for the summit when I climb. Nothing else. And, so far, this hunt is easy pickings.

My fingers slip, and I frown, retreating to my former hold. I try again. The problem is the smooth, knobby bit I'd seen below; the one I feared might be trouble. A third attempt, and I pull back to reassess. I need an alternative, because I can't grip that smooth section without rosin, and I don't have rosin.

Or a harness.

I'm twenty-five feet up with no harness.

This fact hits me square in the chest, and in the span of one breath, my heart turns to a bag of worms. I grip my toes and push close to the wall to steady myself. Panic and stupidity lead to most climbing accidents, and I've already covered the stupidity bit.

"Not smart," I tell myself, and that's all I allow. I'll have to rub this lesson in later, when I'm back on the ground *without* an assortment of broken bones.

When my heart slows to a steady *thud-thud-thud*, I start looking for a better route. I'm maybe ten or fifteen feet from the top. With my adrenaline wearing off, it feels doable. This is not a difficult climb. Once I'm up, the fire escape ladder on the back of the building will make for an easy way down. I just need to do it.

I relax into my feet and start up the path closest to the second-story window. I still have that sill if I need it.

I push off my right foot as I reach up, a good pinch at a comfortable reach. Excellent. Plus, I see a perfect lip for my left hand, so I push up through that leg to snag the next hold. My grip sticks, but something snaps. My left foot drops hard, leg scraping stone. I lurch in the opposite direction, forcing my center of gravity to the right.

Was it the brick? I glance down at the wall below, seeing freshly cracked stone where my foot used to be. Bits of mortar and rock lay in the grass, and my stomach drops into my feet.

I was standing on that seconds ago. If it had broken any earlier, I'd have fallen. I lick my lips, heart pounding. Nothing about that brick looked wrong. There was zero warning.

Which means there might not be a warning next time.

Who's to say the one I'm on now won't snap? My worry ratchets higher with every breath. I don't know anything about this wall. These *bricks* could be painted hunks of mortar for all I know. Every last one could break.

Okay, new plan. I need to get up this wall before it falls apart.

The window.

The sill beneath it will be solid concrete. It'll hold and give me time to breathe. When my body is in line, I swing my left leg up hard. I have to get high enough to catch the window sill.

I overshoot it. My knee hits the glass with a crack. I stop breathing, mouth dropping open at the neat hole my patella punched in the pane. Cracks spider from the hole in multiple directions. For one breathless instant, all I can do is stare, my bare toes resting on the concrete sill while bits of glass clink down from the opening.

Unbelievable. I kicked in the freaking window.

A shard hits my big toe, and it jolts me into action. I drag myself to the right of the mess, my face scraping mortar. The window I broke is tall and wide with arched glass that looks...expensive.

I'll worry about it later. I need to finish this and get down before something else goes wrong.

Nothing does. The rest of the climb passes without incident. At the top, I haul myself over the concrete cornice and drop to my backside, panting in relief.

I should bolt for the ladder, but my legs have turned to jelly. I need a minute to catch my breath. I enjoy the view, which is nothing to sneeze at. Fairview is easy on the eyes from up here. A row of postcard-worthy businesses line Main Street, embellished with flower boxes and understated window displays. Here and there, iron benches rest under neatly trimmed trees—an invitation to linger.

Beyond Main Street, the streets give way to a sleeping patchwork of lush, green lawns with curving gardens and winding paths. And houses. Large, beautiful houses.

One of those houses is yours.

My throat squeezes, and I lean forward, staring at the soft glow of streetlights and curved streets. It is the definition of peaceful and safe, but I'm not feeling either of those things. I feel like I'm peering into another dimension. Like I'm seeing something I've never seen. Which is ridiculous. I live down there. Fairview has always been home.

Always?

A flash of blue and white lights. The police. There's a single cruiser six or seven intersections down Main Street, so someone must have seen me. Adrenaline floods my senses.

Get up. I have to get up.

My body is heavy. Immobile. *What the hell is wrong with me? I need to run!*

But I don't. Moments later, the cruiser turns into the library parking lot, and it's like my body is frozen. My eyes follow the car as it parks, then trail the beam of the spotlight across the library wall. Shrubs and mulch are illuminated. Then, the cherry tree. Next, my discarded socks and shoes.

I wonder what they'll do when they figure out I'm up here.

I wonder what it'll feel like when they take me away.

MALLORY

Friday, November 3, 1:08 p.m.

Whitestone Memorial High School

If I knew I'd never walk down this hall again, it would've gone differently. Maybe I'd grab a last cookie from the cafeteria. At the very least, I would have taken my decent sneakers from my locker. But that's the thing about doing something for the last time. You usually have no idea.

I offer all the typical skipping school excuses. I tell Mrs. Ross I'm going out for lunch. Then I tell Lana I'm meeting Mom so she won't ask to tag along. There's nothing noteworthy about it. I simply walk off campus at 1:08 p.m., figuring it's a temporary exit.

I figure wrong.

As soon as I round the corner outside the parking lot, I break into a run. My bag is heavy on my shoulder, and the cold air burns going in, but I have to hurry. Charlie gets off at two, an hour before school lets out. It'll take me fifteen minutes to get home. That leaves Mom and me an hour to get out. Maybe less than that.

Yesterday's plan was better. We were going to have the entire day to get everything together, but it fell to pieces like everything else in my life lately. The original plan was for me to call off school. Mom was going to cover for me with Charlie, but she was *actually* sick while I was pretending. Which provided Charlie plenty of time to give me the third degree.

How are you sick? You don't have a fever. If you're carrying a virus, it's better to go to school, spare your mother the germs in her condition. You do care about her condition, don't you, Mallory?

He went on and on until I relented, for no other reason than to make him stop talking before my head exploded. So I have no one to blame for this unplanned-school-skipping-sprint-across-the-neighborhood adventure but myself.

By the time I hit the street that leads to my apartment, my armpits are swampy. The sign reads PLEASANT VILLAGE APARTMENT COMPLEX. *Pleasant* and *complex* are both a stretch.

Really, it's six brick shoeboxes arranged in a semicircle around a parking lot that has more potholes than pavement. There are two floors to each building and one apartment to each floor. Our shoebox is the second floor of the third building. It is also the only home I've ever known. Of course, when Charlie moved in three and a half years ago, he made all kinds of promises about a bigger place. A safer neighborhood. A house of our own. Blah, blah, blah.

Charlie is great at making promises. He's even better at breaking them.

I climb the stairs as fast as my rubbery legs will take me and then fumble my keys in the lock. The door opens easily and I push my way in, dropping my coat and backpack in a heap.

"Mom! Where are you?"

I hear the muffled hiss of running water. A cough. "Bathroom."

"Try to hurry," I say, detouring into the kitchen where I turn in a quick circle.

Think, think. Do we need anything in here? None of the plates seem special, and a quick glance at the handful of mismatched pots and pans in the cabinet reveals nothing of interest. I grab Grandma's cookbook from the top of the stove and step into the living room.

Mom is still in the bathroom.

"Are you okay? We have to hurry."

"I'm okay." Her voice is faint from the bathroom. Weary.

I open the door to the tiny coat closet, then pause. "Listen, I've got that number I told you about. It's all going to be okay. I know you're worried, but they will get you to a different doctor. They'll help you. I promise."

The toilet flushes. More coughing. A soft, terrible noise that I know is my mother vomiting. I wince, wishing there was something I could do, but there isn't. Charlie wouldn't let her have the medicine for the nausea. Or a job. Or anything else.

The thoughts push anger up my chest. Correction. I *can* do something and I am. I'm getting us out of here.

My eyes drift to the clock on our old DVD player. 1:29.

Adrenaline thrusts lava through my veins.

"Mom, we've got to hurry," I say, turning my attention back to the closet.

On tippy toes, I reach for her suitcase, figuring we'll need two minutes to throw in the clothes she's set out. It tumbles off the shelf, banging my head, bringing down a rack of winter hats. I see a flash of bright orange and smell gasoline and aftershave. Charlie. Revolted, I flick the hat off my shoulder and jerk the suitcase free.

I stop once at my room, detouring to drag my already packed backpack out from underneath my bed. It's not everything I want, but it's enough for now. I shove the essentials from school inside so I've got only one bag to schlep. Two steps later, I'm in her room.

I pause at the entrance like I always do. The hat was one thing, but this whole room smells like him. Like Mom, too, but mostly like him. The tall dresser by the door is his. All of his stuff is lined neatly in front of the mirror. Cheap aftershave. Stacks of quarters and dimes beside a roll of breath mints. A comb. A cardboard box that holds a pair of cuff links he wears on holidays. There is an empty space for his class ring and, next to that, his Whitestone Memorial High School staff ID badge.

The same logo and background as my school ID, except he gets paid to go.

I tear my gaze away from his dresser to their unmade bed. The frayed bedspread is half on the floor, like someone flung it off in a hurry, but I don't care about that. I care that there are no stacks of clothes.

My throat closes around my next breath.

The bathroom door creaks open. Footsteps shuffle toward me, and Mom appears in the doorway. She's a tiny thing with sloped shoulders, hollowed cheeks, and a softly rounded belly.

"I was too sick to pack," she says. Her smile is still beautiful. *She* is still beautiful. "This was a hell of a lot easier at seventeen, kid. I don't think I can do this."

"It's okay," I say, shifting into action. Forcing my own smile. "I've got it."

I throw the suitcase on her bed, and she flinches. "Mallory, wait. Let's—"

"Get you packed," I say, cutting her off. I jerk open her top drawer and grab a handful of socks and underwear. Then her second drawer. Shirts. Mostly long-sleeved. They go into the suitcase. "Do you want some T-shirts too?"

"Mallory."

I ignore her because she can't change her mind again. Not this time. Three nights ago, Charlie had some sort of system upgrade at school, and I took her to a Bob Evans. She'd picked at her eggs. I'd only ordered dessert because I wasn't there to eat. I was there to make a case.

"You'd eat better if he'd let you have the medicine."

"He's worried about the baby."

"Right, no medicine. No soda either, though it's the only liquid you can keep down."

"Mallory…"

"Is he worried about the effects of TV on the baby too? Because he also won't let you have the remote."

I think that was when it hit her. It *is* worse than she thinks. Bad enough to leave. And in that shitty red booth with the waitress calling us both "honey" and the apple pie congealing on my plate, she said she couldn't stay with him. She decided to leave.

As far as I'm concerned, nothing changes that much in three days.

I open the bottom drawer next, taking two pairs of yoga pants It'll have to do for now.

"You're going to need shoes," I say.

"Mallory."

"We should bring your winter coat too. It's getting colder." I yank open her closet, but the sliding door sticks. I swear and tug it harder. It bumps off track, wedging with about eight inches of open space for me to reach into the closet.

Mom doesn't move.

My body goes still, and I utter a sigh.

She's behind me on the bed. I don't need to look to see that she's taking the clothes out of the suitcase. I don't need to ask to know she's changed her mind about leaving.

"We talked about this." I say it right against the closet door, but she hears me. You can hear everything in this apartment.

"It's…complicated."

"No, it's not. He treats you like a child. Like *less* than that. We can't stay here."

"I'm having a baby." Her hand drifts to her belly.

"Which is exactly why we can't be here. He's going to snap one day, and you know it. It's a matter of time."

"No. He doesn't hurt me." She lifts her chin like she's proud of it. "He never hits me."

"Yet!" My laugh is a terrible sound. "He's getting crazier every day. He took your keys and wallet. He decides every meal, every haircut. He's reads our *text messages*! Who does that?"

"He's worried about money because of the baby. All that data on the phone."

"Mom, this is beyond worried. This isn't normal. He needs help, and he refuses to see that." I march away from the closet, dragging the suitcase to the edge of the bed and grabbing the clothes she unpacked. "You know what? No. We talked about this, and you agreed. You said a break would be a good idea. That maybe he would call someone."

"I felt pressured." She's shrinking in on herself, looking smaller by the second. "You wouldn't let it go. What was I supposed to say?"

"You don't have to *say* anything. Let's just go for tonight. We can talk to one of the counselors at the shelter. If you feel better about things and have a plan, we'll come home."

I can practically taste the lie, but I don't care. I'll say anything to get her out of here.

"I need to think, okay?"

I huff, and her gaze sharpens.

"You're not a mother, Mallory. You don't understand. This baby needs a father."

And I didn't?

I swallow the words down, but something hot wells up in my chest. And snaps. My hand shoots out in frustration, shoving Charlie's dresser against the wall. Change spills, and a cologne bottle tips over, rolling across the dresser top.

"What kind of father is he going to be?" I ask, voice rising. "Do you see the way he looks at you? That weird singsong voice he uses when he gets mean? He's not a good man."

"You don't know what a bad man is. You're too young to know."

"Maybe I'm young, but I'm not blind. He's becoming a *lunatic*."

The front door closes, and I hear footsteps. *His* footsteps. My spine freezes into a string of icy knots. Mom shakes her head, her finger at her lips to shush me, but she's too late. I dropped my backpack at the door.

"You're home from school," he announces. I hear him hang his keys on the hook by the door, just so. "Peter called me. Told me he saw you running and thought I should check on you."

His tone is mild and unconcerned, but fear blooms in my mother's eyes. Charlie crosses the living room, joining us in the bedroom. My heart scrabbles into my throat as he studies the toppled cologne bottle. The suitcase on the bed. His eyes linger on that, and then they turn on my mother.

"Now do you see what I mean, Sasha?"

My mother stays very still. Something passes between them that I don't understand. It catches up with me though. They've talked about this. Or at least about me. I don't need all the details to understand he's going to use information they've already discussed against me.

He picks up the change on the dresser slowly, piece by piece. Each coin scrapes across the wood as he collects it.

"The disrespect," he says softly, eyes flicking back to my mother. "The utter disrespect of this *girl*. Do you see who you're raising, Sasha? Vindictive. Remorseless."

I laugh and catch his attention. Charlie has kind eyes and a soft chin, but both are lies.

"Run out of words to describe me?" I snap at him. "How about rebellious?"

"You snarling little brat." He says it with a voice some men might use to comment on the weather. "You think you can talk to me like that, don't you?"

My anger barely edges out my fear, but barely is enough. "Maybe I do."

He chuckles. "One day, this attitude of yours will catch up with you, and you won't like that game. Do you know what things happen to girls like you? Do you want me to tell you?"

I point at him but look at my mom. "Do you hear him? This is *exactly* why you need to go. We can't live like this."

"Can't live like what, Mallory?" he asks. "With authority in your life? With someone who won't put up with your little stunts? Can't live with a man who won't let you dominate him the way you dominate your mother? You will learn your place in this house."

"Charlie, I don't think—"

He raises a dismissive hand. "I'll handle this. I think it's clear that you've done enough damage."

Mom tries to stand, paling. "Please. We all need to settle down."

He moves to her, big hands on her shoulders, leaning so close that it can't be easy for her to focus. "Why are you like this, Sasha? Why do you let her do this to you?"

My mom's eyes well with tears. He wraps an arm around her shoulders, pulling her close. "My poor girl. I love you. I know what she does to you."

She nods, sniffing. "She's my daughter, Charlie. I love her."

"Of course you do." Then his hand goes to her belly. He makes a soft, sad noise, and bile stings the back of my throat. "Why do you hurt your mother, Mallory? You sulk and you stomp." He gestures at the suitcase. "Now you want to leave and tear our *family* apart?"

"You're full of it," I say, heart pounding. "And I'm not staying here one more second. Mom, you can't make me stay."

"Baby, I—"

"Then go." Charlie's words cut her off. His arm tightens around her, his face turning white. I can tell he's on the edge of something terrible even if his words come softly. "Take your filthy mouth and every evil, sneaking thought in your head out of my house. Leave us be."

"Charlie, please." Mom's plea is breathless. She's gone pale like she'll be sick again. I reach for her, and he jerks her out of my grip, gasping.

"You aren't going to hurt your mother. Not on my watch."

"I wasn't trying to hurt her! What is *wrong* with you?"

"You are what's wrong with me," he says. "You are what's wrong with your mother too! She did her best, but you turned out bad."

Mom whimpers.

"Quiet. I'll take care of this." He presses a kiss to the top of her head, and my face feels cold. Numb. The room tilts to one side, the edges going dark.

"Mom, look at me," I say. I'm shaking all over. "*Look* at me!"

"I can't do this right now," she says, crying.

"Do you see what you've done?" He strokes her back while he stares at me. His voice is mournful, but there's no sadness in his eyes. There's glee. "*Look* at what you've done."

Mom bolts out of the room, and I hear her kick the bathroom door closed half a second before she gags.

We are alone. One wall away, my mother is vomiting, but here I'm breathing in his cologne and watching the awful glint behind his smile. He's enjoying this. Her pain. My fear. All of it.

"I'm going to turn you in," I tell him softly. "I'm going to tell someone."

"Tell them what? Tell them what a monster I am? I pay for your food, your home, your clothes. I'm a nice guy, Mallory, but you keep pushing. Let's see what happens when you push me too far."

Tears sting my eyes, trailing like fire down my cheeks. I keep my voice to a whisper. "I hate you."

"Oh, I don't hate you," he speaks as softly as I did. "You aren't *worth* hating."

I back away until I'm at my bag, and he watches. His smile is nothing but teeth and terror, and it's working on me. I'm afraid of him.

"Go on," he says, like he's shooing a stray dog. "You won't stay gone."

"Yes, I will."

"Nooo." Another flash of teeth that isn't close to a smile. "You'll come crawling back. And when you do, maybe I won't be so nice. Maybe I'll show you what a monster is."

Then his gaze flicks to the bathroom door, and a cold and calculating expression flashes over his face. This is how I know Charlie is more than awful words and obsessive control. He is a yellow sky and leaves flipped backward in July. He is a coming storm.

"You all right in there, darling?" he calls to my mother, so sweet that my jaw aches.

"I'm going to stay with a friend, Mom." My voice wobbles. "For a little while."

"A little while." He nods like this, too, was his idea. Then he drops his voice to a whisper. "And then I'll show you."

"I love you, Mallory." Her voice is muffled. She's still at the toilet, and she's crying.

My stomach twists for her. Charlie's mouth twists, too, a sinister smile just for me as I back toward the front door.

"You'll crawl back," he says again.

It is the last thing I hear before I run.

SPENCER

Sunday, November 5, 9:52 a.m.

This freak is going to mow me down mid-ice. I angle my skates to the right as hard as I can. Snow sprays, and his shoulder connects with mine. I skitter back, digging my blades in as I poke for the puck between his legs. Miss. Miss again. I reach, shoved up against his jersey, smelling ice and sweat.

He grunts, his elbow jamming back into my ribs.

"Be nice," I growl. "You didn't even buy me dinner."

His answering shove is a warning, but I'm good with warnings. I grin around my mouth guard and jab my stick between his skates again. The puck pops loose.

I look up.

"Jarvey!" I scream, passing it hard up the center ice.

Another elbow lands in that tender spot right beneath my shoulder pads. A bruise tomorrow, probably. Doesn't matter to me. Jarvey caught the pass. He's sliding up the ice like a dream, puck glued to the end of his stick.

I shove left and watch the glory boys. Jarvey swinging around the face-off circle, Shawn already at the net, the toes of his skates inches from the crease, and then, Isaac, like a shadow, lingering in that back corner in case Jarvey's shot flies too high.

It doesn't.

They've got gloves up in celebration before the ref even acknowledges the goal. I bump gloves with the trio on my way to the bench, lungs on fire and sweat dripping into my eyes.

Winters, our defense coach, taps my helmet. "Nike poke. Watch your flank."

And then he's back to the wall, leaning over and screaming at Joe. *Out of position. Watch your point.* Alex shifts closer to me on the bench.

"So, is that it? Community service at the library?" he asks.

"How are you still catching up on all this?"

"My parents dragged me to southern France for ten days, remember? I'm still catching up on homework."

"Right. Poor you." I smirk. "But yeah, six months of service, and Dad wrote a fat check."

He shakes his head. "I left with you voted most likely to have a comedy show. Two weeks later, you're most likely to end up in the big house."

"What can I say? Life lost all meaning without you."

“Dick.” He nods at Winters. “You doing the college hockey roundup next week?”

I wince. “I’m not going division one. I just like the game, man.”

“Still need to figure out which colleges will take you. You don’t want to end up not playing, right?”

“True. Info sounds good,” I say, but it doesn’t. It sounds like everything else: a high-pitched static hum about college and the future and the things we know we should be doing.

Someone smacks my helmet. “You’re up, Keller. Look smart!”

I slide on my joker face as I leap over the wall. “But, coach, we both know I’m an idiot!”

I hear the team laughing behind me. My blades bite ice, and the blue lines stretch out before me. From this angle, even I can see where to go.

SPENCER

Monday, November 6, 7:58 a.m.

I pull my badge out of the glove box before I lock the car and lope up the library stairs. It's still dark inside. A benefit to doing my mandatory community service early, I guess. I usually have to do it after school, but it's a teacher workday, whatever the hell that means. It used to mean Froot Loops and video games until Mom got home, but then I decided to break a four-thousand-dollar window, so now I'm here.

It's different inside when it's closed. I didn't notice the first time, but I figure the library would seem different when the police escort you in with your father.

We'd met with the library director, Mr. Brooks. He and my dad had talked about Fairview and boys and the history of public institutions. I sat on my chair trying to figure out how some guy twenty years younger than my dad winds up in charge of a library and listening to Frank Sinatra at 4:00 a.m.

It was ten or fifteen minutes before Mr. Brooks had turned to me.

"Climbing the library is a new one. What's the appeal?"

"I like to climb." I shrugged.

"Buildings in general, or do you usually stick with libraries?"

"No, that's a first."

"So, what inspired you?"

"Higher knowledge for our best future?"

My father sucked in a breath, ready to reprimand me. But Mr. Brooks laughed. That's when he recommended community service at the library. Six months for me to get exactly what I'd asked for. Higher knowledge.

Who knows? Maybe there's a book in here that will tell me what to do when all the smart choices feel wrong.

"Good morning, Spencer!" Gretchen greets me like I've won a prize. She says everything like that, so she's either hitting some very powerful drugs in the back room or she dreams of hosting a game show.

"Hey, Gretchen."

"How was your game Sunday?"

"Game?" I feign panic. "I *knew* there was something I missed."

"Funny! How would you feel about lending a hand on a desk this morning? We've got a couple of call-offs, so we need the help."

"Sure thing."

"Thank you." Another big smile comes with the thanks. "We've got some time if you want to shelve a cart or two first."

She thanks me a lot, and I don't know how to respond to it. This isn't some do-gooder effort because I'm such a swell guy. This is penance being paid by a pseudo criminal, and she shouldn't really be thanking me.

The carts are waiting for me in the circulation office, each one separated by section. I drag two nonfiction carts out and into the stacks. The space is dark and still, so I search for the lights, running my hands along the wall.

Someone gasps behind me, high and shrill.

"Gretchen?"

Footsteps rush down the aisle. Not like heels or sneakers, but the *patter-slap* of bare feet. I turn, expecting to see Gretchen, or—someone. Barefoot from the sound of it.

The aisle stretches out, dark and empty.

"Hello?" I ask, my voice wooden and strange in the quiet.

Goose bumps rise on the back of my neck. I stare at the shelves, endless colored spines staring at me. Did I imagine it? I push one cart back far enough to enter another aisle. There's no sound. Nothing out of place to make me think it's anything but my mind playing tricks on me. But I feel tense, like someone's near. Watching me.

The lights flick on with a clunk. I jump, blinking in the sudden brightness.

Gretchen's voice floats from a location near the main entrance. "Sorry about that! Can't shelve books without light, huh?"

Whatever I thought I heard in the dark is gone, so I get to work. I tug the two carts into the first aisle. I follow the numbers, pushing books into their proper slots and moving on. It's the kind of mindless task I like best these days.

Twenty minutes later, I drag both empty carts to the front and check the clock. Ten minutes until the library opens. Gretchen jogs up, bright-eyed and grinning. The usual.

"What's shaking in the shelves?" she asks.

"The travel guides were getting rowdy in the seven hundreds, but I warned them if they didn't settle down—it's withdrawn for them."

She laughs, so I haven't lost my touch.

"So what do you think?" she asks. "Can you staff the browsing room? Mostly, you'll need to help people find DVDs."

"Sure. No problem."

"Do you remember how to give out the guest passes if they want to use a computer?"

"I do."

"I think you and browsing are going to get along really well, Spencer."

Now she's got me grinning. Honestly, I don't think it's drugs. It's just her. I can make people laugh, but I don't think I've ever smiled the way Gretchen does.

Inside the browsing room, I hop up on the tall, rolling chair at the desk and wonder how this constitutes community service. I could be picking up trash on the side of the road. Technically, I could be on probation and suspended from hockey, but I'm not. It's the cushiest version of a punishment I could have dreamed up.

Mom thinks I've learned an important lesson. I think I got off too easy. Nothing new there, I guess.

The library opens at 9:00 a.m. and patrons trickle in. A gentleman takes a newspaper to a leather chair in the corner. A woman who I often see walking her dog in the neighborhood brings in coffee and a laptop.

I shift in my chair and resist the urge to spin. It's not the kind of space that invites spinning. The room is like my grandparents' house—all dark wood and leather in that way that makes me think of market reports and cocktails after dinner.

I tip my head back to stare at the brass chandeliers hanging from the arched ceiling. There are six enormous skylights positioned around the room for light. I wonder how big of a check my dad would have had to write if I broke one of those.

"Excuse me?"

I jerk in my chair hard enough to topple off of it. Luckily, I land on my feet. I reach to steady myself, and knock three books off the tall desk. My visitor doesn't laugh when I stoop to pick them up. She's so quiet, I'm half convinced I conjured her like the footsteps in the dark—some kind of boredom-induced hallucination. But when I rise, she's there. Waiting.

I don't recognize her, but she's around my age. Maybe a year younger. Given her ridiculous red shoes and the obviously drugstore-dyed streaks in her hair, she wouldn't blend into the crowd of manicured nails and straight-ironed hair at my high school.

So she's probably not from Fairview. A city school, maybe. Or a homeschooler. That would explain her being here on a school day. No one skips school to go to the library.

"Can I help you?" I ask, because she still hasn't said anything.

"I'm not sure." She looks reluctant, nodding toward the doorway that leads to the main lobby and the book stacks. "Is that lady a librarian?"

I glance at Gretchen, who's currently deeply in conversation with another patron.

"She is, but she might be a minute. Are you looking for a DVD?"

"No." She hesitates again, shifting a heavy-looking blue backpack higher on her shoulder. "I need some information about alternative schooling."

I open up the library catalog to search. "Like homeschooling?"

A laugh. "Definitely not."

"Vocational schools?"

"No." She frowns. "I'm looking for traditional high schools in an alternative setting. Like online schooling?"

"Oh! Sure." I fumble through a couple of internet searches, coming up dry. "I'm not finding much that looks legit—oh, wait. Are you interested in an online dog grooming certification?"

The joke doesn't just fall flat; it dies in bloody agony. She grimaces, like I offered a class killing puppies, not grooming them.

"Hey, I'm probably searching wrong," I say, extending a hand. "I'm Spencer. Not a librarian, a volunteer."

"Mallory," she says, but she's already glancing around, like she doesn't know what to do with herself.

"If you want, I'll give you a guest pass for a laptop so you can try until Gretchen is done. You could search online schooling. Dog grooming. Jambalaya recipes. Whatever."

She still doesn't smile, but she nods. "Okay. Thanks, that might help."

I watch her get settled to make sure the guest pass works. Then I watch her because I'm bored. Then I watch her because it's either watch a cute girl with bad hair or an old guy who's dozing off in the arts section of the paper. The options are far from mind-blowing.

She types in machine-gun bursts, clicking no keys at all, and then clattering out what sounds like the entire Gettysburg Address in four seconds. When she uses the mouse, though, she's feather soft. More banging on the keys. More gentle mouse sweeps and clicks.

Ah, she's found something.

I can tell by the way she leans forward, wrapping her feet around the front legs of the chair. Like gravity might fail soon. Or maybe the monitor is trying to suck her in. I consider an ancient *Poltergeist* joke about staying away from the light, but resist.

She fumbles with the back of the desk behind the computer, and I don't know why. I don't understand what she's doing until it pops open. A hinged compartment. Like a tiny cabinet in the back of the desk. I've never seen it before, so I doubt there's anything in there, and if there is, she probably doesn't want it.

But lo and behold, she's got something. She pulls out a blue pen and starts jotting notes on one of the provided pieces of scrap paper. Unbelievable. There's practically a secret compartment in that desk, *and* she found a working pen inside. It's easier to find a hundred-dollar bill than a functional pen in here.

As soon as I think it, she stops writing and shakes it. Shakes it again, trying to get the ink flowing. She bangs it on the desk then tries the writing-a-million-little-circles trick.

I have to bite back a laugh when she gives up, dropping the pen in disgust. She unzips her monstrous blue backpack and snakes an arm inside. When she finally pulls it back out, I see the yellow barrel and pink eraser of a typical pencil.

The second she presses the pencil to the paper, I hear the telltale snap of breaking graphite. I laugh, and her shoulders hunch. I'm sure she'll laugh too, but she doesn't. She looks like she's about to cry.

I yank my hands off the desk, a sudden burst of heat rushing up my neck. I turn away, eyes on my shoes even when I hear her get up.

She's probably leaving. Maybe she'll tell Gretchen, and I'll definitely catch hell if she does. Not that I don't deserve it. I *should* have offered to help. I was raised to—

Tap, tap, tap.

The sound startles me, and my arm bumps the edge of the desk. The books I just picked up go flying again. I collect them from the floor with a sigh. When I'm upright, Mallory's still there. Glaring at me.

"I need to invest in glue," I say, waving the books before I set them down. Finally, I remember myself. "Is there anything I can help you with?"

"Bet you can guess," she says.

I grin and finally, *finally* she smiles. It makes her even cuter, though I'm not exactly sure why. Her lips are chapped, and close up I can see chunks of faded purple in her hair along with the streaks of bleach. But her eyes are so wide and green that it's hard not to stare into them.

"I bet I have a pen or something around here," I say, digging around the top drawer. I find several library pencils, which I tell her not to bother with because I'm convinced they're shipped to the library dull to the point of being unusable. I find nothing else. Not in the first drawer, the second, or even the third. "Wow, this is ridiculous."

She laughs a little when I open a fourth drawer and come up dry. Finally, I lift my own keyboard in desperation and find a single, uncapped ballpoint pen. I hand it over with a flourish.

She takes it. "I thought I was going to have to tap a vein and write in blood."

"If it came to that, I'd suggest a quick trip home for a pen. Bodily fluids are frowned upon in the library."

"Right." She tugs at the hem of her jacket like she's uncomfortable, then holds up the pen with a weak smile. "Thanks. For the pen."

"No problem," I say, but her smile is gone. I don't know exactly what I did, and I definitely don't know how, but I pissed her off. She doesn't look at me and abruptly sets down the pen I gave her. It sits at the edge of the desk, far from the computer and her bag.

Gretchen relieves me ten minutes later, so I head back into circulation and grab another cart. I move faster than usual. The circulation manager, Ruby, notices and raises her eyebrows at me from where she's checking in books. But I ignore her and head for the supply cabinet.

This is a stupid idea, and I know it even before I unlock the supply cabinet and grab the box of pens from the second shelf. I also know it when I march back into the browsing room.

Mallory isn't there, but her blue backpack is still sitting by the chair. Gretchen is chatting merrily with the newspaper-reading gentleman I ignored. I should go.

Screw it.

I grab a Post-it and hurry so Gretchen doesn't bust me out for offering half of our staff pens to a patron. Thankfully she's still busy, so I scrawl a quick note.

These better?

Then I pop open the little hinged compartment and cram every single one of the pens inside. It shuts with a soft click and I press the sticky note to the top, leaving quickly.

Just outside the browsing room, the bathroom door swings open. Mallory emerges, stopping short, and I give her a quick nod and keep walking. I don't need to watch her find the pens. It already feels like a win.

Ruby walks past me wearing latex gloves and holding bottles of cleaner. I assume she's heading to clean a bathroom, but she turns into the stacks near the browsing room.

I chuckle. "Wow. Do I even want to ask?"

"Just a little barefoot cookbook browsing."

"What?"

She doesn't answer, so I follow her without being invited.

She gestures to the floor, and the footprints are obvious. Dirty and narrow and definitely bare—five round toes and a high arch.

"Of all the damn rules we have, is wearing shoes so difficult?"

I swallow hard, staring at the tracks, because I was near the cookbooks this morning. And I heard footsteps. "Ruby, I thought I heard someone in here this morning. Someone barefoot."

She sprays and swipes the area with a wad of paper towels, not pausing when she replies. "Did you tell Gretchen?"

"I…no."

"If you see them again, let us know, okay? Gotta wear shoes in the library."

"This was early. Before we opened."

"Then our cleaners missed something. That or we have a barefoot ghost checking out Crock-Pot recipes."

MALLORY

Thursday, November 9, 7:14 a.m.

Four school days. That's all it takes. Four days and I am no longer a student at Whitestone Memorial High School. I'm a Success Academy Scholar in the Success Online Academy Program.

I wonder almost instantly if they couldn't have come up with an *R* word that would have turned *SOAP* into the much more encouraging *SOAR*. I mean, why not *Routine* instead of *Program*? Or *Regiment*? *Revolution* maybe?

Lana boots up her laptop, which takes a while. We're sitting in her bedroom, which is, impossibly, smaller than mine, and for the last several nights has been my sleeping space too. It has not been an easy fit. Lana's single bed takes up all but a narrow strip of wood floor, and a dresser and a nightstand are crammed into that strip. It's practically a game of hopscotch to get out of here without hurting yourself, and getting comfortable on a flimsy sleeping bag in the space between her bed and the wall? Impossible.

Still, I'm grateful that she's been cool about me staying a few days. We told her mother, Maria, that my mom was out of town. I called my mom and told her Maria was working a lot and wanted Lana to have company, so it just made sense. One phone call and this whole house of cards will fall, but Lana's mom is working nights for two weeks, and my mom likely won't check in. She's usually too focused on keeping Charlie happy, and right now, Charlie doesn't seem too interested in keeping tabs on me.

"So how does the school thing work?" Lana asks, brushing her hair. We'll both head out in five minutes. I'll walk with her until we hit the corner where her mom can't see. Then I'll switch and head another direction. Her mom has no idea I'm not at Whitestone. She'd flip if she knew.

"It's all online. There are a few live chats and lectures, but mostly I do it when I want."

"But aren't you, like, a dropout now?"

"No. I transferred to another school. The people at the online academy made it easy. Mom had to sign a few things, and I had to fill out an application, but once I was enrolled, everything was smooth sailing. I don't even think it'll be very different."

She looks at me like I've lost it. I don't blame her, but I haven't lost it. School via laptop is not the same as running from class to class and hanging out at our table at lunch, but I have to stay positive.

Regular high school is not an option. Charlie works on the computers for the whole district, and we have only one high school anyway. He could turn up in any hallway and see me.

"I can't believe your mom went for this," she says, typing her password.

"I told her it was temporary. A break to chill things out in the house. She was leery about the online stuff, but you know she's not much of a fighter. Especially since she's pregnant."

"God, I know." Lana frowns. "Can you imagine? She's so old."

"She's only thirty-four. A lot of women don't even start having babies until after that."

She scoffs. "Not around here."

Lana pushes her laptop over to me. There's a crack in the corner of the screen, and the *Q* is missing. But she's sharing with me, and I'm grateful.

"Thank you so much, Lana," I say, and she scoffs at that too. I open a browser and navigate to the website they gave me, logging in without issue. I show her the home screen.

"See? Easy peasy."

"I just don't get why you have to leave school. I mean, you live in the district and—" She cuts herself off and tilts her head until her long dark hair slides over her shoulder, shadowing her face. Her eyes narrow as she pieces together the fragments I've given. "Oh my God. You convinced her to leave him, didn't you?"

Lana and I have known each other for a long time. Long enough for me to be honest.

"I thought I did. He changed her mind."

"I hate that bastard. Why don't you report him?"

"There's nothing to report him for. Believe me, I've checked. The school loves him. He's got everyone there snowed into thinking he's great."

"What about the police? Isn't there something they can do?"

"Like what? '*He's weirdly controlling, Officer,*'" I say, pretending to place the complaint.

She smirks. "Says the teenager who ran away."

"*Exactly.* You know how he is. It's not only what he says."

"It's the creepy stuff he doesn't say," she says with a wise nod. "He's what I think a serial killer would be like, you know? Always calm and cold."

I swallow hard, because she's right, and it's exactly why he scares me. Three and a half years ago when they met, I would've said he seemed quiet, but decent. The quiet part is still true, but decent? Deranged might be a better word.

A memory snaps into focus in my head: Charlie was reviewing a document on the computer, a notepad beside him. I stepped closer, a knot growing in my stomach, and saw a list of familiar names in his precise writing. Mom's friends. My friends. Teachers. There were dates and tally marks. A couple of cryptic comments.

Tracking our calls wasn't the worst thing or the only thing he did, but it was the first time he scared me.

"Wait, what about the steakhouse? He made your mom quit her *job*," Lana says.

"She went along with it. It's not against the law to be an asshole husband. They can't do anything to him unless he directly threatens or hurts us."

"Maybe he won't, and it'll never be worse than him being a freak."

His words come back to me. *Maybe I won't be so nice.*

"I think he's capable of worse," I say softly. "Something awful."

"I hate him." She says it bitterly, but shakes it off fast. "So what do we do?"

I smile because I love this about Lana. She's so logical. When her father and brother were sent back to Venezuela last year, I was the angry one. I was ready to take to the streets, but Lana and Maria dove into paperwork and attorney websites. Lana told me she wasn't going to whine when she could spend her time trying to do something that might make a difference. It's still not over, but they're getting closer.

Which is why I need to learn from her lesson.

"I'm going to wait it out," I say. "Charlie thinks I'll come back with my tail between my legs. When I don't, Mom might change her mind. I think she'll go when the baby comes. I just need to lay low until then. Mom's due New Year's Eve."

"That's a long time." Lana's face falls. "Are you sure you can't go home and avoid him until then? Then you can be at school. Things can stay the same."

I shake my head thinking of the way he looked at the bathroom door, the cold threat in his eyes. "Something happened that day. He said I'd come crawling back, and it felt like he'd be waiting for it. He gave me chills."

"So where will you go? You can't stay here forever," she says.

The regret in her voice is genuine. She's my friend. And Maria is a good lady. But she's not the kind of mom who won't start asking questions if I don't go home soon.

Still, that's the one piece of this I haven't resolved. I've enrolled in a new school, I have the schedule for the next SAT (February) and the next ACT (March), and I'm going to petition for early graduation. I even have a week-by-week study schedule. What I don't have is a place to live.

Lana scoots away from the headboard, touching her sock-clad toes to my arm. "You know I wouldn't care. You could move in if it were up to me."

"I know."

"When we're in college, we'll get an apartment. You and me."

"Sure," I say, and I cover the way my voice cracks with a smile. I don't tell her that all those plans we talked about feel a million miles away. My future is boiled down to the essentials. Getting my mom and the baby away from Charlie. Working because we'll need both of our incomes to afford anything.

I can't say that to Lana, though, so I hug her tight and tell her how much I appreciate her help. It's the truth, even if it's not every truth.

We shower and dress and head out. I thank her for the laptop again. Then I walk the twenty-two blocks to the Fairview Public Library. It's farther away, but it's quiet, and there's less chance of running into someone from Whitestone.

I spend my whole day working through classes, attending the scheduled lectures, and working ahead in every class I can. It's so much easier when I'm not on a library computer.

I don't know what I'll do when I have to return Lana's laptop. The library computers require guest passes with a two-hour maximum. A stone formed behind my ribs the first time I saw the "time expired" message, and it hasn't entirely gone away. I need more than two hours or I'm going to start missing scheduled lectures.

And I need more than time. I need a new plan for where to stay. Lana's mom is almost done with her night shift weeks. I need to figure out something long term.

Lana thinks I could come again after Thanksgiving, but that feels a long way off. I could try Aneela, but her parents have never been big on overnights and *always* want to talk to the parents personally. I'm not really close enough to my other friends to ask. Plus, I don't have a phone to call, which makes this all even trickier.

Maybe I should have brought my phone. He couldn't track me if I leave it powered off.

I slip the laptop into my backpack and roll my stiff shoulders. My stomach growls. It's been doing a good bit of that, but with eighteen dollars on me, I need to be frugal. The original plan, of course, included more money. Mom had a couple hundred on her, but that's blown to smithereens now.

I'm sick to death of sitting, so I take a stroll. I get a drink from the fountain and check the programming calendar for something to do. A mock-up of an old movie poster catches my eye. *Pizza, Popcorn, and Rebecca? We'll see you Thursday.*

That solves one meal. I don't want to think about how many are still a problem. I'm still not ready to sit again, so I head downstairs where the technology center and children's books live. There's a vending alcove there, a couple of machines set across from a table and chairs. Beyond the glass walls of the alcove, a bulletin board stretches above a padded bench.

Tour time's over. I need to do something. The boredom is not something I accounted for, and it's already wearing me out. Upstairs, I stop in the restroom and go through my bag in the stall after I pee. Laundry will be an issue soon. I fish through my pockets, hoping I'll find a few bills I missed, but I come up dry.

Okay, think like Lana. What's my plan?

1. Call Mom—somehow—or go check on her so she knows I'm fine.
2. Call the women's shelter for options.
3. Brainstorm ways to make money?

I'm in the stall rolling my dirty jeans and T-shirt tightly when the bathroom door opens.

I freeze like I'm doing something wrong, which is silly. It's a public bathroom. I'm allowed to be here.

Someone enters with slow, slapping steps. Do shoes sound like that? Have I ever paid attention? Probably not, but I'm paying attention now, because there's something wrong about that sound, especially when the footsteps stop.

I slow my breathing, holding myself utterly still. I can't be sure, but I think whoever this is, she's near the sink. Why is she just standing there?

Goose bumps rise on the backs of my arms. I want to pick up my feet, in case she looks under the door, but I don't dare risk the noise. I curl my shoulders in instead, my breath shaking in and out.

What is she doing out there? Does she know I'm in here? Can she see me?

My gaze darts to the thin space around my stall door.

Oh, God, wait.

What if a *man* saw me come in here? What if Charlie found me?

A quiet snap interrupts my thoughts. The soft brush of fabric. Another plastic rattle, something being snapped open. Makeup? It sounds like someone messing with powder or a tube of lipstick. I strain my ears, catching the barely there groan of the countertop under pressure. I can picture someone leaning against it to see the mirror more closely.

Probably because that's exactly what's happening. I close my eyes and sigh. A little old lady probably shuffled in to powder her nose, and I'm in here convinced Charlie is about to burst into my stall with a knife. I am such an idiot.

I sag back, feeling ridiculous as I flush the toilet. If she did notice me, I don't want to be the creepy silent girl who sits in the stall for no reason. I shove the rest of my stuff in the bag. I have to get a grip.

The footsteps—still strange—*shuffle-slap* back toward the door. It bangs open and I hear someone exhale loudly.

"Thank God."

A muffled whimper and a comforting hush answer. The first woman whispers, then two sets of footsteps retreat. The door swings closed again, and I wince in the sudden quiet.

The person with the makeup was probably just a lost kid or

someone who needed help. I'm not sure I could feel crappier about my suspicion at this point. Paranoia is not a good look for me.

I secure all my zippers and heft my backpack onto my shoulder. Out the stall, I stop dead, a sudden chill zipping through the center of my chest.

On the mirror, in red-brown lipstick smears, is a message that was *absolutely* not here when I walked in.

Stay Hidden.

SPENCER

Sunday, November 12, 9:19 a.m.

"How much more community service can you have?" Dad asks, looking incredulous.

"Dad, did you forget the meeting with Mr. Brooks? I broke a giant, sixty-year-old window."

He mumbles something about remembering bits and pieces. I'm not surprised. Dad spent most of that meeting being relieved he wouldn't have to pay his lawyer to get involved.

"You're going to be busy with college visits and hockey tourneys soon. You did your bit. We paid for the damages. All this is getting ridiculous."

I flash back to my knee buried in the window, glass raining down. "Community service doesn't feel ridiculous."

"Just tell me if it gets in the way. So, where are you on your essay?"

"What essay?"

"Very funny. Your college application essay. Stop acting like you don't know this deadline is coming fast. Where are you on scheduling tours?"

My stomach balls up tight. "Haven't started."

"Private schools pay attention to visits. You're not going to win any points if you don't bother to make the trip. Did you think about that?"

"Currently, I'm thinking of running away to join the circus," I say.

Dad laughs. "My son. The comedian."

Allison settles a small hand on my shoulder. It's one of those big sister gestures she developed when her Amherst acceptance letter arrived two years ago. "Dad's right. Now's the time to get your lists together. Reach schools, good bets, a couple of safeties."

Dad points his sandwich at me, brightening. "I've got people at UChicago and Dartmouth. If you want something bigger, we can talk Duke or Northwestern."

"Don't rule out Amherst," Allison says with a smile.

"I think my C minus in English will rule out Amherst."

"Pull up your GPA. What are your strong subjects?" Dad asks.

English usually is my strong subject, but he's not really looking for answers. When we drove home from the library the night of my climb, he answered all his own questions. What was I thinking? I wasn't thinking. Who was I covering for? Probably Jarvey and Shawn. Those two are a nightmare. Did I even think about my senior hockey season? Obviously, I didn't. But the next time I get a wild hair up my ass, maybe I could do it in the off season.

Maybe I should have cleared it up then, but how the hell do I bring it up now, two weeks later? *Oh, heads up, Dad. I was alone that night. Also, my GPA is currently at a 2.3, so I think we can rule out any top schools. And sitting up on the roof—with a broken window and the police en route—made me wonder if I have any business at all living in Fairview.*

"Jokes aside, you've got to make a list," Dad says.

"Not this morning, Dad," Allison says, standing up. "He's going to be late. Doesn't your shift start at ten, Spencer?"

"Library opens at ten on Sundays. They want me there at nine thirty."

"I've got to pick up a couple of books I've got on hold. I'll give you a ride if you can convince them to let me check them out."

Allison's good at diffusing awkward family crap. She's good at a lot of things: a swell big sister, former class treasurer, and currently on the dean's list. She's also freshly back from some summer/fall study abroad thing with the university, which means she's here until January.

Allison takes the lead out the door. Her pale eyes are bright, and her face is Mediterranean-tanned. She's wearing a gauzy pink sweater and leather shoes she bought in Milan. I don't know if I'd call my sister a snob, but she dresses the part.

We head down the stone steps outside our house. There's a landscaping truck on the curb, and a couple of guys strapping on leaf blowers. We still have a couple of maples left to drop, but already the yard is carpeted in red leaves. We used to build forts in those leaves when we were little. Now Mom has them scooped and blown into bags and carted away before she gets home from work. The homeowners' association prefers the neighborhood's lawns leaf-fort free.

It's maybe a ten-minute walk, so I'm not sure why she's really offering this ride. She clears it up the second we get in the car.

"Are you ever going to tell me why you did it?" she asks. "The library, I mean."

"The voices in my head?"

"Don't be a jerk. You don't hear voices, and you don't break laws. You're also fast enough to not get caught."

She's not wrong.

"Maybe I'm slowing down in my old age," I say, deflecting. "Is this why you only took third in your last cross-country meet? Is there early aging in my DNA, big sister?"

She smirks. "You're adopted, you little turd."

"*What?* What are you saying, Allison?" I make my eyes big and round like I used to when I'd trick adults into thinking they'd spilled some adoption secret.

Allison laughs, because she remembers too. "I can't believe how often you pulled that stunt on teachers. You were terrible."

"I'm still convinced that's why Mrs. Gates retired."

"Could you blame her? You had her convinced she'd contributed to your emotional devastation."

I sigh dreamily. "Good memories."

"Spence, I know thinking about college is stressful, but don't be afraid of it. There's so much opportunity."

Opportunity. I swear to God it's everyone's favorite word these days. I don't reply, so Allison keeps going. "You can't do this much longer. You're a senior. You need to think about the future."

"Duly noted. I also need to think about getting inside before the volunteer coordinator hands me my ass."

"Fine, let's go."

We lope up the marble steps, and I scan my badge to open the heavy brass door. The quiet inside is suffocating. Most of the lights are still off, which makes it worse. The few staff members gathered around the circulation desk have a coffee-hasn't-kicked-in glaze in their eyes. I doubt anyone is missing me.

Ruby comes out of the office to boot the checkout computers. "Two volunteers for the price of one? Good to see you, Allison."

"You too! Though I'm hardly a volunteer. It was only a few weekends."

"We'll take any time people are willing to give. I thought you were off at school."

"Amherst," she says, beaming. "I was studying abroad so I'm on a break."

Ruby brightens. "Wow, Amherst! That's great. What's your major?"

"Economics, but I think I'll go for my master's in statistical science after that."

"Well," I say, clapping my hands together. "As much as I love a little econ talk in the morning, I should get to work."

Gretchen slips out of the back office, as if on cue. "Hi, Sunshine! Can you turn on the browsing room computers and then grab the key to the back door and check for donations?" Then she turns to my sister with a smile. "Hi, Allison! I thought you were away at school."

I practically burn tracks getting out of there before the Amherst talk can start up again. The lights are out in the browsing room, but the rows of skylights keep it bright. My shoes pad lightly on the dark carpet around the perimeter of the room.

I stop to get the keys, but my eyes are drawn to the patron desk with the compartment. Mallory's desk. My note is gone, which makes me wonder. Did she get the pens? Did it make her laugh?

I stroll over and pop open the compartment. The pens are gone, but there's something in their place. A single well-used glue stick wrapped in a sticky note sits in the middle of the cubby. I pull it out carefully. It's my note, but looping blue handwriting leaves a message beneath mine.

You said you needed glue.

I grin. I said that when I dropped the books. She was paying attention. I drop the glue stick in the staff desk drawer, but I pocket the note before I leave.

The library lights are still out in the stacks, but I can hear Gretchen and Ruby telling Allison goodbye and I don't want anything to do with that lovefest. I'm sure they'll get the lights in a second, so I follow the red glow of the exit sign toward the loading dock.

I don't actually need the light, but the darkness is eerie. Probably because I'm thinking of the footprints and that gasp I heard the other day. Just keep moving. I make my way along the back wall until I find the electronic lock. Beyond the door, there's a small storage room for deliveries. I cross to the exterior door in two strides, eager for the sunlight outside.

It's a bright, cold day. I pick up some trash that blew against the door overnight—and head for the stack of donated books left by the corner of the dock. Way better than the folks who leave heaps of shitty old encyclopedias down in the driveway to get rained on. Still, a box would be nice.

I check the covers and spines of every donated book before it goes in the crook of my arm. We have to do this, to make sure they aren't water damaged or, worse, carrying bed bug hitchhikers. I open the bigger books and check the pages for telltale "ink" spots or other damage. Like I'd know a telltale bug sign if I saw it. Most of these books are merely grungy.

"I didn't really take you for a knitter."

I jump at the voice, but this time, I don't drop the books. I consider dropping them for show when I see Mallory at the end of the driveway. In the daylight, she looks small and pale—still sporting those glaring highlighted chunks in her hair and the same awful shoes.

I smile. "Actually, I was going to put this on reserve for you."

She glances back at the alley where she's standing, wavering like she's not sure she's allowed to be back here. Her hair is hanging in her eyes, and the knees on her jeans are dirty. She seems out of place, against the white fences and perfectly trimmed hanging baskets. Then she smiles, and I forget about the flowers.

And the fact that I'm technically at work.

Which is technically *not* work, but criminally earned community service.

"You're not reserving that for me," she says.

"No? But I'm *sure* you asked me for..." I turn the book over, reading the title. "*Knitting Your Way through the Holidays.*"

"And in a fit of service commitment, you decided to deliver it to me outside?"

I feel myself grinning. "Of course. What kind of library associate do you take me for?"

"One who drops books."

"Guilty. But I didn't drop this beauty."

"Maybe not, but you still can't check it out to me."

"Clearly you don't know the magnitude of my library powers."

"Clearly you're forgetting that you don't know my name."

"Your name is Mallory."

"Yes, but Mallory what?"

She waits expectantly. I open my mouth and close it again. Then we both laugh.

She looks right at me. Most of the girls I flirt with—because I know what I'm about here—play this game with the coy dialed all the way up. Batting eyes and tugged hair. But Mallory stares me down like a dare: chin up, eyes bright, and her shoulders back like she could take on a wayward truck and maybe do some calculus while she's at it.

"Okay, I give," I say. "What's your whole name, Mallory?"

She hesitates, her grin sliding off her face. "I should go."

A ripple goes through me. It's stupid, but I want her to stay and talk to me. About yarn. Or pens. Anything, really. But she's already walking away.

I step to the edge of the dock, raising my voice.

"But I have your knitting book! How can you walk away?"

"I'm going to the entrance. You're opening soon," she says. As she disappears behind the library wall, I hear her laugh.

I'm laughing too, when the dock door swings open behind me. My smile withers the second I turn. It's Gretchen, but I've never seen her like this, so pale and drawn I can only think she's sick. Or gotten a phone call with terrible news.

"What's wrong?" I ask, crouching to collect the remaining books.

"Is your sister still in the lot?"

I glance out, but the car is gone. "No. Why?"

She lifts a hand, and her fingers are shaking. "Come inside. Leave those."

"What's wrong?" I repeat, feeling itchy and strange. She's scared, and it's freaking me out because I've never seen her look anything other than happy.

"We found—" She stops herself and presses her lips together like she's lost the words. Or doesn't want them to come out. "Just come inside, Spencer."

I drop the books and follow her in. The door shuts behind us with a soft whump, and then we're stuck in that tiny room between the dock and the library. I take a breath that smells like cardboard and musty books.

Gretchen stays in front of me when she opens the door to the stacks. She's blocking most of my view, but the lights are on now. There are whispers in the aisles. The air feels heavy. Wrong. I swallow and my throat clicks. Clicks again.

Gretchen isn't moving and doesn't turn to face me when she speaks.

"Stay behind me, do you understand?"

It isn't a question. I hear sirens in the distance, and they go silent close to the building. The last time I saw a police car here, I was sitting on the roof, but this isn't like that. My gut tells me this is much worse.

"Do you understand?" she repeats. "*Right* behind me."

"Yeah," I say, and my heart flies like I'm running suicide drills on the ice.

How long was I outside with Mallory? It couldn't have been more than ten minutes. What could happen in ten minutes?

Gretchen steps into the library, turning right to follow the back wall toward the circulation desk. I follow her, looking around. Trying to figure out what the hell is going on.

More whispering draws my gaze down one of the aisles. There's something big on the floor, between the 840s and the 920s. A couple of staff members are standing over it, and it isn't a pile of books.

I see a sweep of fabric and a tangle of long blond hair.

Terrible pieces come together in an answer. It's a person. There's a person—a girl—crumpled on the floor between two shelves. She's facing away from me, arm bent awkwardly behind her back.

She is perfectly, horribly still.

My heart climbs with every beat, until I feel it in the back of my throat.

"Spencer."

I startle at Gretchen's voice, hurrying to catch up. I don't let myself look again, but it's too late. The image of the dead woman is burned into my mind.

MALLORY

Sunday, November 12, 10:08 a.m.

This is how I know something happened. They don't unlock the doors at 10:00. By the time I make it from the dock area to the front of the library, two fire trucks are parked at the curb. The firefighters hop out and I hang back, hoping it's a false alarm. It's an old building. Fire alarms can be weird. But then four staff members spill out, including Spencer.

All four look distraught talking to the firefighters. Ten minutes ago, Spencer was outside laughing with me. Now his dark skin is the color of a February sky. This isn't a false alarm. Something bad happened inside.

Two staff members lead the firemen in. When the ambulance comes, I expect the paramedics to rush, but they don't. They emerge slowly, opening the back doors and easing out the gurney.

My shoulders hitch.

If someone was hurt, they would hurry. Someone would go

in to check. I've seen enough squad runs in my neighborhood to know.

My mind is buzzy when a familiar staff member approaches me. She introduces herself as Gretchen and tells me the library is closed for some reason I don't catch.

I shake my head. "I'm sorry. Can you repeat that?"

She nods, but then swallows hard like she's got to brace herself to say it again.

The word she uses is *emergency*, but I think she means someone died. I can't be sure, but the thought comes with a terrible stab of certainty. That's why they need the gurney, but they don't need to rush. That's why the library is closed. Someone died inside.

We both go quiet. The world does not change. Traffic lights switch. Birds chirp. Everyday life continues, bobbling along the film of this awful scene.

Gretchen smiles. "Keep an eye on our website or social media pages for when we plan to reopen."

"I'll check. I hope everything's okay." The first bit is a lie. I can't check. I don't have a phone, and I won't have access to the internet unless I go back to Lana's, which I can't do in the middle of the day.

Now what? Gretchen slips to the other side of the stairs to meet with other alarmed-looking patrons. I linger on the steps, trying to think. After finishing my timed paper, I was planning to register for the SAT. Or at least start studying some of the vocabulary. The library was the beginning and end of my plans for today.

A police cruiser pulls up to the curb without flashing lights, and my shoulders sag with guilt. Someone walked into the library alive, and now they're not. This feels so much bigger than my school assignments.

Except that these assignments are the best way to keep Mom and me safe. With good grades and test scores, I might get into a fast-track college program. Maybe I could get a job. With us both working, we could afford an apartment on our own. She wouldn't need Charlie.

"Hey."

I whirl around, but it's not an officer or a fireman. It's Spencer. He's taller up close like this, without the desk between us. He tries a smile, but it doesn't quite land.

"Are you okay to get home?" he asks me.

"I…"

He's caught me off guard, and my heart trips over its own beat. I'm still looking at the ambulance parked at the curb. The people whispering near the library entrance.

"I could take you."

I startle. "What?"

"We'd have to walk to my house first. To get a car."

His grin works this time, revealing perfect and expensive-looking white teeth. Spencer is attractive in a way that makes me think of tropical islands and kaleidoscopes. That last part must be about his eyes, which shift between green and gray and back again. It's not something I should notice. I have zero time for this kind of nonsense right now.

"I'm sorry. I have to go."

"You don't need a ride?"

"A ride?"

"A ride home."

My stomach binds up. I hitch my bag higher on my shoulder. "No. I'm good."

He nods, face wan. "We'll be open tomorrow I think. If you're coming."

"Okay."

"So I'll see you around? I'll be here after school. At four."

I can't tell if he wants me to have specifics or if he wants to fill the silence. The latter would make more sense. If we're talking about nothing, maybe we can stop thinking about the awful thing that happened here. An awful thing he might have seen.

Part of me wants ask him. Or make him forget. But I don't even know this guy. How would I help?

I sigh. "I really have to go."

"Sure. Of course."

There's nothing else to say. I want to turn, *need* to turn, but I can't. I'm staring at the lights behind him. Wondering what he saw. Feeling like I shouldn't leave him.

"You saw something, didn't you?"

I direct the question to my shoelaces, but when I meet his eyes, all the hard angles in his face go soft. "Yes."

"I'm sorry."

"Yeah," he breathes. "Me too."

I feel a pull to him in that moment, a connection. There's something so close, so personal about the space between us now. But I can't trust those connections. Spencer seems nice, but Charlie seemed nice too. I've learned the hard way not to trust how anything seems.

The Mom issue is solved by Sunday updates. Charlie works two Sundays every month to run system updates while school isn't in session. Which is exactly when I decide to pay her a visit.

I take a bus, reluctant to spend the money, but eager to shave fifteen blocks off my walk. I still check for Charlie's car in the parking lot, but once I confirm he's gone, I take the stairs two at a time, my heart dancing at the sign of our rusty door knocker.

Mom is surprised to see me on her stoop at 12:30 on a

Sunday afternoon. She's wearing a wrinkled shirt, and her hair is limp and greasy, but her belly… Is it already rounder?

I touch her stomach in the open doorway and smile. "Baby's growing."

She smiles back, but her face pinches. "We should call Charlie if you want to stay. He said we needed to—"

"I'm not staying." My chest clenches. It's hard to see her like this, small and quiet and afraid. Before Charlie, she was different. We rode our bikes and cooked hot dogs on grills in Fenimore Park. Before Charlie, my mom was *alive.*

She's always been guy crazy, and there'd been a few steady boyfriends over the years, but none of them stuck. She sometimes cried, saying she was easy to leave. Until Charlie. Charlie got his claws in fast. Looking at her now reminds me that those claws are in deep.

I smile, trying to soothe her. "How have you been?"

Her eyes fill with tears. "I'm worried about you. I don't know what to do. You call from Lana's, but then you email that you might stay with another friend. You've been so vague."

She's right, and it's not unintentional. "I've been at Lana's. Her mom doesn't mind."

"Maria has her own troubles. You can't stay there forever."

"It's not forever. I'm staying with another girlfriend tonight," I lie. "Hey, I'm doing great in my new school. I'm already a week ahead on all the work."

She sniffs. "Charlie is *so* angry about that. Said I let you talk me into dropping—"

I flinch and grab for her hands. "Can we—let's talk about you, okay?"

Because I don't want to hear about him. I know what Charlie wants. He wants my mom under his thumb, and he wants me to come crawling back to tell him how right he is. I'm sure he wants us both on a very short leash, and if he doesn't get it, I don't know what he'll do.

"How are you feeling?" I ask, because she hasn't answered.

"Better. I'm able to eat a little at supper. He's been bringing soup. I thought I could eat a sandwich, but he says lunch meat is bad for the baby."

I punch a cheery voice right through my bitterness. "Soup is great!"

Mom isn't fooled by my bright tone. She sighs and walks farther inside, where she sits heavily on the couch.

"I don't know what to do," she says, voice cracking. "I love you, Mallory. I hate that you're gone. I worry. All the time."

I rush to her side when she sniffs. Pull some tissue from a roll of toilet paper on the end table. Probably not the first time she's cried since I left, I think with a guilty twinge.

"It's okay," I say. "There have been good things about this break. I'm already starting to study for the SAT. I bet I can start community college this summer. And I can get a job."

"I know he's got his issues," she says, ignoring me. "He's hardheaded."

My smile stretches tight. I can't keep this up much longer. "It's beyond hardheaded."

"You never make it easy on him to be the head of this house."

"Why does he need to be the head? Why do you put up with this, Mom?"

"You don't understand because you're young," she says. "He's been very sweet, honestly. He even apologized for getting so upset. He's worried about you too."

I don't snort, but almost, and she sees it. I sigh. "The man said I'd come crawling back and that he wouldn't be so nice then. He hates me, Mom."

"I'm sure he didn't say it like that. And he doesn't hate you. Why do you insist on villainizing him no matter what he does for us?"

Villainizing. I step back abruptly because that is not something my mom says. That is a word Charlie would use.

I feel like I can't get any air, like the room is getting smaller. Mom is still talking, but I can't hear her because I'm too busy imagining him pulling strings attached to her jaw. She's sitting here spouting all the lines he's fed her. He's doing this, and he's not even here.

"I need some answers," she says. "When are you planning to come home?"

"I think we should wait until the baby comes. You're feeling better, and I'm doing great. When the baby comes, we'll talk. We'll work it out."

"That's in January!"

"It could happen sooner."

"You were five days late," Mom says. "Before your Nana died, she told me I was two and a half weeks late. Halston babies come late, and she will too."

She. The word is a sharp hook at the base of my throat.

My mom flushes, and her eyes go bright with mischief. "I'm not gaining enough weight, so the doctor took a peek yesterday," she whispers. "Ultrasound. It was supposed to be a surprise, but I…wanted to know."

My chest fills with emotion so light and bright I'm sure I'll float away on it. "It's a girl. I'm having a sister."

Her laugh is unexpected and warm. She almost immediately shakes it off, eyes flitting at the door.

"Don't tell Charlie. He said it wasn't right to know. That it steals the joy."

Her words have the effect of a bucket of ice water. "I won't be here to tell him."

It wouldn't matter if I was here. If I could, I would hide this from him forever, because suddenly, this baby isn't a helpless, faceless thing. She's a girl. My sister.

And Charlie will treat her exactly like he treats the two of us.

A shudder rolls up my spine as I imagine the doctor passing a squirming pink bundle into Charlie's hands. My stomach rolls so hard, I think I might be sick.

I stand quickly. "I really should go. We'll figure this out, okay?"

"Take your phone. Please. I have to know you're safe. One email a day isn't enough."

We find a compromise. I take my phone and tell her I'll call her some, but I'll only power it on once a day. I tell her it's so I won't be distracted or tempted to text friends, but it's really so Charlie can't track me. He'll definitely try, so I can't turn on my phone anywhere near Lana's or the library.

I hug my mom before I go, pressing my forehead to her shoulder. "It's going to be okay."

"Do you think so?" she asks.

For the first time in a while, I do. I can feel her belly between us, round and firm—a timer ticking down to when my mother won't be sick and exhausted. She'll be my mom again.

And I'll get her to leave him for good.

SPENCER

Sunday, November 12, 4:18 p.m.

It's probably best that Mallory didn't take me up on that ride because I wasn't allowed to leave for two hours. Mom had to come because a parent has to be present for a minor to be questioned by the police. I should have remembered that from my climbing adventure.

Mom shows up in a suit with a firm handshake for the officers and a gentle hand for my shoulder.

"Are you all right?" she asks.

"Fine. Really. I didn't see anything."

"What do you think happened? A heart attack?" Mom asks the police, absently stroking my shoulder.

Her pale hair is pulled into a neat knot at the nape of her neck. I have no idea how she keeps it fastened because you can't see anything other than carefully coiled hair.

They're talking in low voices, but I pick up a few words. *Autopsy. Pending. Paraphernalia.* Mom relaxes, but her frown deepens.

Then it's my turn. Officer Schooley asks all the general questions. When did I arrive? Where did I walk? Did I hear anything, see anything, notice anything? I tell him about the footsteps I thought I heard, and he jots that down, but otherwise I have nothing for him. I wish I did, but he thanks me for my time and turns away.

So that's it? I just leave with all this happening here?

Mom squeezes my arm. "Head on to the Audi. I'll be there in a minute."

I nod, but linger on the steps and watch her talking to him, concern creasing the corners of her eyes. Once in a blue moon, the creases will appear between her brows, but the Botox fairy takes those away every three months.

Up on the second floor, the administration staff must be in. I can see someone standing at the window, a vague smear of shadow near the curtain. It makes sense, I guess. If someone dies at a library, it seems reasonable to call in the cavalry.

Still, I feel mesmerized by the figure behind the glass. I have a flash of myself climbing, of my knee going through the pane of one of those upper story windows. The figure is barely visible, just the vague outline of a shoulder and an arm. The curtain bunches and twists where a hand might be, and my eyes fix on that movement. Bunch and twist. Bunch and twist.

"There you are," Mom says.

I smile. Back at the window, the curtain goes still. Whoever was there is gone.

"Sorry," I say. "I was too antsy to sit."

Mom rubs my shoulder on the way to the car. She doesn't harp on me for waiting and doesn't ask me much when we settle into the immaculate leather seats.

"Now I don't want you to worry," she says as she starts driving. "The police don't suspect foul play, and I don't think it was someone local."

A strange laugh comes out of me. "You think someone from out of town drove in to die in the Fairview Public Library."

"I mean they weren't *from* Fairview."

"Okay," I say, wondering how she's sure and why it would matter.

Classical radio plays softly in the background. The car smells like my mother—high-end perfume and the heavy gloss paper from her real estate flyers.

"How are things there usually?" she asks.

"What do you mean?"

"Libraries are a public space. There's no controlling what kind of person comes inside."

"Yeah. There could be criminal kids who kick out windows in their spare time."

"Not funny, Spencer. Someone died. Normal people don't wind up dead in libraries."

My jaw clenches, and I hold the armrest a little tighter. I want to ask her where the hell normal people die, but I don't. I want to ask her why she stopped raking the leaves and why her forehead doesn't move and if she really thinks she's better because she's from this stupid town. But I don't ask because I don't think I actually want the answers.

I should shut up and be glad it's a stranger. I should, I don't know, send some kind of silent prayer for a peaceful passing or whatever the hell you're supposed to do when you run into a dead person. But I don't know what I should do. This is the theme of my life these days.

I get to the library at 4:30 the next day, which is early, but it already looks like nothing happened. Mr. Brooks is wandering the lobby, escorting anyone concerned upstairs to chat. Gretchen is smiling, and Noah is working on a music display. I guess I'm playing that nothing-happened game too because I have knitting needles in my pocket—and let me tell you, buying knitting needles in hockey gear raises plenty of eyebrows.

I leave them in the desk compartment, but second-guess myself right away.

If she knows what happened in here, she might not come

back. A dead person in the library would be enough to keep someone away. Whatever. Worst-case scenario, someone else finds knitting paraphernalia in a library desk. I could inspire a new wave of yarn enthusiasts.

Two-thirds of the way through my second cart of shelving, I find her. I do a double take, but it's definitely her. She's at a table near the gardening section, working on an ancient-looking laptop with a notebook beside her.

From the stack of papers next to her, it seems like she's been at it for a while. We exchange a weird wave, but I have no idea where to go from there. Waltzing up to explain the gift waiting for her feels ridiculous, and I suspect she's not in the mood for ridiculous. Her eyes are ringed with dark circles, and her hair is twisted up into a messy ponytail.

It reminds me of the dead girl's tangled hair. Three days ago, it could have been Mallory on the floor, and I wouldn't have known or cared. She would have been a stranger, then. And Mom still would have told me it was no big deal, because hey! She's not from Fairview.

I finish the fiction cart and grab another one. Nonfiction this time, because it'll keep me closer to her table. I linger so long at the ends of the rows, I'm probably edging into stalker territory. Not that she notices. She's clicking away and jotting down notes and scrunching up her nose like something on her laptop is weird. Or slow.

After a while, it seems more than slow. She taps several keys, growing frustrated. Then she checks cords and swears under her breath, pink blotches rising on her pale cheeks.

I step out from behind the shelf I was essentially hiding behind and walk closer.

"Excuse me, ma'am," I say, voice deep and super servicey. "Having trouble?"

She spares me only the briefest glance, still clicking away. "The stupid connection keeps failing. I'm probably ten minutes from finishing this assignment."

"That sounds frustrating. Are you aware that the library offers public computers? They're hardwired to our connection, which is often more reliable."

She frowns but the ghost of a smile lights her eyes. "I'll have to look into that."

"I have a particular desk I'd recommend."

She arches a brow. "Do you have a pen as well?"

"I seem to have given all my pens away."

She laughs, and it's hard not to pump my fist. It's also hard to stay put when she shoves everything in her backpack and heads for the browsing room. Once upon a time, I was not the weird guy who flirts with girls at his community service gig. I guess times have changed.

I finish my cart and restock the staff picks before I find her again. Mallory is at the desk typing away. She has the needles tucked in the front pocket of her backpack, and as soon as she sees me, she gets up.

She heads straight for me, tipping her chin up. "Hey again."

"Hey."

"Are you on break soon? I want to talk to you. Alone, if possible."

I laugh. I can't help it. "Well, don't beat around the bush on my account."

She takes it all wrong, her face screwing up like I've pissed her off. Or maybe even hurt her. I step closer with a smile, trying to make it clear I'm not teasing.

"No breaks," I say, "but I'm off at seven."

"Okay," she says, flushed but determined. "Can I talk to you then?"

"Absolutely."

"Just like that?"

"Just like that."

She doesn't smile and doesn't say anything else, but suddenly the space between us is electric. We're not talking and we're standing beside a display of books on the Great Depression, but I feel like she's so close we might as well be touching. I can't figure it out. I can't figure *her* out.

I clear my throat. "I could give you my number."

She shakes her head. "That's okay."

Neither of us moves to leave but my heart speeds up, and

my throat tightens. It feels like climbing, when I'm perched on the side of a bad ledge, no foothold in sight and no easy way up. Every muscle tenses and my breath catches. Anything could happen from here.

"Hey, Spencer!"

I turn at the familiar voice behind me. Alex is in the doorway to the browsing room. He's holding a stack of books on the War of 1812. Isaac's got some on President Grant, and Jarvey's standing there, sucker in his mouth and a don't-give-a-shit expression on his face.

They move in with grins and quick fist-bump, shoulder-slap greetings, Isaac disappearing when his cell phone rings.

"How much longer are you stuck in this hellhole?" Jarvey asks, looking around.

"Show a little class," Alex says. Then to me: "When are you off?"

"Seven." I glance over my shoulder, thinking I should say something. Introduce Mallory. She's already back at the desk. She waves me off, and Alex gives her a brief glance.

"You should skip last period and come to the rink early tomorrow," Jarvey says. "Your long passes need work, and Shawn said he'd pay for the ice time."

"My last long pass got you a goal, didn't it?" I turn to Alex. "What do you think? Am I tainting the ice for Gretzky here?"

"Shut up," Jarvey says, but he's grinning around his sucker. "Just be there, all right? You good for that?"

"If you want, I can drive," Alex offers.

"I can drive," I say. "I'll be there."

"You better," Jarvey says. "Worthington is looking tight. We need to be ready."

"I said I'll do it."

Jarvey flashes a filthy grin at Mallory. "Whatever else you're *doing*, do it fast."

He disappears, joining Isaac in the lobby. I feel myself pulling back as I watch them. These are guys I've hung out with most of my life. I'm one of them. So why the hell do they feel like strangers?

Alex nudges my shoulder and I smirk. "Is it just me or are they getting worse?"

Alex nods. "Definitely. They're only here to get some scoop on the dead body."

"There's scoop?"

"Yeah, from one of the librarians. Jarvey's not a total idiot. He pushed the freedom of information shit, and the guy caved. Told us she was a Jane Doe, and that the police aren't ruling the death suspicious."

"Dying in a library feels pretty suspicious."

"It was a drug overdose," Alex says, shrugging. "Or that's what my mom thinks."

She'd have the best guess, being a trauma specialist at the hospital downtown.

"Not surprising," Alex says. "We're a heroin highway or whatever. She's not from Fairview though."

I wince. "Man, everybody keeps saying that."

"Excuse me, gentlemen. Spencer," Gretchen says. "May I have your assistance?"

"Course." I wave at Alex and follow her around the corner and down a short flight of stairs to the lower level. The Youth Services Department is down here, along with a small kitchen and vending area and some benches. A staff member and a girl I don't recognize are talking to a mother and child. The child is sniffling, and there is worry on the mother's face.

"What can I do for you?" I ask Gretchen.

She sweeps her hand toward the bulletin board. "Help me get this all down. It scared her half to death."

"Okay," I say, starting at the top. I'm about to ask why when I see the words scrawled across the brochures and flyers. *Where are you?*

"It hasn't even been two days," she says, sounding angry. "Already somebody goes for a cheap scare. Like this isn't a tragedy. That woman was a real person."

Gretchen cuts herself off abruptly, but she's moving fast, ripping down everything she can reach. I do it too, noticing it's all the same. The handwriting. The marker. The words.

Where Are You?

It's not that scary, but the kid in the vending area is sobbing. I wad up the flyers and head to the trash can near the glass wall.

"That's not it!"

It's the little girl, obviously. She can't be older than seven or eight.

Gretchen joins me and we stand shoulder to shoulder, just out of sight. I guess we both want to hear, but we don't want to intrude either.

"Did someone tell her about the woman?" I ask softly.

"They sure did." Her voice is a sarcastic singsong. "Guy with a sucker. Your friend?"

Jarvey. I close my eyes, my stomach sinking. "He's..." There are a lot of things I want to say, but there's a little girl crying, and Jarvey's responsible. "Yeah, he's a shit."

The girl's sobs ramp up again. "You won't listen! It's a ghost! I heard a ghost!"

Her mom tries to hush her, a stern tone layered beneath her whisper as she gathers her purse. She's getting ready to move this whole scene upstairs and outside is my guess. But the girl flings herself out of reach, red hair swinging.

"I heard a ghost crying, Mommy. I heard a ghost in the walls."

MALLORY

Monday, November 13, 7:05 p.m.

I have a laptop on the fritz, a phone that's essentially a tracking device, and nowhere to sleep tonight. My options are suck and suckier, but asking a cute, rich boy for help still makes my insides squirmy.

I wait inside, watching him from the windows by the front door. Honestly, I'm trying to think of a better option. Because trusting any guy feels stupid given my present situation, but a guy from a neighborhood like this? One who seems unusually nice? I think Mom and I are living proof that if a guy seems too good to be true, he probably is.

Plus, I know nothing about Spencer. I don't even know what he does in his spare time. Football probably, if his enormous, muscular friends are any indicator. He has zero reason to help someone like me. If I say too much, he might even run and tell a manager, and then…

Could they kick me out for—I don't know, for being here too much? Would they try to call my mom?

I sigh and press my knuckles into the windowsill. He's standing near the bushes, looking tall, dark, and put together in a way that advertises his zip code. I turn my back on the door and close my eyes.

Spencer is my best option. Maybe my only option.

"Is there anything I can help you with?" I open my eyes and spot curly hair and a wide smile. Gretchen. "You look like you're a million miles away."

"Oh!" I laugh. "No, it's...school. I'm in a new online program."

"Ah, that's why you're riveted to the keys so much," she says. "Is there a project you need help with?"

She's coming closer. I hold my breath, reminding myself to not panic. I'm not in trouble. I'm a student. Studying. Still my laugh dribbles out on a wave of nervous energy.

"No, I'm good. Thanks," I say. "I should get some fresh air."

"Fresh air helps!"

I don't answer because I'm already walking outside. Spencer watches me descend the stairs. I'm not so dense that I miss the way he looks at me. Or the fact that I'm looking, too. When he grins, dragonflies take flight in my chest. I take a breath to push them down, because I already decided I don't have time for a boy. The only male I should be thinking of is the one I need to get away from my mother.

"I was beginning to think you'd changed your mind," he says.

"Why?" I smirk. "Because I didn't come running?"

"Well, I wasn't expecting *running* per se."

"Rushing, maybe?"

"*I* rushed."

Rushed to see me? Heat blooms in my stomach, rising through my neck and face. He steps closer, and I smell something clean and woodsy. It's him. He smells expensive.

Probably because he is *expensive.*

"So what do you do at the library?" I ask.

"Most of the time I check books in, shelve them, and sneak pens and knitting needles into desk compartments."

"I thought you worked the desks."

"Not usually." He quirks his head. "Am I being interviewed?"

I grin. "Maybe."

"So what do *you* do at the library?" he asks.

"School. Why?"

"I didn't want to be the only one answering questions."

"Now I am beating around the bush."

"I know. It's comforting. I wasn't sure you were capable."

His smile relaxes me. Spencer pushes at my guard without even trying. I'm afraid I'll tell him more than I should. Which is why I need to be careful.

"I was hoping you'd be able to help me with something. In the library."

"Like math homework?" He grimaces. "Because despite all the bullshit rumors about guys being good at math, I suck."

"It's not homework. I need more time on the internet."

"There shouldn't be any limits with our wireless connection since you have a laptop."

"That's the problem. Lana's—" I stop myself. "My laptop is screwing up. Keeps losing the connection."

"And the public computers have a two-hour max," he says.

"Right. Some days that's fine, but on others I have live lectures and tests. I need three or four hours to be safe."

His face grows thoughtful, and my stomach squirms. I barely know this guy, and I'm asking him to bend the rules for me. This isn't who I am. I handle my own crap.

"Forget it," I say with a weird, breathy laugh. "I shouldn't ask you to do this. I'm sorry. I'll sort something out."

He holds up a hand. "I didn't say no."

"You didn't?"

"I'm working it out. I can put you on the staff connection, which isn't limited, but I've got to figure out the schedule. You'll need to move around so people don't realize you're using the internet for more than two hours."

"Of course. Are you sure about this?" I shake my head. "You could get in trouble."

"Let me let you in on a little secret, Mallory. Trouble isn't *exactly* new to me."

I laugh. He doesn't make me feel like a girl wearing dirty

socks and eating nothing but granola bars I found on clearance at the Dollar Tree. I feel close to normal with Spencer.

"So you'll help me," I say, needing to be sure.

"I don't know," he says, obviously teasing me. "It's a risk."

"This is where you roll out a list of demands," I say. "The staff password for your history paper."

"I'll have you know I'm great at history." He wrinkles his nose. "Usually."

"Math, then?"

"I'm beyond help there," he says, "but I might have one tiny request."

"What?"

"Your phone number."

His words pull the oxygen out of the air. How stupid can I be? I'm not a normal girl flirting in the library parking lot. I'm a runaway with a cell phone I can't power on without my stepfather tracking me. Currently, I don't even have a home address.

I can't explain my world to Spencer.

"I..." My mouth feels dry and hot, and my fingers go cold on my backpack straps.

His face falls, confusion giving way to embarrassment. He takes a step back, and my insides ache. "Wow. Holy misinterpretation." He laughs, hand at his chest. "The male ego is a heavy yoke to bear."

"I'm sorry."

"Don't be. I misread," he says, clearly humiliated. "Sorry. Really, I am. I didn't mean—I'll get you the connection. No problem."

"It's not—it's hard to explain."

"No, it's my bad. I'm always delusional after work. Sometimes I think I'm the Pope."

I laugh, but it hurts. "I have to go. Will I see you tomorrow?"

He nods, hands in his pockets as he walks away. And maybe I imagine the slump in his shoulders. I probably do because I *want* him to be disappointed. More than that, I want to yell after him and tell him he wasn't misreading anything, that I would give him a number if I could.

I don't say any of that because it's pointless. It doesn't matter how he interprets me. Any way you slice this, we will always be heading in different directions.

The red clock on the bus reads 7:24, but I don't know if that's good or bad. How late is too late to stop by the Women's Crisis Center? Hopefully before 7:30 at night is cool.

I ring the doorbell, chewing my lip while I wait. There's no obvious sign or parking area. For the women's protection, I'm sure, but I check the address four times, just in case.

A woman with short, tight curls and an ample bosom opens the door.

"May I help you?"

I recognize her voice immediately. It's Ruth, the lady I spoke with on the phone.

"I'm Mallory. My mom, Sasha, and I were supposed to come a while ago."

"Of course. Would you like to talk inside?"

I nod, and she leads me in. It's like a house, but bigger. I'd think a college dorm might look like this. Inside the front door, there are living rooms on either side of a large entryway and wide stairs leading to a second floor. Nothing is fancy, but there's plenty of space.

A group of kids play video games in one living room, and the other is quiet. Ruth leads me through the quiet room, which isn't empty. A mother and toddler are playing with plastic dishes in the back. The toddler is mostly bald and giggly. The woman has a tired face and a yellow-green bruise under her left eye.

Ruth says hello but doesn't introduce me. Instead, she leads me into a small adjoining office. There are stacks of papers on her desk and floor and several pictures of a very fat pug on the shelf behind her. She closes the door, and I sit, waiting for her to settle behind her desk.

"Make yourself comfortable. I'm glad you came."

"I'm sorry my mom isn't here with me."

She smiles, clicking something on her computer. Opening my file, I guess. It worries me that I even have a file in a women's crisis center.

I hadn't considered this piece of my plan. What if Charlie found out? What would he do? More of the same berating lectures? No. Appearances are everything to him. Me being here, or anywhere like it, would tip him over the edge. Having a runaway stepdaughter? A wife considering a split? That's his worst fear—proof that he's not in control.

Ruth looks up from her screen. "You were originally planning to come on the third? Is that right?"

"Yes. I'm sorry about that."

"No apology needed."

"My mom changed her mind. You don't seem very surprised by that."

"It's not uncommon," she says simply. "Is she still considering it?"

"Not right now. It's just me."

Her smile drops, and her eyes search the screen. I'm not sure what she's reading until she says, "Remind me how old you are, Mallory."

"I'll be seventeen next month."

"Are you currently still at home?"

I barely hesitate, but it's enough for her to guess the

answer. She's probably professionally trained to read through girls like me.

"I'd like to put you in touch with the Mulberry Manor," she says. "They're a group home, like us, but for teens. They can provide a temporary residence and great resources."

"They'll call my mother." This part is very clear on several websites. Within twenty-four hours, they'll inform my mom, and then Charlie will hear all about it. And with Mulberry Manor so close to his school, the news could get out to other people he knows. Coworkers. Maybe his boss. The backlash of that terrifies me.

I shake my head. "I'm sorry. Thank you, but I can't."

"Mulberry Manor deals with situations similar to yours every day. They're very skilled at these conversations with parents. Talk to them."

"No. If they call her, he will know. He'll—" I take a shuddery breath. "It *can't* happen."

"Has the situation escalated?" A glance at my file. "You mention a lot of control issues, but has he become violent or threatening?"

I sigh because this is the problem. How do I explain a monster that hasn't fully shown his face? "He isn't like the men they talk about on the website. He doesn't scream or hit us."

"Abuse comes in many forms."

"Yeah, well Charlie's form is tricky to explain. If I go

somewhere like that, everyone will find out. He'll be humiliated and he'll snap. Right now, she's safe, but if I embarrass him…"

Ruth wants to ask me more questions, but I hold up my hand and take a step back toward the door. "I appreciate everything you're doing, but I need some time to think."

"Where are you staying?"

"I have friends. I'm okay. And before you ask, yes, I'm in touch with my mom. She knows what's going on."

"Mallory, if your mother won't leave, and the situation has become dangerous, then you need to consider what's best for you. I want to help if you'll let me."

I tell her I'll think about it, but I'm lying. I don't think about Mulberry Manor or Ruth's comments at all. I head south to the bus stop and use my pass to get to Lana's house. It's 7:55 when I arrive, the dark porch lit by a single yellow bulb.

I ring the doorbell, but it isn't Lana or her mother who answers. It's her younger brother, Finn. Fernando, actually, but he was so frightened after his father was deported, he insisted everyone start calling him Finn.

He was a reedy thirteen-year-old then, but now, only a year later, he's broader at the shoulders and grouchy in the face.

"She's not here," he says without greeting. Finn traded in his smiles when his father left. Now he's quiet and sometimes a little mean.

"Okay, will she be back soon?"

"She's with Mom and Abuela," he offers, which is obvious and offers zero information.

"I need to give her something."

"You were here for over a week. You couldn't give it to her then?"

I swallow hard around the sudden fist-size lump in my throat. If Finn's noticed—then Maria's mom has noticed. They might have talked about me; how I'm here too much. If I stay again, she might grow suspicious enough to call my mom.

"Do you need to wait for her?" he asks.

"Nah, just give her this, will you?" My hands shake as I hand over the laptop, my smile as wide and flat as a magazine ad. I tell him to have a good night, and my voice cracks. Then I turn and pad down the steps, my knees like wet sponges.

What am I going to do?

Night has swallowed up the last warmth from the sun, leaving a biting wind behind. I pull up my hood, my fingers waxy and cold. Lana's duplex is only four blocks from my apartment, but when I get there, Charlie's car is in the parking lot. I see two splotches of shadow against the glow of the living room window. Charlie and Mom are on the couch. Probably watching TV.

My insides ache with cold watching them. After a while, I've almost convinced myself to climb the stairs and put my key in the lock, crawling back—just like he said I would.

But then I see his hand through the window. It comes up slowly from the back of the couch to rest on the back of Mom's neck. My skin goes cold, a memory flaring to life: Four years ago, at a movie theater. Mom and I filed out behind a couple. The man did that, reached up and cupped his hand around the nape of her neck and my mom had shuddered. Revolted.

Men like that. Might as well put a collar on her.

My mother might as well be wearing a collar. What would she think of herself if she remembered those words in the theater? My shivering stops, and my sore shoulders go numb as I turn away. She might have forgotten her own lesson, but she raised me better.

I walk the twenty-two blocks to the library and climb the stairs to the entrance at 8:43. The air is warm and smells of old paper and wood polish. I immerse myself in the wonderful atmosphere, grateful for the heat and the familiarity.

Absurdly, the warmth makes me shiver harder. I duck behind a book display before the lady at circulation can see me. My body is racked with cold, hands stinging and teeth chattering so hard that I shove my tongue between them to keep down the noise.

I tuck into the corner by the display window, letting myself warm up. No one greets me. The associate at the desk steps into the circulation office to retrieve books and then across the lobby to restock one of the tiered book displays.

I slip quietly through the front and into the tall rows of shelves. The first closing announcement sounds overhead and instinct takes over. I move quietly through the stacks, sticking to the less frequented sections, avoiding the sound of any approaching carts. Ten minutes before closing, a guy takes a call at the browsing room desk. His head turns toward his monitor, the phone propped on his shoulder, and I cross to the restroom like I'm on autopilot.

Inside, I drink from the faucet and then quietly lock myself in the back stall. When they make the final call before the library closes, I rethink my hasty plan, unlatching the door so that it can swing open a few inches. The stall will look empty. They won't see me unless they come all the way down the line.

And they won't.

They won't have any reason to do that.

I pull my feet up on the toilet and rest my forehead on my knees. Two staff members call out to one another in the hall beyond the door. They walk through the rooms. Voices murmur.

The bathroom door swings open, and my stomach shrinks into a baseball. A walnut. Footsteps. The *swing-bang* of the first stall door. My heart is a bass drum. A frantic beat that rattles my bones.

Say something! Tell them before they find—

The footsteps retreat. The lights click out, and darkness

swallows the room, shrinks it down to the space of my breath against my knees.

I open my eyes and see nothing but blackness. I'm alone in the dark, but I am not afraid. I am relieved.

SPENCER

Friday, November 17, 6:02 a.m.

I wake up in terror, tumbling out of bed and searching for my phone. Late. I'm sure I'm late. To what, though? Practice? School? A game?

I find my phone on the nightstand behind a half-empty bottle of Gatorade. It says 6:02 a.m. It's Friday. We've got testing, so juniors aren't due in until fourth period. I've got a shift at the library, because every night this week was nothing but hockey. But I'm not due in until 8:00.

There's plenty of time. I'm fine.

My hands are shaky, and my heart is still pounding, so I say it out loud. "I'm fine."

Nice try. When's the last time I felt fine?

I strain my senses, in case a weird instinct is trying to alert me to danger, but there's nothing. No smell of smoke or strange footsteps thumping up the stairs, though that makes me think about the dirty footprints in the library. And that little girl in the vending area.

I heard a ghost in the walls.

Creepy, but I don't think I can blame the little girl for me waking up. This is my new daily routine. Some people do yoga or drink lemon water. I start my days with a crippling panic attack and cold sweat.

It wasn't always like this.

And that's just it. Why *is* it like this? In August, when school started, I was normal me. Now, it's like I spend half my time floating six feet above my own head, going through the motions of a life that feels like it belongs to someone else. Nothing has changed, and it's not depression. I took general psych last year, so I know the signs. I'm just...I don't know. Floundering?

Maybe.

It's pathetic. I'm pretty sure kids with real problems don't use words like *floundering*.

I jump in the shower before heading downstairs. I'm halfway through a bowl of smuggled Cocoa Puffs—Mom's all organic—when Allison comes in from a run. She pours a glass of water and bellies up to the table next to me, chugging.

I push my cereal over. "Don't drip in my milk."

"Good morning to you too, sweetheart."

I flip her the bird, and she sits across from me, stretching her calves. For a while, it's companionable silence, which I've missed. It's always been easy with Allison and me. Mom calls us flip sides of the same coin. Allison's serious, and I'm a clown. She runs cross-country in shorts and sneakers, I play crash-'em-up hockey in ten thousand pounds of gear. She's blond and short like our father, but my DNA made me dark and lean.

"Did you see Mom before she took off?" Allison asks.

"No. How early did she go?"

"Six twenty? She wanted me to talk to you."

"Yeah?"

"She wanted to see if we could schedule a weekend of visits together. She thought you wouldn't mind me tagging along."

"I haven't scheduled any."

"That's kind of the point. You're cutting your time really close, Spencer."

She drops the big sister hand on my bicep again, and I resist the urge to slap her away, because she's Allison. My sister. I force myself to remember my worst skateboard wreck. Allison showed up like a flag-carrying knight, scooping my wailing seven-year-old self off the ground. She was only nine, and we were probably the same weight, but she piggybacked me all the way home with blood dripping down my knees onto her new Abercrombie shorts.

She's a good sister, and whatever's wrong with me, I have no right to take it out on her. So I listen. She tells me about my bright future and encourages me to make plans. Take on leadership roles. I tune a lot of it out because she's using words like *potential* and *aptitude*.

"Zoned out yet?" she asks.

"About five minutes ago."

She sighs. "You know I hate this."

"If by hate, you mean you love it more than anything."

It's a joke with teeth, and Allison feels the bite. Her smile fades. "You're worrying Mom. Your grades are slipping."

"I'm fine. I'm passing everything."

"You're passing, but last year you were on the honor roll. You got arrested for God's sake."

"They didn't press charges." I turn away from her, my gaze dragged to the backyard beyond the window, everything in its place. Everything the way it's always been.

"You're quiet a lot," she says. "It makes me wonder if something is wrong."

"I'm fine," I say, though we both know I'm not. But what should I say? How do I explain that all the familiar things and smart choices I've ever known feel like shoes that don't fit?

"I won't get in the places they want," I try, because it's a start. "It feels pointless."

"Your grades aren't that bad."

"Come on, Allison."

"Well, you still have the ACT and the SAT. Your scores are good. Plus, Mom and Dad have plenty of strings they can pull. If you want something, you've got to try."

"And what if I don't?"

"What do you mean?"

"What if I don't want Dartmouth or UChicago or any of this?"

"You want to go to a state school?" Her brow furrows. "Are you shooting for division one hockey? Spencer, I don't think—"

"It's not about hockey," I say, pushing a hand into my hair. I don't know how to say any of this. All I know is that all this stuff—the plans and the colleges and climbing the library and feeling like a stranger in my own damn town—adds up to something.

But what?

"Mom and Dad aren't going to go for a gap year if that's what you're getting at."

"It's not." I sigh because this is a losing fight. "I'll schedule some visits. Let's drop it."

"Hey." She kicks my shoe with hers. "I know you missed early admissions, but I promise it's fine. You're smart. You'll make the right choices."

"Sure," I say, and I kick her shoe back.

I know she's trying, but she's never been further from the mark. And as for the choices I need to make? I've never been less sure of anything.

I'm at the library by 8:00, but I'm not the first one here. Gretchen's car is in the lot, and someone's up on the top floor too. It creeps me out for a second, that quick glimpse of slim shoulders and flash of a female profile stepping away from the window. I think of the person I saw in the window before. Then the little girl's cries of *Ghost!*

Of course, there's a whole second floor of staff. The director, the marketing team, and an executive assistant doing whatever it is those people do all day. It's weird to think there's more to the library than books, but there are offices and supply rooms and collection rooms where old books are repaired and new materials are processed.

Still, it's odd the way she's just standing there, mostly hidden by the curtain. Her fingers curl, pale and stark, against the bunched fabric. It's like the woman I saw the day we found the body.

Gretchen's in the front office, coat shrugged onto the chair behind her. She offers me a bleary-eyed smile and a scratchy greeting.

"You're early," she croaks.

"Couldn't sleep. No offense, but you look like crap."

"Allergies," she says, and coughs so hard I'm sure she'll have bruises.

"It sounds like tuberculosis," I say. "Or consumption."

Her red nose wrinkles. "People don't actually get consumption anymore."

"They will if they hug you today."

She laughs, and it sets her coughing again. Then she frowns at me. "Why are you here so early again?"

"Putting my immune system to the test, apparently. Mind if I get a soda before I start?"

"Knock yourself out."

In the vending area, I buy a Coke and notice half a dozen cheese and crackers wrappers sitting on one of the tables. Did the cleaning crew miss this room? A smear of black marks the floor near the cabinet door. A vague impression of toes.

Ruby was cleaning up prints like this in the cookbook section. It's bizarre. Who the hell keeps walking around the library in bare feet? There are smears on the cabinet door too, and come to think of it, that door is usually closed. It's open a couple of inches now.

I sigh as the reality sets in. The wrappers on the table aren't from the vending machine. They're from our cheese and cracker packs, the ones we give out at special story times. We keep them in that bottom cabinet, and apparently someone found the stash.

Better tell Gretchen.

First, I clean. Gretchen is feeling too shitty to deal with a mess, so I wipe up the black and scoop the wrappers into the trash.

Cleanup done, I grab my Coke and head out. Halfway out

of the room, I almost slam into someone. A strangled yelp gets caught in my throat.

It's Mallory.

She's got her shoes in her hand and her eyes are wide. How is she here? Did Gretchen let her in early? I'm open my mouth to ask when she holds up her hand. A deep flush starts at the collar of her shirt, rising quickly to the roots of her messy hair. I don't get why she's embarrassed or why she's stopping me.

And then I do.

Messy hair. Rumpled clothes. Sock-clad feet. Gretchen didn't let her in early; she's been here all night.

Why the hell would anyone stay in the library all night? To pilfer crackers and read the reference books you can't check out? It's weird.

I hesitate, glancing up the stairs. Gretchen's in the office, entirely ignorant that I'm not the only other person in here this morning. If she finds out, Mallory will probably get in pretty big trouble. Strange as this all is, I don't want her in trouble.

Mallory tucks her bottom lip between her teeth, her face still deeply scarlet. It hits me low in the gut because that's where shame always hits me. I'm embarrassed that I caught her like this, and that it took me so long to put together the pieces. Her constantly being here. The stuffed to bursting backpack. The cracker wrappers on the table.

She wasn't pulling a studying all-nighter or a stupid prank like me. She's here because she doesn't have anywhere else to be.

Mallory still isn't moving. She stands there, in the space between the stairs and the hall, her breath coming hard and fast. I want to say something so badly, but what?

"Spencer?"

We both jump at the sound of Gretchen's scratchy voice from the top floor. Mallory starts turning in a circle, her eyes panicked.

"Just a sec!" I shout up, and at the same time I reach for Mallory, my fingers grazing her sleeve. She's so different in this moment, so uncertain. I've never seen this girl so much as drop her gaze, and I hate it.

"I won't say anything," I whisper.

She lifts her chin, worry and fear jockeying for position in her eyes. I don't think she believes me, but I'm not sure she has much of a choice.

"Sorry," I holler. "Machine was stuck, but I got it."

Gretchen coughs again. Distantly. "Would you bring me one of the Earl Grey tea bags?"

"Earl Grey. Sure thing."

I pluck gently at the fabric of Mallory's sleeve, tugging her toward a quiet study room down the hall. She follows, reluctantly. The room is still dark save the meager morning light leaking through the half window.

"She won't come down here. They'll turn on the lights when they open Youth Services. You'll have to slip out then."

"Okay." Her voice is strangled like she might cry.

"Try to make your way to the front. I'll distract Gretchen if I see you."

She nods, sniffing. Then, she asks, "Why?"

I don't have an answer, but when I take a step back, my legs feel loose and rubbery. It's like coming off the ice after a long shift. I feel as likely to fall down as I am to stay up.

"Why?" she asks again, stepping closer to me. Her eyes pin me to the spot. They peel back my bullshit, and I have no idea what she'll find underneath.

"I don't know," I admit.

She swallows hard, and there's a shuddery breath. It's hers, not mine, and it makes me want to touch her again. I resist the urge and bite down all the questions I want to ask.

"You won't get caught," I say, my voice thick though I don't understand why.

She gives a sad laugh. "Maybe. My name means bad luck."

"Mallory?" I ask. When she nods to confirm, I shake my head. "Not to me it doesn't."

MALLORY

Friday, November 17, 8:36 a.m.

He leaves me shaking and crying in a dark study room. I hate myself for letting him see me like this. I sag against the back wall, my red sneakers dangling from my hand. They're scuffed and obnoxious. My jeans are dirty. I'm sure I don't smell good, and I shouldn't care about any of this because it doesn't matter. But I do care.

I don't want to be this girl, the one three days from a shower with grit under her nails and a pack of mostly used diaper wipes serving as her hygiene staple. I don't feel like that girl now, even though all of those things are true.

The sobs shake my shoulders, but I press my fist hard at my teeth, like I'm trying to punch the noise down. Maybe I am.

Eventually, that works. The tears stop, and my breathing steadies.

And I take stock of what's happened.

Spencer found me in the library. I should be grateful that it was him and not the night cleaning crew. They were a near miss my first night, arriving an hour after closing with a jangle of keys that all but launched me off the bench in Youth Services. I learned fast. They come every other night, and they don't vacuum behind the puppet theater. So far, at least.

Hiding in the theater and waiting for them to finish was the worst part of the last three days. That and trying to find things to do in the mornings. I make it a point to never be around too early.

I'm lucky no one found me before. In addition to cleaners, I've heard other staff here once or twice. Footsteps. A voice, once. Honestly, how did I ever think I wouldn't get caught?

I touch my cheeks, surprised by how cold my hands are. I sigh and close my eyes. They feel hot and gritty from crying. I grab a tissue from a box and swipe at my snotty nose. I turn to rest my forehead in the corner of the room.

And something scratches the wall.

I'm startled and step away, but after a brief pause, the noise continues.

A scratching and then a thump. I shift my gaze. It sounds like it's coming from the floor above, drifting down through the walls.

It's probably a mouse. We had them once. Mom couldn't buy traps until she got paid a week later, but by then, it was a full-scale infestation. Awful doesn't begin to describe it.

Tap, tap, scratch.

Tap, tap, scratch.

Tap, tap, scratch.

A cold shiver slides up the back of my neck. I don't remember the mice tapping, and I don't remember them sounding like this. This noise is different. Rhythmic, like a song.

Tap, tap, scratch.

Tap, tap, scratch.

Goose bumps line my arms as I step closer, trying to find the source of the noise. Is it mechanical? Wiring or pipes? My mind isn't conjuring images of bumping pipes or frayed wires, though. I'm picturing fingers tapping at drywall. When the noise stops, the picture's even clearer in my mind, a hand drawn back, a head tilted to listen, maybe.

I edge out of the room, unnerved. Out of the corner of my eye, I see a flash of blue hair under a gray knit cap. I stop dead as the girl passes right in front of me. A staff member. I've seen her at the desk in Youth Services.

I duck behind a wall, my heart slamming against my ribs, my eyes squeezed shut. There's no way she didn't see me. No chance. But when I open my eyes, I see her strolling slowly into the children's area, an open book in her hands.

That's the second time I got lucky. Am I really going to count on a third?

I need to get my head together. I stormed out of my home with a backpack and less than twenty bucks, and now I'm sleeping in the library? This isn't a real plan. It's a knee-jerk reaction. I can't do this until the baby comes. There has to be a better way.

The minute the library lights flicker on, my emotions settle. I don't know what it is that moves me calmly from the study room and up the stairs, but I'm grateful for it. I slip into the stacks and hover close to the tall bookshelves, waiting for people to trickle in.

Spencer is shelving DVDs in the room where we met. I can tell he's looking for me. He said he'd help, and I think he meant it, but I'm not taking any more chances. I press my hand to the shelf and wait. It's not the best section to be stuck in. Cookbooks, so lots of pictures of delicious looking meals for the girl who's existing on granola bars. My eyes shift to the sleek, wood floor.

A pattern of dark smudges sullies the gleaming planks. I lean back to study it. They're footprints, filthy and bare. The five toes on the print closest to me are nearly black.

Who walks around barefoot in a library and why are the prints still here? The cleaning crew mopped last night. I heard them filling the buckets and dumping them back out.

These are recent. From this morning. They lead from the carpeted area near the stairs, like someone strolled here from the browsing room with filthy bare feet.

I guess I'm not the only strange one in the library today.

A clatter at the front catches my attention. Someone gasps, and then a child begins to cry. I look up to see a toddler amid a pile of spilled books at the foot of the check-in desk. A mother is trying to help pick them up with a baby strapped to her chest. Gretchen is already coming to meet them, cooing at the toddler and crouching down to help.

In other words—she's distracted.

I move so quickly and quietly you would think I am made for sneaking and hiding in the shadows. I'm across the lobby and through the entry before anyone sees.

The door opens easily when I push it. Outside there is a mixture of cold wind and bright sun. I heave a sigh and close my eyes. The warmth from the sun is meager, but I drink it in. Even if I'm good at hiding in the dark, the light feels good on my face.

Since there's no way I'm spending my day at the library, I head to Suds and Fluff to wash my clothes. Mom and I used to come here before our apartment building put in a laundry room. The pre-Charlie era.

We used to come on Sunday mornings and it'd be busy. Today it's only me and a rumpled woman with a dog-eared romance novel and a bright pink kerchief on her head. She sits on a cracked orange chair, snapping gum and turning pages. Four loads of clothes tumble dry behind her, small socks and lots of towels. The windows of the dryer offer a glimpse at her life—a full house, at least some little ones.

I slug my backpack off on one of the long white folding tables, rubbing my finger along a yellow-brown cigarette burn in the Formica. Then I jump up to sit with my pack on the table, sorting dirty socks and emptying my pockets.

Before Charlie, Mom and I spent almost every Sunday here. The apartments hadn't put in the tiny laundry room then. She'd pick up the Sunday paper and two apple fritters from the Yo-Ho-Ho Doughnut Shop. I'd sit on a table—often this one—with my legs swinging while we passed the crossword puzzle back and forth, waiting for the dryers to finish. The one with our jeans was always the slowest.

In a million years, I wouldn't have dreamed I'd miss those slow mornings, the smell of dryer sheets, and my fingers sticky with doughnut glaze. Now they are precious, bittersweet memories of my mother before Charlie.

The bus rides added up and so did my stop at McDonald's. After checking every nook and cranny and pocket, I collect nine dollars and seventy-eight cents. One packet of soap and a ride for my clothes in the washing machine and dryer will cost me more than half of that. I buy the cheapest box of detergent the vending machine offers, and after a brief thought of saving some, decide I'll only end up with white powder all over my backpack.

I dump the whole thing in and slot in my quarters carefully. I pause before I shove them in the money feeder, awkwardly zipping my coat so I can pull my arms inside and get my shirt and bra in the load too. I peel off my socks, sliding my bare feet back into my sneakers.

The romance reader is folding her first load when I head into the bathroom with a bottle of baby shampoo from my backpack. It was all I could find when I packed, a free sample from one of my mom's pregnancy visits.

I run the freezing cold water for several minutes, hoping against hope that it will warm up. It doesn't. I check the bathroom lock and strip down. Wash my hair and everything else I can. It isn't easy—drying off with crappy paper towels, shivering with my hair dripping when I zip my coat over my still damp torso.

The woman in the kerchief is eyeing me above the pages of her novel. I can't decide if it's horror or pity in her eyes, but I give her a long hard stare that dares her to keep judging my wet hair. She returns to her book, and I move my clothes to the dryer, checking the return change slot, just in case.

The washer grumbles to life. Now there's nothing to do but wait and think. I return to my perch on the table to do both.

Money is becoming an issue, but the more I think about getting a job the less likely it seems. What address do I put down? What phone number? As a minor, I'm pretty sure they'd have to call my mom, and then...then, nothing, that's what. There's no chance Charlie will let her sign another document without his permission.

I pause, imagining Mom sitting on the couch with her dark-ringed eyes and round belly. Is she really the same woman who sat on this table with me, drinking lukewarm coffee and filling in the crossword puzzle with a green pen?

My mother isn't stupid. How did she end up with a guy like Charlie?

He was different in the beginning. When I met him, he took both of us out for ice cream and mostly listened while we talked. He was quiet and polite. When I asked, he told me he worked in computers. Back then, he wasn't working at the school. He actually took a pay cut when he moved to Whitestone, just so he could be closer to us.

Is that really why?

I straighten my shoulders, the ugly possibility dropping like a hard clap. Did he get that job for better access to us? Mom worked at a steakhouse, so no IT jobs there, but her daughter's school? I can't think of a better way to keep tabs on us.

I shudder at the disturbing thought. He got the job before

they got married. Could he have really planned that meticulously and snowed us so well?

He could if he knew what he was doing.

Charlie's older than Mom. I've never thought about it much before, but he's forty-one. Old enough that Mom can't be his first girlfriend. Maybe not even his first wife.

My heart pulses faster in my chest. Why don't I know more about his past? Does my mom? Something tells me she doesn't, but she should. The more I think on it, the more I'm sure I should have considered this earlier.

Charlie wasn't single his whole life.

There had to be someone before Mom, but who? Because that woman isn't with him anymore, and I want to know how she got away.

SPENCER

Friday, November 17, 6:35 p.m.

"Open! Open!" I hear the words and the frantic smack of Jarvey's stick on the ice, but all I see is a moose in a black jersey coming at me. He checks me so hard my mouth guard flies and my skates come out from underneath me. I hit the ice, stars bursting in my vision as I roll to the side, reaching blindly with my stick. I catch a skate, another stick. My vision clears, and I jab the puck free.

Doesn't matter. It's a sloppy mess that not even Jarvey can turn into a goal.

On the bench, he's on me before the next line moves to the face-off circle.

"What the hell is wrong with you?"

"Sorry," I say, shaking the clouds out of my vision. Sweat streaks down my face.

"You need to wake the hell up!"

"Hey!" Coach Tieger grabs Jarvey by his jersey. "Get to your side of the line."

Then he turns to me. "You need a skull check?"

Concussion check is what he means. I've got most of the symptoms, head spinning and vision blurred. If I puke, it'll be a trifecta, but I shake my head. "I'm good."

"You look like you're going to hurl," Alex says.

"Well, maybe if you'd clean your gear and keep down the stench…"

Tieger laughs and moves on, but Alex doesn't bite. His eyes are dark and narrow behind his face shield. "Big hit."

"Yeah."

"You could have dodged it."

"Thanks."

"Seriously, you'd normally dodge that. Something's up. You were weird at school too."

I smirk like I'm about to deliver a comeback, but it's Alex. In the eighth grade, when I still wanted to play Legos and didn't want anyone to know, he was the guy I could call. I can't lie to him, but I can't tell him about Mallory either. So I stay quiet.

The buzzer screams on a loss. Everyone's banging helmets and sticks all the way to the locker room, pouring out a stream of sweat and swearing that usually has me hamming it up. It's my job to make us all laugh, so we don't drop gloves and throw around blame.

Except today, I can't. Because all I can think about is Mallory.

Why doesn't she have somewhere to sleep? What happened? I can't help feeling like I should do something about it. Help her. It has to mean something that I'm the one who caught her.

Not that I meant to catch her.

Shit, does she think I'd tell someone?

The coach is dressing us down for a lackluster performance, but I'm in outer space. Or, more accurately, in Mallory space, worried she'll think I'd rat her out. Wondering how I'll find her if she doesn't come back to the library. Plotting ways I can fix all this for her.

Why the hell is this girl under my skin so bad? Because she's funny? Because she's in trouble in a way I've never seen before? Or is it because she's from a whole different world, and some broken part of me is currently pulled like a magnet to all-things-not-Fairview?

Who knows.

I roll my shoulders, feeling edgy. Alex is right. I've been like this all day, and though it's 6:40 and there's practically zero shot of her being at the library this late on a random Thursday, I have to try.

I don't even take off all my gear. I yank off my upper body pads and sling my half-empty bag in the back of the Audi. I drive twice the speed limit all the way to the library, reeking to high hell and fumbling for the pedals in my bulky leg pads.

I take the stairs to the door two at a time. Phoebe, who works at the desk, gapes the second I hit the lobby, a mix of shock and distaste on her face. I get it. I have helmet hair, I smell like a hockey bag, and I'm wearing pads that look like clown pants.

"Hey," she says, trying to be polite. "Are you here about the news?"

My body goes tight with fear. What news? Did they find Mallory? Is that why I didn't see her leave this morning?

"What news?"

She beckons me forward. Risky move on her end with the way I smell, but I take a couple of steps closer.

"We think someone's been looking for that lady." She drops her voice to a whisper. "The woman who died. Gretchen called the police because we're finding messages."

My heart squeezes. "The police? You found the person?"

"No, we found messages."

"The *Where Are You?* stuff on the bulletin board?"

"There are new ones." She brings me to the back where a cart of crisp, clean books is set aside. The yellow stickers we use for new releases are pasted on each spine.

Phoebe opens one and taps at the message scrawled on the inside cover. **Where Are You?**

"Whoa. Inside all of these?"

"*All over* them. The inside of the covers, the pages. Look at this one."

She flips through the pages of a picture book, and I can see the words over and over. They're on every page, front and back. Furthermore, the pages are filthy. The plastic covers hid it well, but gray-black stains smear most of the pages.

"I've seen that black stuff before in here."

"Ruby, too. She said she cleaned up footprints that looked like that. The police took the worst books to do testing."

"So what happens next?" I ask.

"A detective is coming in tomorrow morning to talk to Mr. Brooks about next steps."

"The police are coming again?"

"Before we open so we don't create alarm." She cocks her head. "Wait. Why are you here again?"

"Looking for a book," I lie.

I depart with a brief trip through the stacks, like Phoebe would expect. In reality, I'm not looking for a book, but I'm checking every single table and sitting area for Mallory. No dice. I take the stairs to the lower level. I last saw her down there, so you never know. I have to try.

The technology center is a bust, and Youth Services isn't looking better. That's when I hear the murmur of music and amplified voices nearby. The auditorium. My eyes flick to the poster on the wall, an advertisement for classic movie night and free pizza. If the cracker wrappers on the table are any indicator,

Mallory might be hungry enough to suffer through whatever they're showing.

I follow the noise and the smell of popcorn down the hall to the auditorium, finding it dimly lit and sparsely filled. A black and white film is playing, and Mr. Brooks is seated in the front row. Other than him, it's mostly older patrons clustered in small groups around the room.

Then I spot Mallory. She's sitting cross-legged on the floor beside the food table, a mostly empty pizza box in her lap and a plastic cup beside her.

She's not wearing what I saw her in this morning, and her hair is wavy. She seems more relaxed. Probably because she's not scared to death someone will turn her in or call the cops.

She watches the movie like she's never seen one, her eyes wide and fixed on the moving images, her idle crust nibbling stalling every few seconds when some bit of dialogue grabs her.

Someone shrieks in the hall behind me, and I turn, spotting a middle schooler who quickly realizes he's in the wrong place and doubles back up the ramp. When I look back, Mallory's not by the table. The empty box and her cup are in the space where she used to be.

"You've got to be kidding me."

Movement by the far door catches my eye. It leads directly from the auditorium to the parking lot, and I know who just used it.

I jog across the room, ignoring people swiveling in their chairs to watch me. As soon as I'm out of the auditorium, she's halfway down the alley. I lurch into a sprint, chasing her, then stop short. What the hell am I doing? I'm going to scare her.

"Mallory, wait!"

She hesitates, her run stuttering to an awkward walk. I half expect her to tell me to leave her alone, but she doesn't. She stops in the middle of the alley. No, not in the middle—she stops *there*. Beside the bricks I climbed. Beneath the window I broke. Maybe it's all coincidence and irony, but I don't think so. I think it means something. Everything in me is screaming: *Pay attention. This matters.*

"I didn't say anything," I tell her as I inch closer.

"I know," she says.

"Then why are you running?"

Her shoulders heave up and down. Up and down. I barely ran at all, but my heart thuds hard behind my collarbone, my gaze drifting between the scene of my crime and the girl who knows well enough to run when she's in trouble.

"Why are you following me?" she asks.

She's Mallory again. Direct and clear, and when she turns to me, her eyes are bright.

"Why. Are. You. Following. Me."

"That's a super valid question." One I don't know how to

answer. Direct approach is not my thing. My conversational style includes throwing comebacks and witty asides until whatever I mean is so lost in translation even I can't figure it out.

But I can't do that with her. Or maybe I don't want to. "I wanted to know why you were in the library all night."

"I didn't take anything," she says, defensive.

"I'm not worried about you pocketing a dictionary. Knitting needles, maybe."

"This isn't funny."

"I know." I step forward. "I'm sorry. I'm not good with this."

"With girls who sleep in the library?" She sounds incredulous. "Is this a common problem for you?"

"I'm not good with being serious. Or direct. All the things you're good at."

"Well, you asked a pretty serious and direct question," she says.

"Which you didn't actually answer yet."

She flushes but doesn't flinch. She also doesn't reply.

"I don't know how to say this without sounding creepy," I say. "I've been thinking about you. Honestly, I can't get you out of my head, and I want to help. Tell me what's going on."

"I can't."

"Can't or won't?"

"I hate that question," she says. "When is there ever a difference?"

"There's always a difference," I say. "Two entire letters, for starters."

"I'm here because I don't have anywhere else to go." She crosses her arms over her chest.

I nod like I understand, but I don't. I try to imagine a scenario—*any* scenario—that would leave me stuck sleeping in a library on a random weeknight.

There isn't one. If my parents are out of town, they march me over to my grandparents like I'm eight years old. If I'm pissed or annoyed or drunk or whatever other stupid thing—I text them and crash with Alex or Isaac. Hell, if I'm desperate, there's Jarvey or even Ava next door.

"Nowhere at all?" I ask as gently as I can. "What about your..."

"Parents?" she asks, tilting her head, her voice lilting like her answer is an indulgence. "It's *parent* for me, and it's complicated. I don't want to talk about it."

"Actually, I meant friends."

"Yes, I have them, but it's not an option. Let's not talk about this, okay?"

"Why not?"

"Why should we?" she asks, her voice shaking a little. "What does *any* of this have to do with you?"

"It doesn't. I'm sorry. I know I'm being nosy, I just... What can I do?"

Her anger dissipates, leaving confusion behind. "Why do you want to help me so badly?"

I feel the *why* is written in neon lights across my forehead. I obviously like her, but is that really all this is? It's stupid to admit right now, regardless. There are clearly a million other things in her life that are obviously a bigger fish to fry than some dude with a thing for her.

"I can't explain it. But is it so awful that I want to help?"

"You are helping. You agreed to get the staff password, which I need."

"I'm not talking about the internet. The internet is everywhere."

"Not if you aren't a paying customer," she says. "I don't have a laptop now."

I wave that off. "If it's broken, I have a friend who could check it out."

"It's not that. It wasn't mine. It's my friend's computer."

"I'll bring you one," I say.

She laughs. "Oh. Sure. You'll *bring* me a laptop. Drop it off with a car, okay? I prefer something red. Convertible."

"You're funny," I say, smiling. "Seriously, though, my dad's a business finance consultant. He gets free laptops as a thank-you all the time. We have loads of them."

She blinks at me. "I can't take a laptop from you."

"Then you're *really* not going to like my next offer." I take a breath. "I don't think you should stay here."

"Well, it was either here or there," she says, gesturing to a bench at the edge of the parking lot.

I open my mouth, and all manner of barely contemplated craziness pours out. "You should stay with me. You can use the pool house and the laptop and our internet, and then there aren't any problems with the connection expiring or whatever."

"I'm sorry. Use your what?"

"Pool house," I say. "I mean, sort of. It's not like a full-fledged apartment or anything, just a little lounge area for changing and storage and a bathroom. But the internet works out there, and we closed the pool in September, so no one's ever in it. There's a TV and a couch. A foosball table."

"A foosball table." She laughs, clearly incredulous. "Thank God."

I flinch. It was a stupid thing to say. "I didn't mean to list amenities."

"How did you mean it? Poor little homeless girl, I guess I'll play the hero and sweep her off the streets and into my pool house. I'm not a charity case, Spencer."

"I know that."

"Do you?"

"I do. But it doesn't mean I want to sit here and do nothing about your situation."

She throws up her hands, and I can see that she's close to

crying. "It's not your problem! And for the record, I'm not some needy, crazy girl who ran away. I had compelling reasons."

"I believe you."

She sighs then, shoulders drooping. "Some days I don't."

She goes quiet then, and I want to reach for her. I want to touch her cheek, where it's going pink again. But I definitely shouldn't do that.

She inhales sharply and it's clear she's reached some kind of decision.

"I'm sorry I'm not being receptive or grateful. It's a nice offer. But I can't walk off with you into Mansion Land. We're practically strangers."

"Where will you go? Because you can't stay here tonight. They're bringing cops in the morning."

"Cops? Wh—" She drops off abruptly, gaze moving above my head like something's caught her eye.

She frowns. "There's someone up there. Watching us."

"What?"

She bumps her chin up and takes a step back. "In the window by the curtain."

The hair on the back of my neck prickles. There's a woman again, inside the window I broke. It's quick, an unmistakable but blurry impression of long hair and a pale face—and then she's gone. I think of tangled hair on the library floor. An arm twisted behind a back.

Stop.

There are offices up there. Including Mr. Brooks'. It could be his assistant.

I scan the upper floor hoping to confirm some activity. Lights and computers. People hard at work on a Tuesday night.

"Did you see it?" Mallory asks softly.

"Yeah."

I don't excuse it with second floor offices or staff working late. The windows paint a different story. None of the second-floor lights are on. Not even the office where the woman was standing. It was dark the entire time.

MALLORY

Saturday, November 18, 7:02 a.m.

I wake to the murmur of conversation, and for a minute, I flail anxiously. Where am I? Memories whirl back. Pizza at the library. Spencer's ridiculous offer. The woman at the window. I open my eyes to Lana's cracked bedroom ceiling and remember my long, cold walk to her house last night.

I'm sweaty and stiff, tangled in Lana's ancient *My Little Pony* sleeping bag in the narrow space between her wall and the door. My mouth is tacky and sour, and the crick in my neck promises to be with me all day, but I am so grateful. She didn't even ask me questions when I tapped on her window. She snuck me in, locked her door, and pressed her finger to her lips so I wouldn't talk.

We traded notes back and forth in her diary instead.

Lana: I've been so worried.

Me: I'm okay.

Lana: Did you go home? Did he do something to you?

Me: No. But I have a plan. I think I know where to go.

Lana: Where???

I didn't tell her and she didn't press, which is good because I was flat-out lying. After a while, she touched my hand and it was all I could do not to cry. She tucked the diary under a picture of her dad, and we fell asleep.

Now, when I sit up in the narrow space between her wall and bed, Lana isn't there. I rub my eyes with the heel of my hand and listen, catching bits of her mother's voice in the hall.

"...broken! Do you think we have the money to pay for another?"

"No, Mama. I'm sorry."

"Sorry won't pay for a new laptop."

"I know that. I'm sorry. I am."

"I know you're sorry, *mija*," her mother says, voice softer, "but we can't afford carelessness right now."

More apologies and my stomach twists. She wasn't careless, and she didn't cause this. I was using her laptop when it broke. She's in trouble because of me, and if her mom finds out she snuck me in here...

I move fast, rolling the sleeping bag tight and staying low on the side of her bed. I push it under the dresser where we found it and slip the second pillow she offered back under hers. Then I drag my backpack out and pull out four dollars and twenty-five cents. It's all I have left.

I place it on her bed and consider leaving a note promising her more, but how would I get it? Even getting through this week is impossible. But I have to try to fix the damage I've done.

It's the worst kind of November weather, a cold and rainy day that clings to my coat and dampens my jeans by the time I reach the library.

I lurch when the doors are locked, then remember it's too early. Worse still, there's a sign.

Thank you for your patience! Due to a last-minute all staff meeting, we'll be opening at ten today.

The police. Spencer warned me, so I should have remembered.

I have too much time and no money. Sitting on the steps to wait feels conspicuous, so I descend to the sidewalk. I look up, wondering why the police came today. I saw someone upstairs in the window last night. Maybe they were watching from the window the day the woman died too. Maybe they know something that could help.

Not that it's a crime to be solved. I heard a few staff members talking the other day. They mostly whispered, but I picked out the word *heroin* more than once, along with *overdose*. It happens. I guess I could see it happening here.

With the rain picking up, I tug on my hood and retrace my steps down the library stairs. Not sure where else to go, I walk the long blocks back to the women's shelter. Ruth answers the bell with a smile like she's been expecting me.

She doesn't ask me any questions before inviting me in. She takes me to the kitchen and makes me hot cocoa and an egg and cheese English muffin with a little cluster of grapes on the side. I don't talk until I've eaten every bite, even the little not-quite-ripe grape that bursts in my mouth, a sour shock on my tongue.

"I'm glad you came by," she says.

I make a noise between a cough and a laugh. "You're glad?"

"I'm hoping it means you're thinking of talking to my friend at Mulberry Manor."

Footsteps thunder overhead. The squeal of a child laughing. The bell jangles above the front door, but none of that racket distracts Ruth from waiting for my answer.

"I'm not ready for that," I say, but I really mean I'm not ready for Charlie to find out about that. If I'm at Mulberry Manor, I won't be there to protect my mom if he loses his mind when that call comes in.

"I thought about going back home," I admit.

"And?"

"And he's still there."

Ruth takes my plate to the sink, and I sit back. I was so cold and miserable I followed her in without paying much attention to the kitchen at all. Now I notice the table I'm at is one of three. There are baskets with coloring sheets and assorted crayons. Little-kid drawings plaster the front and sides of the enormous fridge.

"I know it might be difficult to put into words, but can you tell me about the incident that prompted you to leave without your mother? Was there a fight?"

"There was an escape attempt." I mean it to be funny, but it only sounds sad. "Mom hesitated, and Charlie came home."

"Did he become threatening? Violent?"

"He's not like that," I say. "I tried to explain it before. He has to be in charge. Not of normal stuff, of everything. He manipulates things, convinces my mom she's weak and stupid. And he tells her I'm every bad thing you can imagine."

"Did the words become too much that day?"

I shake my head. "No. We had both decided to go, but Mom got scared. I stuck to my guns and left. I sort of thought she'd come, too, but she was getting sick when it all happened."

Off her shocked expression, I shrug. "She's still got morning sickness. Which is really all-the-time sickness. Anyway, while she was out of the room, he told me to go but said I'd come crawling back. He said he wouldn't be so nice when I did."

Her eyebrows lift. "He believes his behavior is nice?"

"He's a real hero in his own mind. Providing *such* a great life for us."

There's concern on her face I haven't seen before. "Mallory, how long has your mother been with Charlie?"

"They've been married about three years."

"Did you know him before that?"

"No. When I met him, he was nice. Quiet. It started with little stuff. He was picky about curfew. One minute over was as bad as not coming home at all. He got jealous with my mom over nonsense. Baggers at the grocery store. Her doctor. When she got pregnant, it got worse."

"But you don't know anything of his past. Former relationships?"

I think back to my string of thoughts in Suds and Fluff. "I don't. I wondered about that the other day. But he works for the school, so it can't be bad. They do background checks."

She spreads her hands. "It's beyond my area, but I imagine a public school would run a fairly thorough background search."

She doesn't say anything else, but her mouth tenses. She probably doesn't want to tell me that a background check can miss things.

"Do you think something could slip through?" I ask.

"I think it's understandable that you're concerned," she says. "It could be there is something there, or it could just be a difficult relationship."

"Some days I feel like I'm crazy for being so afraid of him. It's a feeling, not cold hard facts and evidence."

She reaches across the table, touching my arm with a severe expression. "I've seen some terrible things walk through this door, Mallory. For a while, I thought I could tell, but I've learned

I don't know *anything*. I never know. Sometimes the ones I'd guess to be killers can head to counseling or rehab and turn out all right. Sometimes the ones I want to give the benefit of the doubt trade in their fists for knives or guns. The only thing I know for sure is that it is *never* stupid to trust your gut. That's your instinct."

"My instinct told me to run away from my mother," I say.

"No. Your instinct told you that you were not safe."

I arrive at the library a little before noon and scan the whole place before I get started. First, I look for the police, and then for Spencer. There's no sign of either. Logic tells me Spencer will probably have hockey practice or a game. Logic also tells me it's a relief that he isn't here to distract me, but my heart disagrees.

I set up at my regular desk in the browsing room with a guest pass. On a hunch, I check the hidden compartment and find a small white envelope with two words written across the front: *Knitting Tips*.

Inside is a note card with eight consonants, three numbers, and a punctuation symbol. I grin, my face going warm all over. Spencer got me the staff password. Beneath it, in much smaller writing, there's another number, an area code and seven digits. I don't need a name to know it's his phone number.

My heart clamors again.

Call him.

I think about it. I could do it. Run ten blocks east, power up my phone and call the guy. And then Charlie will have one more number in his arsenal of information. Who knows what he'll do with it. Would Charlie call him? Search for details attached to Spencer's number?

Calling Spencer is way too dangerous.

My priorities are crystal clear. First, school. Second, researching my creepy stepfather. Third, trying to figure out a better sleeping arrangement.

I have no idea where Spencer is on the priority list, but he's certainly not hitting a top slot. I put my headphones on for focus and set a timer so I remember to move to a computer downstairs in two hours. My school account is quiet, but I leave responses for every single message and leave comments on the lecture videos. One test later, my timer rings. Two hours down. Nine to go.

I browse the stacks until 3:00, and then I can't ignore my growling stomach any longer. Ruth sent me with a plastic bag filled with protein bars and little boxes of raisins, so I nibble on one of those and head outside of the library for a long stroll. I wander the aisles of Walmart. Stop briefly in a Starbucks, like I'm waiting for a friend. Then I walk the blocks aimlessly, counting the minutes until I can safely go back inside.

The day staff leaves at 5:00, and the part-timers who work nights come in around the same time. It's a hassle, but a hassle is fine if it means not alerting the staff to the fact that I'm a girl with nowhere else to go. The less they can compare notes, the better.

I return, sure that I'll find Spencer. But I'm wrong. So I spend my last two hours in Youth Services with a study guide and head to the downstairs bathroom after my 8:30 timer.

I use the same trick down here, staying in the back stall, door cracked and my feet perched on the toilet. It feels like I'm there forever until the lights go out, and then there's nothing. No voices. No staff checking the bathrooms.

Surely they have to check the bathrooms, right? But they don't. I wait long minutes, with the silence pressing hard on my ears.

Maybe they're still down here. They could have an after-hours meeting or whatever. I can't sit in here forever. I have to check.

The sound of my own blood rushing behind my ears is threatening to drive me over the edge, so I lower my feet to the floor and stand. I have to see for myself. Every movement *screams*, the scrape of my shoes against the tile, the soft clunk of the stall lock. Finally, I reach the outside bathroom door.

I push it open a crack. The hall is mostly dark, with a faint glow in the distance. I wait one breath.

And another.

The water fountain hums across from me, and the soft whir of the heater drifts in from unseen vents. Otherwise, the library is utterly silent, but it isn't dark. Not entirely. That glow wasn't a trick of my eyes from the bathroom. There's a light on.

I slip out of the bathroom and peek around the corner, spotting the glass-walled vending area, still brightly lit. And still occupied. I catch a glimpse of someone bent over the table before I pull into the shadows, pressing my back to the wall.

My heart pounds so hard I feel it in the tips of my fingers. Long minutes pass, but there's nothing. No noise. No talking. Is it a librarian hanging out after hours?

My imagination?

I look slowly around the corner again and spot the back of a dark head on top of shoulders. I'm ready to run when I recognize him.

Spencer. My shoulders slump with a sigh, but then tense almost as fast.

Why is he still here?

I walk in to find him at the table with an open can of Coke and a sleek phone in his hand. He doesn't acknowledge me, but I'm 100 percent sure he heard me.

"What are you doing here?" I ask.

"Waiting around to see if you'd show. I lost track of you around closing."

"You were watching me? I didn't even know you were here."

"I wasn't working, so I was trying to keep a low profile. I was hoping you'd call."

"I couldn't. But I wanted to," I admit, the words out before I can fully consider them.

Surprise softens his features. "Good. Because honestly, I've been wondering if this is a good idea, me imposing on your space."

"It's a public library. I don't own the space."

"But I'm here *because* you're in the space. So the question remains."

"What question?"

"Do you want me to go? Because I'm thinking my optimism that you want my company is probably verging on arrogance."

I feel fluttery, like I'm balancing between panic and giddiness. Which is about right. "You think you're optimistic and arrogant?"

"In this case yes." He meets my eyes. "I like you, Mallory. If you want to use the word *crush*, I'm pretty sure it would apply, but it would also make me feel like I'm twelve years old."

I laugh, my heart speeding up again. This time it isn't fear. Spencer is manageably cute, but his crush confession changes the playing field.

"How did no one catch you?"

"Clearly we're both ninjas. Seriously, are you comfortable with me being here?"

"Yes," I say softly, but when his face lights up, I add, "But you could get in trouble."

"Eh, it's a calculated risk. I actually have an important purpose for being here."

"What's that?"

"You said you didn't know me." He reaches for a messenger bag I hadn't spotted. Pulls open a heavy canvas flap and tugs out two thick photo albums. "Here you go."

I sink into a plastic chair across from him. "What is this?"

"Seventeen years of my mother getting her craft on."

I run my hand over the leather cover. It's thick and heavy. Obviously expensive and absolutely nothing like the cheap pastel baby book my mother has for me.

I open the cover and bite back a grin at the soulful-eyed baby with a mass of dark curls nestled in some sort of basket.

"Why are you in a basket?"

He waves his hands. "Oh, just wait. There are pumpkins and giant pillows. Our family photographer was obsessed with putting me in the weirdest crap you can imagine. There's one of me in overalls hanging from a clothesline."

My fingers glide under the gold scrolling letters of his name. Spencer James Keller. He lets me peruse without comment. It feels a little like spying, flipping through the pages of a life that isn't mine. One-year-old Spencer coated in frosting from his hair to his belly, his grin not so different than the one he wears now. Toddler Spencer in an oversized hockey jersey, tiny ice skates laced onto his feet. The years pass, and I watch him grow as the backdrops change. Enormous Christmas trees and a velvety backyard. Beaches, mountains, and clustered buildings and brick streets that have to be somewhere in Europe.

I tap a finger on a picture in a pumpkin patch. Spencer with a girl who's been in lots of the pictures. She's close to his age, but blond with pale eyes.

"Who's this?"

"My sister. Allison."

I flip another page and see a family photo—the first one had been in full ski gear, so it was hard to see. But now I spot his mother's pale hair and blue eyes. Allison has her coloring. His father's hair is darker, but not like Spencer's. And none of them have his bronze skin.

"You don't resemble them much."

"I'm adopted. Sadly, the blond and blue-eyed beauty wand passed me by."

"Please. Like you're hurting in the beauty department."

"A compliment? Wow, that's a surprise."

I eye him. "Don't try to pretend you don't know this."

He grins. "You are unlike any girl I've ever met."

I feel electrified when he gazes at me with a hint of a smile. It's not a good idea to get carried away with this guy, so I return my attention to the photo books. The second one becomes more sports-focused as he grows older. His awkward phase in junior high didn't last long, though there's a solid year of smiles with braces that explain his perfect teeth.

There are several photos featuring hockey equipment, jerseys, rinks, and adorably mussed hair. I watch him turn into the Spencer I know in these pictures, shoulders widening, cheekbones cutting through his boyish face, his long-lashed eyes turning from cute to mesmerizing in the picture where he's holding up his first set of car keys.

"Ah, my license," he says.

"You look thrilled. Did they buy you a car?"

"No, but we have enough of them. Mostly, I was thrilled I passed. Took me three tries."

"Parallel parking?" I guess.

"Hit a cone every time."

I flip through the last pages, noticing him strapped into ropes and clinging to the side of a cliff. It's a shade of orange I've never believed rocks could be, the kind of orange seen on TV from the southwest, contrasting so sharply against the blue sky it seems impossible.

"Where is this?" I ask.

"Moab, Utah. Close to Arches National Park. That's my third climb. I went eighty feet."

"Ice hockey and rock climbing," I say softly, closing the book and pushing them back. "Well, now I know your hobbies. And I know that you had a serious affinity for Batman Underoos when you were in kindergarten."

He wags a finger at me. "Batman is the shit. I still wear those sometimes, you know."

I laugh, and he takes the books, stacking them in his bag.

"Now do you know me?"

"I know more," I say softly. "Thank you."

"You're welcome."

I lean back. "I don't mean to stereotype, but you seem more sporty than bookish. How did you end up here?"

"Yeah, funny thing. I don't actually *work* at the library in the traditional sense."

Before the question can make it to my lips, he goes on.

"I'm here on mandatory community service. A nice-guy version of probation."

"You're on probation?"

"No, but close enough."

"What did you do?"

He swallows hard. "I climbed the library. Not my best life

choice, but it might have been no big deal if I hadn't broken a window on my way up."

"Wait…you climbed the library. Like, the building?"

"Yeah."

"On the outside?"

He palms the back of his neck. "Hearing you say it out loud, it does sound strange."

"Do you often climb buildings?"

"Nope. Usually I climb at a gym, because I'm in Ohio. If I'm somewhere with mountains, outside is way better. I started in Colorado when I was thirteen. We went on a late skiing trip, but it was a weird, early spring. The snow was crap. Dad went to the bar, Mom went shopping, and Allison and I took a rock climbing class. It didn't stick with Allison, but I loved it. I've climbed on every trip I could since. Utah, California, Switzerland."

"You've been to so many places."

"Only the touristy parts," he says with a shrug.

"That must be tough." I only mean to tease, but there's a sharpness to my voice.

"Okay, that was a jerk thing to say. I *have* been to a lot of places. I just feel like I haven't seen them, you know?"

I don't know because I've never left Ohio. But I nod, and he goes on.

"Besides, no matter where I go, I always end up back here."

"Oh, sure. How can you bear it with the pool house and all?" I smile, trying to get him to laugh, and failing.

"I'm the luckiest guy around," he says, but he forces out the words like they hurt. "Seriously, I have it way too easy—the world on a proverbial silver platter."

"You don't want it," I say, wonder filling my voice.

"I don't think it matters," he whispers, and then he shakes his head. "But whatever. I'm being an asshole. I have a good life. A nice family. These are *not* real problems."

His smile is wide, but there's nothing but hurt behind it, so much pain that my chest constricts with my next breath.

"You should be able to make choices about your life," I say.

"Don't." He says it so softly that I freeze, feeling I've broken some unspoken rule. "Don't feel sorry for me. Please."

He reaches for me slowly, and I'm powerless. Hypnotized by the graze of his fingers against the side of my thumb.

My chipped nails make me feel cheap and ragged. But then he runs two fingers over the back of my hand, and I don't feel anything but his touch. It's nice. More than nice, if I'm honest.

"I'm sorry," he says. "I did not mean to veer into full-bore narcissist territory."

"Don't be sorry," I whisper.

His finger is still moving against mine, sliding to the crease between my thumb and forefinger. I can't remember any time I've been aware of such a mundane part of my body.

My breath catches when he looks at me.

"So will you talk to me now?" he asks. "Even if I can't help, I can listen."

I don't have to think about my answer this time. I trust him enough to tell him at least some of the truth.

So I do.

SPENCER

Saturday, November 18, 10:28 p.m.

She pulls her hand away from mine before she starts. It's like she's giving an oral test, hands clasped in front of her as she unfolds the facts in careful, measured sentences.

She talks for twenty minutes, and I don't interrupt. It's not because I'm such a polite conversationalist either. It's because I'm freaked. What the hell do you say when someone tells you their stepfather tracks your calls? Threatens your mother? Tells you to leave? It's the kind of story you hear about on talk shows, but it isn't a story. It's her life.

Mallory doesn't deliver the details breathlessly, amping up the drama. She lays out the facts in simple, unemotional succession.

"So you left," I say when she's finished. "You haven't been home since."

"Twice. My mom had to sign papers for the school to unenroll me."

"I thought he worked at your school."

"We had to go to the district office. Thank God."

"When was the second time?"

"I visited her. I didn't want her to worry."

I drop my gaze, afraid to ask but unable to hold the question in. "Why didn't she come with you?"

"It's hard to explain. She's been really sick with this pregnancy."

"What about him? Can't you call someone? Some kind of..." I don't really know what word to use, but there has to be a professional or expert for this situation.

"They can't do anything unless he breaks a law. It's messed up."

"Even if you prove you're in danger?"

"I've thought of that. I'm going to research Charlie. Maybe if I can prove he's hurt someone before..."

"Has he?"

She sighs. "I have no idea. And if he hasn't, then I'm right back to square one. Waiting for the baby to come so my mom hopefully comes back to her senses."

"I'm hardly a pregnancy expert, but doesn't that take a while?"

"She's due New Year's Eve."

"You're going to live in the library until after Christmas?"

Her face crumples in a way that tells me she's already considered the gaps of logic in this plan, and doesn't have a better solution. The crap of it is, I don't either. What could I possibly do about her situation? I've never even *heard* of something like this in real life.

She makes a noise somewhere between a sniff and a sad laugh. "I know. It's stupid."

"Not stupid," I say, and I leave it at that.

I reach across the table again, and this time our eyes are locked when I graze her hand, pushing the pads of my fingers against hers. I go slow, giving her every chance to back away because I don't know if this is a good thing to do. Is anything good when a person's world is falling to pieces?

Her fingers flex against mine, and she bites her bottom lip as our palms come together. All the words floating around in my head feel small and insignificant, but this doesn't. This feels right. Important even.

Listen to me. When did I turn into a guy like this?

Abruptly, her jaw tenses, and our connection breaks. "Spencer—"

Scrape. Thump.

It's above us and faint, but Mallory jerks, and I stroke her thumb again. "It's okay. Probably just old building—"

Thump, thump.

"Cleaning crew?" She sounds doubtful.

"Not their night. The custodian and volunteer shifts are on the same calendar."

Another scuffle upstairs cuts me off. Now my pulse jumps.

I want to say it's nothing, but I'm not as convinced now. The police were here this morning and suspected the writing in the books was another prank, part of a copycat pattern. But what if they're wrong? Could they have missed someone hiding in here?

More vague noises drift down from a floor above us. I look up. The sound is distant but internal. Not a car door slamming or other disturbance outside. Not somebody jimmying open a window.

Whatever this is, it's already inside.

"It's the building," I say.

Something mechanical could do this, right? This is an old building with old pipes and wires—old *everything*. One of those things has to be making this noise.

Another scuffle, softer than the first. And then a loud one. It isn't reassuring. There's no rhythm to this sound. No *click-click-click* of a stuck fan or *gurgle-bang* of a straining pipe. This is *random*—less like a machine and more like something alive.

When our gazes meet, I can tell Mallory's thinking the same thing. She disentangles her hand from mine.

"I don't think that's the building," she whispers.

I nod, and we stand up slowly. The single fluorescent light in the vending machine room feels like a spotlight. Nothing but darkness lies beyond. Anyone on the lower level—even on the stairs—could see us. I eye the light switch, and Mallory slowly eases her way around her chair, careful not to bump it.

I move too, feeling like eyes are following me from the darkness beyond the glass. My heavy boots make tiptoeing all but impossible, but there's no noise now, so I do my best, inching to the switch. I flick it off, and we're swallowed in darkness.

I feel, rather than hear, Mallory approach. Her arm brushes mine, and she stays close.

I take her hand again, and her palm is as sweaty as mine.

We wait one minute, then another, my ears straining to pick up any remnants of sound. There's a prickle at the back of my neck, but the noises I pick out of the quiet are nothing out of the ordinary. The heater fan whirring softly, the plink of water dripping from a faucet, the shuddery rhythm of my own breath. But here and there I think there's something else.

We leave the alcove, removing the barrier of the glass walls. Less muffling for my ears to contend with. Mallory's hand goes stiff in mine, her arm taut with resistance. She follows in the end, pressing close to my side.

The sound isn't as faint here. It's coming from the floor above us, in the hallway if I had to guess. I press myself to the wall and run schematics of the building through my head. Scanning my memory for a way out. I tilt my head and the noises start again. Soft thumps move up the hallway and back. Up and back.

Footsteps.

Someone is pacing.

I think of the footprints Ruby cleaned. Barefooted prints. Mallory was wearing socks when I found her, and there's nothing black or sooty on her. Those prints belonged to someone else.

But the police searched every nook and every cranny. They even checked the tapes for the entrance camera for any barefoot patrons that day. So what the hell is this?

"What are they doing?" Mallory asks, voice barely a breath, her gaze fixed on the ceiling, where the footsteps are coming from.

I don't know, so I shake my head, listening to the footsteps. Up and back. Up and back.

The police should have found this person. They *would* have found them, wouldn't they? Unless that little girl was right, and there wasn't a live person to catch.

I heard a ghost in the walls!

My throat tightens as I think of the woman stretched out between the bookshelves. The tangle of long blond hair and pale arm bent in a sickening angle. I don't believe in ghosts.

Do I?

The footsteps pause suddenly and my heart stutters. A new noise, soft and high, drifts down from the second story, sending all my hair on end.

"Do you hear that?" Mallory asks.

I incline my head, not because I don't hear it, but because I wish I didn't. Dread pours like lead into my legs and arms as the sound grows louder. A rhythm that lifts and drops like laughter.

Or sobbing.

Someone is sobbing.

Time to go. We can't be in here with this...with whoever or whatever this is. I need to get us out of here. Right now.

"Spencer." Mallory's voice is a harsh whisper at my shoulder.

I squeeze her hand in response, easing up the first step. She tries to pull her hand free, but I hold it fast and lean down until our heads bump.

"No," she whispers. "They'll catch me."

"We can't get out down here," I reason softly. "The exits all lead up the stairs. I'm ninety-nine percent sure this person is on the second floor. We can get out, but we need to *go*."

"We can hide," she says. "That person isn't here for me. It has nothing to do with me."

Pattering thumps move across the floor above. I jump like an eight-year-old caught out of bed at a sleepover, my eyes tracking the dark ceiling blindly to follow the now unmistakable rush of footsteps. Down the stairs. They're closer now—moving into one of the rooms directly above.

The browsing room.

The crying continues, so much louder that I have to resist covering my ears. They're running now, every step sending a chill up my spine. Wood scrapes and something bangs. Like a door slamming shut.

My joints tense, ready for a sprint. But there is silence.

No voices. No footsteps. Nothing.

I tell myself to breathe in. Force myself to let it back out. I come to my senses to find that Mallory and I have tucked in to each other instinctively. We're mashed together, her hands twisted in the side of my shirt and my fingers too tight on one of her wrists. Neither of us speaks.

After a minute, an hour—hell, I have no idea—Mallory jerks me hard from the stairs. She's not shaking now. There isn't an ounce of fear in the steady pull of her slow steps. This is the Mallory who looks me in the eye and says what she means. I'm still a wreck, but she's on a mission, and I'm all too happy to follow the leader.

She moves slowly, deliberately along the back wall. I hear the soft hiss of her hands dragging along the wall. Then the barely there squeak of a door opening.

She leads us into a restroom. There's a pearly glow from the streetlight beyond the small window. Enough to let me see the curves of her face and the outline of three stalls. That light, or maybe the distance from the noise, brings me back to my senses, shaking the ghost stories loose.

I need to get a grip long enough to figure out what is going on. Who would be in here? An upset employee? Possibly. Maybe someone in administration is working late and having some kind of library crisis.

I check my watch.

At 11:14 p.m.?

Okay, it's not *that* likely. But despite my sweaty hands and racing pulse, I know the chances aren't high that a murderer would sneak in after hours for a good cry.

"I don't like this," I whisper. "We wouldn't hear if they came down here."

"Yes, we would. I could hear people going up and down the stairs."

"But those people weren't trying to be sneaky."

"I thought that through. Whoever this is, they aren't trying to sneak either."

"I still don't like it." But I can't argue with it because she's right. And heaven knows the police are less than three minutes away if we're wrong.

"I can't get caught, okay?"

The desperation in her voice convinces me. I press my back against the cold porcelain of the sink and eye the window in the back corner. Too small to be of any use. Mallory joins me at the sink, shoulder against my arm.

"Don't you need to get home?"

"Alex is covering for me. I told my parents I was staying with him."

"And what did you tell him?" she asks.

"Not much. He's cool, though." Actually, I told him I was going to see a girl. I've covered for Alex plenty since he's been dating Ava, so I knew he wouldn't push for details.

"That woman who died in the library," she says. "Do you think whoever was in here tonight was looking for her?"

"Maybe. It's a screwed-up way of trying to find her. How would they *not* know?"

"Easily. This probably showed on only one newscast. Unless you're from Fairview, it'd be easy to miss."

I wince. "My mom told me that she wasn't from around here." The words taste bitter coming out. "The woman who overdosed. Like that was supposed to be a comfort."

Mallory sighs. "She could have been from anywhere. No one plans to turn out like that. It's just bad luck."

I take Mallory's hand because it's easier than telling her I think she's right. It's easier than explaining I'm afraid I'll always see that woman's body when I close my eyes. And it's definitely easier than admitting I'm scared there's nothing else to me—that I'm a nobody rich kid with luck he doesn't deserve.

MALLORY

Sunday, November 19, 6:39 a.m.

We creep up the stairs and through the still-dark library. The circulation team arrives by 8:00, so we agreed leaving at least an hour earlier would be safest. I'm glad we figured it out early, because I fell asleep.

I had zero intention of it when we sat down, side by side across from the sinks. For a while, we were tense and wary, on high alert for footsteps or voices. It's not like the fear vanished. I don't think that's how fear works.

As the minutes stretched into hours, I think we got used to the fear.

That's what happened to me at least. Boredom crept over the edges of my terror until I found myself in a blurry haze, nudging Spencer's shoulder and whispering how I wished we'd grabbed a book or something.

He pulled up his phone, scrolling through various, mostly

unfamiliar, options until he settled on something similar to sudoku. It was a game I could picture a middle-aged woman doing in waiting rooms.

When I told him as much, he shrugged and said maybe he *was* a middle-aged woman in another life. I laughed out loud. In that second, I forgot all about the pacing and the crying and the footsteps we heard. My world shrunk into the space in that bathroom, the solid heat of his shoulder against mine, and the comfort of his soft voice in the darkness.

My eyes grew heavy and my legs went cold on the tile floor. Then I don't remember anything until he woke me up, hand on my shoulder and the barest gray promise of sunrise lighting the window.

"Are you ready?" Spencer asks me now at the bathroom door. He's quiet, but not whispering. His voice is the only sound I hear. The footsteps and crying—it all feels like a moment we dreamed up in the night.

His silence reminds me I haven't answered.

"I'm ready."

We move quietly through the downstairs and past the eating area, where Spencer collects his bag, and then we pad softly up the stairs, pausing at the main floor. The stairs keep climbing to our left, and I shiver, thinking of what we heard up there last night.

It's still dark in the library, but there's a different quality to it—the promise of morning pushing danger to the back of my mind. Spencer is still cautious, scanning the stairwell.

His breath goes tight, and I follow his gaze up the stairs. Along the stairwell wall, I see it, a message scrawled in black ink.

Where Are You?

My stomach bottoms out, and my face goes cold. "We have to tell someone."

"We can't. Not without them knowing we're here. We need to be very careful of the cameras when we head out."

"There are cameras?"

"At the entrances."

We walk along the back wall, past the tall shelves toward the red glow of an exit sign. Spencer unlocks the door and cracks it open. The streetlights and waning stars leave the world shockingly bright compared to the darkness of the library.

"The camera's up on our left," he says softly. "It's aimed at the parking lot and the back dock. There's another aiming for the opposite corner. We're going to go straight out, until we hit the fence, and then make a sharp left behind the dumpster alcove. See that brick wall?"

I do, and I see the dumpsters in front of it. My instinct is to stay to the wall, but I do exactly what he says, and he follows right behind me. We huddle between the fence and wall, inching our way to the alley. He tugs me right, away from Main Street, but also away from the cameras.

I'm surprised when Spencer cuts east a couple blocks later, doubling back toward Main Street. "Wait, where are you going?"

"To my place."

"I can't—"

"I'll get you set up in the pool house. Or my room. At least for today. My dad's in Sweden this week, and my mother and Allison leave by seven. No one will be home."

"I told you I can't go to your house."

He stops and turns, dark circles under his eyes proving I'm the only one who slept.

"After the scrapbook and everything?" he asks, grinning, but when his smile fades, his expression is almost tender. "We're not strangers anymore, Mallory."

He's right, but it doesn't explain what we are now.

I follow him anyway because I'm not sure what else to do. Traffic is already starting to build on Main Street, sleek European cars purring to a stop at the row of traffic lights. Spencer leads us across the street, to the part of Fairview I never visit.

Proud stone and brick houses perch in well-spaced rows, with green lawns stretching out before them like velvet skirts. The trees are bare, but hardly any lawns sport more than a couple of dead leaves. It's as if the whole autumn shed never happened at all.

Spencer seems unaffected, but I'm gawking as we walk. The houses grow larger and more imposing with every block. He turns left on a wide, divided road, with a narrow strip of shade trees and lush grass between the lanes.

Everything smells crisp and clean, and I'm painfully aware of my dirty jeans and bright shoes. The house to the left sits like the homecoming queen of the block: eight tall paned windows across the front and an honest-to-God turret on the left side. A winding brick walkway leads to a porch with potted mums and artful arrangements of gourds in large wicker baskets. Stone benches nestle in the flower beds, beneath carefully trimmed evergreens. It's like the cover of a magazine.

I'm still gaping at it when Spencer turns in, not sparing a glance for the magnificence. It takes a second for my brain to wrap around what he's doing and what it means as he bounds up the steps to the front door. He lives here. The boy that spent the night with me on the floor of the library bathroom *lives* in this house.

I hang back, feeling out of place on the sidewalk—in this neighborhood altogether. He motions me forward, pulling out a key that he fits in the ornate brass door handle.

"Aren't they still here?" I ask.

"Doubt it," he says. "And it wouldn't matter. I have friends over all the time."

I hesitate, feathering my hands over my hair again. Then scoffing at myself for the effort.

Sure, Mallory. Smooth down the flyaways and you'll blend right in.

"Are you coming?"

I force myself to march my feet across the pristine bricks and up the steps. The door is enormous. Three times as wide as the one that opens into my apartment, this one has glass inserts and an elaborate brass knocker.

Spencer is already inside, shuffling through some mail he finds on a table inside the foyer. *Foyer* isn't a word I'd normally use, but there is nothing else you could call this room. It's sure as heck not a plain old *entry*, not with the giant chandelier hanging above us and gleaming wood tables flanking the door.

A staircase leads up the center, splitting left and right to separate sections of the upstairs. To my left I can see a room with an expansive fireplace and plush leather furniture.

I shift my bag. My shoulders are tense, and sweat trickles from my armpits. Spencer toes off his shoes so I follow suit, but I pick mine up, feeling painfully conscious of every move. Like even my socks will mar the stone tile beneath us.

Spencer separates the mail that isn't his on the table and flips through a magazine with hockey players on the cover. I follow him through a living room that could seat twenty, a widescreen TV above the fireplace and built-in bookshelves nestled between the windows. Everything is coordinated; the lacquered pots with houseplants and the sleek wood frames around the monochromatic art.

I've never been in a house like this. I've never even seen one from a distance. It doesn't feel like a place someone actually lives. There's no afghan flung over the sofa or forgotten water glass on the end table. Even the wastebaskets I pass are entirely empty, clean, plastic liners glaring up at me.

"There might be some leftover pizza," Spencer says, his voice echoing from a place deeper in the house.

I follow the sound into a sprawling kitchen with marbled countertops and dark cabinets. There are two sets of sinks. I stare at this, dumbfounded. Why would you need two—well, technically four—sinks in a kitchen? Spencer's rummaging around in drawers, and then pulling open a cabinet under the counter. Except it's not a cabinet. It's a dishwasher in disguise.

The entire house is insane. Beautiful, yes, but in a way that borders on uncomfortable. I knew he was wealthy, but something tells me this house is over the top, even for here.

Spencer's oblivious though. He slides two plates across the long, counter-height bar and heats pizza in a toaster oven. I watch him mutely, nodding when he offers water and then fills our glasses from a fridge twice the size of mine.

When the pizza's done, Spencer takes a seat across from me and starts devouring. I ease myself onto the edge of a stool across from him, setting my shoes carefully on my lap. My stomach is so tense, I can't imagine eating, so I pick at the cheese and glance around. More house unfolds to the right, an open dining room with a fluted glass bowl in the center. Beyond that, a second living room holds couches and chairs in earth tones and a vase of fresh cut flowers.

Spencer is picking up his second piece when he stops, eyes wide. "Wait, do you have an allergy or something?"

"To pizza?"

"I don't know. Dairy or gluten or whatever. I didn't ask."

"No." I force myself to take a bite, but now he's watching, and as much as I try to school my face to nonchalance, I think he's figured it out. I swallow the chunk of pizza, but I didn't chew it enough, and it hurts going down. I take a drink of water to help, and Spencer's still watching me when I put the glass down carefully.

"I'm sorry. It's just—" I gesture around, a little lost for words.

He glances around himself, looking vaguely embarrassed. "Yeah, I know. Mom's a real estate agent. She lives to stage houses."

I don't really know what that means, but I nod and take another bite. Spencer rolls his eyes in the general direction of the living room.

"I swear to God, I could build a second Everest with the number of throw pillows that come through this door. You should see her bed."

I laugh, my shoulders easing down from my ears. I manage a full piece of pizza and half of another before I push my plate away, thanking him.

"You mind?" he asks, then finishes my piece before taking both dishes and our napkins. I shift on the stool, careful not to touch the shiny counter, my shoes still propped in my lap.

"Come on. I'll show you the pool house."

"I'm not staying. Remember?"

"The library is either occupied or possessed. Remember?"

Unease prickles under the skin at my nape. "You don't really believe that, do you?"

"What?"

"That it's haunted."

"Logically? No." But then he sighs. "But I can't figure out who would have been in there. The police already searched the building. And I watched everyone leave last night."

"Maybe they were quiet," I say.

"So they could run around sobbing later?"

"I don't know," I say, my stomach rolling uneasily. "They're going to find that message. Do you think they'll close the library again?"

"Probably not. Why? You eager to get back?"

"The library open and full of people seems less scary. I still have tests to finish."

"Do you mind if I take a quick shower? I can drop you off there when I'm done."

"Okay," I say, not moving from the stool.

He comes around the island to face me, his gaze dropping to the shoes in my lap. An expression like pain flashes over his features, and I flinch.

"Mallory, you don't have to hold your shoes. And you can take off your backpack."

"It's fine," I say, hating the way my voice squeaks. I swallow against the lump rising in my throat.

He reaches for the shoes, and emotion snaps, electric hot in my chest. "I said it's fine."

He watches me for a moment and then leads me out on the patio without a word. It's not ridiculously big like the kitchen, but it's beautiful here by the pool too, bird feeders and a round table with eight chairs grouped under a large umbrella.

The pool is covered with a clean, white tarp, but he leads me toward it, curving left at a stack of poolside loungers, to enter a small brick building with paned windows—a perfect match to the house.

"It's not much," he says with an absent wave at the barely

worn plush couch. A small fireplace sits in the south wall, and two windows overlook the pool. There are no windows facing the house. Logically, I know this is a plus. I also know he's giving me this tour trying to convince me to stay. And I feel irrationally angry about it.

I swallow down the emotion and nod as he points out the floor to ceiling cabinets where they keep beach towels and the small, but nicely appointed bathroom with a shower. Soap and shampoo wait in large pump bottles on the floor, and I practically salivate at the memory of warm water sluicing through my hair.

I should say something. I really should. But what?

"I really can't stay," I say softly.

"You can," he says. "And you can put down your shoes. And you can take off that bag. Please, Mallory. I *want* you to stay."

"I told you that I can't."

"What if you stayed for the morning? You could work here while I run to hockey, and then I can take you back to the library. Will you at least take off your backpack?"

"I don't want to take off my backpack!" My shout is a shock to us both, but it's too late to take it back.

I'm suddenly breathing harder. Faster. Why am I doing this? Why am I angry with this guy who's been nothing but nice to me?

"What's going on?" he asks softly.

"I don't need you to tell me what to do, and I don't need you to save me, okay?"

"Carrying your bag means I'm saving you?"

"No, this. *All* of this."

I walk outside quickly, past the pool and up the patio stairs. I'm being a jerk, but I don't know how to talk to him about this. Spencer's family doesn't want guests to see they own a dishwasher, and I'm going to explain why I need to stand back up on my own when the world knocks me down? The world *doesn't* knock people like him down. It pushes them higher.

Spencer catches my elbow gently, and I turn, shamed by the tears I feel gathering.

"It's just a pool house," he says. "I know it doesn't solve anything."

"Do you?" My voice cracks. I gesture up at the house behind me. "Look at where you're from!"

I shake my head, angrier with myself by the moment. I have no reason to take this out on him. He got dealt a better hand at birth, but that's not his fault. *None* of this is his fault, and I want to stop being this way. I do. But all this pain is gushing out. Terrible words are coming out of me no matter how hard I try to hold them in.

"I know you mean well, Spencer, but you don't have a clue of what I'm going through or how to help me."

"I agree," he says softly, and then his hands are on my face, his index fingers tracing the swell of my cheeks, his thumbs resting under my chin. It diffuses me, turning my anger to anguish in the span of a breath.

I don't know his touch to crave it, but it feels like craving when he traces my jaw, lifting my face until our eyes meet. My vision is blurred with tears, but I can still see the shift of his irises, blue, then green, then a shade too pale to name.

I swallow hard. "I don't want to be your hero project. The sad girl you helped that one November."

He laughs. "Mallory, in the last six weeks, I've served twenty-six minutes in a penalty box, three separate sessions in morning detention, and I've been arrested."

"I don't follow."

He plucks at one of the straps of my backpack, and I move my shoulders, letting him sling it off me.

"I'm not really the hero type."

The patio door opens and I jump back so fast, it's a miracle I don't fall down the stairs. My heart is pounding, and it's all I can do not to sprint from the scene like a thief.

"Isn't it a little cool for patio entertaining?"

The sun is behind the house, so it's hard to make out who's at the door. I cup my hand over my eyes. I catch a glimpse of cashmere sweater and long, blond hair, and I instantly remember the photo albums. It's his sister.

SPENCER

Sunday, November 19, 9:05 a.m.

Mallory jumps like Allison showed up with a badge and a gun.

"Hey. I thought you and Mom were at that museum opening," I say.

"We are. Well, we were at the pre-tour breakfast. I forgot my wallet."

"I thought it was an all-inclusive thing since Mom's on the board."

"I need my wallet for the fund-raiser after," she says, and then I see her face shift when she looks at Mallory. The vague new-friend interest in her eyes sharpens, and my stomach clenches because I know why.

It's barely 9:00 a.m., and I'm wearing yesterday's clothes and standing next to an equally rumpled girl. If I know my sister—and I do—it will take about three seconds before she makes the mental leap from our appearance to the fact that I wasn't home last night.

She thinks I spent the night with her, and she's not wrong. But she's not right either.

I'm about to say something when Allison smiles and extends her freshly manicured hand to Mallory. "I'm so rude! I'm Allison, this charming guy's older sister."

"It's very nice to meet you," Mallory says politely. She shakes her hand, but doesn't offer her name, which doesn't go unnoticed.

Allison is quiet for a few long seconds, but instead of the suspicious questions I expect, her eyes are all mischief when she asks, "So what are you two up to?"

I glare, and she takes the hint with a cough that covers her laugh. "I should get back before Mom flays me. It was really nice to meet you."

"You too," Mallory says, still not offering her name.

"See you later, Spencer."

It's an awkward departure. Allison walks slowly, and I half expect her to march back and start drilling me. Only that's not her style. She'll ask me later.

I wonder what Mallory sees when she looks at my sister. Her fresh-from-Italy sunglasses and boutique dress? A pampered Fairview princess?

Her words from before come back to me like a slap. *Look at where you're from.*

For all I know it's what Mallory sees when she looks at me

too. Spoiled rich kid. Mommy on the board and a pool in the back. It's funny because it's not even an exaggeration. But one roll of the dice, and this all could have been different.

I feel myself on top of the library again, gazing down at a world that has always been mine and has never felt less like me.

"I'm going to go," Mallory says, jarring me out of my head.

"You don't have to leave."

"Thank you for the pizza," she says, taking her bag back and hitching it on her shoulder. Her eyes drift downward. "I'm sorry. I was awful, and you've been so kind. Thank you."

"Don't thank me, stay. This isn't about charity. You're better than this, Mallory. You're the kind of person who should have *all* the opportunities. You know what you're doing. You probably have a ten-year plan."

"Ten-year plan?" She laughs, and it sounds sad. "I don't even know what I'm doing next week, but that's my problem. I'll sort it out."

I feel like a bowling ball has been dropped into my chest. Mallory has a choice between bad and awful, and she's settled. I have *all* the options—a golden ticket to make any choice I please, and instead of using it, I'm choking on it.

Even though I don't say a word, Mallory reads my eyes. Her chin comes up. No smile. "Sometimes I wonder if you're obsessed with helping me because it's easier."

"Easier than what?"

"Then figuring out what *you* need."

"With my kingdom of throw pillows? What else *could* I need?"

She doesn't bite the joker's hook I toss. Her eyes turn sad. "Maybe something that makes you happy," she says. "Because clearly none of this does."

I arrive at the library at 3:00. I'm sore from a bad check in the 11:30 hockey practice and startled by the detective in the circulation office. For one ridiculous minute, I consider bolting, and then I realize I'm probably not going to prison for staying overnight in the library. If I'm caught, I'm caught.

Though if I am caught, I'm going to have a hell of a time explaining that yes, I was in the library all night with a runaway girl from Whitestone, but no, we did not write the creepy message on the stairwell wall. That was *another* library trespasser who disappeared in the middle of the night while we were cuddling on a bathroom floor.

Gretchen pops her head out, no trademark smile in sight. "Spencer? We had another incident. Would you mind trying to help us fill in any pieces you might have?"

I'd rather eat my own jock strap, but I follow her into the

office. Besides the detective I saw through the open door, Ruby, and Mr. Brooks are there. I step in, my knees loose and weak.

"Good morning, Mr. Keller," Mr. Brooks says, lifting his coffee cup off the clipboard in his lap. "You helped with the messages on the bulletin board, right?"

"Yes, with Gretchen. Were there more?" I'm not sure if a lie can be posed in the form of a question, but I feel guilty all the same.

"Did you see the stairwell?" Mr. Brooks asks.

My heart trips itself, but I shake my head. If they've got me, this is going to backfire badly. But if not, I can't say anything that would indicate I was here last night. Because all roads involving last night lead to Mallory, and she can't be anywhere near this.

"There was a message on the stairwell," Mr. Brooks says.

"Like the last ones?"

"This time it was much larger. And written on the wall in permanent marker. Do you remember any patrons behaving unusually?"

I squirm because I don't want Mallory to get caught, but I don't like the idea of someone being in here, roaming the halls and writing on the walls. "I thought I heard footsteps one morning a while back. And I saw black footprints in the kitchen—maybe a week ago?"

"What can you tell us about your last shift specifically?" the detective asks. "Did anything out of the ordinary occur?"

Like sneaking in the library near closing time? Or sitting on a bathroom floor all night with a patron you've got a crush on? My throat feels Sahara dry. It clicks when I swallow.

"Nothing that stands out."

"Spencer didn't work yesterday," Mr. Brooks says as an aside, then to me, "You'll keep your eyes open?"

"Of course. Do you think—" I turn to the detective. "Do you think it's someone dangerous?"

"No way to know at this point," he says.

"Either way, I'd like to talk about security measures," Mr. Brooks says. "The recent tragedy is being used as a springboard for all this, and my patience is wearing thin."

I nod, half waiting to be dismissed and half expecting them to get to the accusation part. There could be a bigger reason I'm here with all of them. They could be testing me to see what I admit. We tried to be careful, but we could have screwed up. They might already know I was here last night.

"Spencer." The detective flips back through his notebook, tapping his pen on an earlier page. "You were here the day the little girl mentioned hearing a ghost, right? There were three gentlemen in the library that day," the detective says. "One of them told the little girl about the tragedy. Gretchen believes you're acquainted?"

"I didn't witness it. But, yeah, I know the guys."

"What are their names?" the detective asks.

I tense. There's no way this won't send Jarvey over the edge. Worse still, I don't want Isaac or Alex mixed up in it. But refusing to help the police? There are some lines I'm not willing to cross.

"Hey." I'd barely noticed Ruby before, but now she's leaning in, her eyes narrowed. "I could pull the records. I could go through the security tapes and then through the circulation for the day. You'd just speed it up, but if it helps, we'll say I gave the names."

I nod and give them the information. "For the record, I think it was Jarvey. He had the sucker, which Gretchen mentioned. Is it… Will he be in serious trouble?"

The detective gives a wry grin. "Unfortunately for all of us, there's no law against being a pain-in-the-neck teenager. We're simply looking for more detail. We want to talk to anyone who might know something."

Truth is, Jarvey is a jerk. He probably did scare that kid and, in some scenario, might have pulled a note prank on a bulletin board for kicks. But he was not pacing and crying in the library last night, and I doubt he knows a thing.

The question is, who does? Because someone has been getting in and out of this library in a way that none of us have figured out. It's spooky.

I restock the displays in the front until Ruby comes out. She heads right for me, looking relieved to be out of the inquisition room.

"Weird and intense, right?" she asks.

I laugh. "Yeah."

"Come on. Let's go do some heavy lifting."

"Huh?"

"We need register tape and copy paper. They're in the big supply room upstairs."

"There's a supply room upstairs?"

"Just for big items. We use it for orders. Or to restock our supplies down here."

We follow the smell of fresh paint to the stairs where a maintenance worker is rolling over the message. I lurk a step behind Ruby, my shoulders tensing as I glance at the still wet coat of primer over the words I saw earlier. Every step I take brings more doubts to focus.

They should know about the noises we heard last night. This is a crime. The police are involved. We never even heard that person leave last night. For all we know, they could still be in there, and I should have said something.

I still could.

By the time we reach the top, the hair on the back of my neck is standing upright. Ruby heads straight down the hallway, past Mr. Brooks' office and the fiscal officer's area. We turn right, and I flinch, half convinced that some sobbing, marker-wielding person will burst through one of the closed doors.

At the end of the hall, Ruby unlocks the supply room door and pushes it open. The smell of familiar cleaner assaults my nose. Ruby coughs, and I step in behind her, nostrils burning with a sting of cleaning wipes, the ones that come in those giant tubs my mom always sent me to school with when I was young.

The heavy door swings shut behind us, amplifying Ruby's voice in the small, shelf-lined room.

"Are you freaking kidding me? Someone uses half a canister of the damn things and just leaves them in a dirty pile?"

She's stooped over a veritable mountain of cleaning wipes. She's not wrong. There has to be at least half a can of them, and they're filthy, stained black-gray like they've been used for wiping tires. I shift back on my heels, searching for a trash bag.

"Who *does* shit like this?" she asks. "I need a trash bag."

I turn to find one. There's got to be a box of them because there are certainly boxes of everything else. Paper clips, staples, binders, rubber bands, Sharpie markers. My focus sticks on that. The box is knocked over and empty.

I turn around, spotting a marker on the floor, not far from the door. Caps litter the floor.

"Ruby, I thi—" I cut myself off the second I see the wall.

"Ruby, you need to see this."

"See wha—"

She doesn't finish because she sees it too. Endless lines of black handwriting cover the inside of the door and the wall around it. The writing is a heavier, cramped version of the writing I saw last night. Slanting black words bunched so tightly together it's hard to pick one word from the next. But it's the same pattern, over and over, the same strange but beautiful writing, all narrow loops and sharp diagonal lines, spelling out the same three words.

whereareyouwhereareyouwhereare
youwhereareyouwhereareyouwhereareyou

MALLORY

Sunday, November 19, 2:29 p.m.

Lana hid me in her room most of Saturday while she ran errands with her mom, but I slipped out of her window at six the next morning, too afraid of being caught. It's a drizzly morning, so I spend several hours aimlessly wandering Walmart and the local drugstore, waiting for the skies to clear. Finally, the rain eases and I head out. It's time to check in with my mom, and I need to be as far from Fairview as possible when I call.

I avoid Main Street and take all the side roads out of Fairview. As I head south, the houses and yards shrink, and at Bartlet, the spell breaks. The trimmed lawns and power-washed sidewalks abruptly give way to tired strip malls and streets with faded lines.

I'm considering heading another block south when I spot the Krispy Kreme Hot-n-Ready sign glowing in the window. My stomach lurches. I'm all too happy to try to get a free doughnut, though I'm pretty sure you're supposed to buy a drink or something.

The guy behind the counter doesn't even ask what else I want. He shovels two hot donuts into a bag and off I go.

It's not the last gift of the day either. Halfway down the road I spot a crumpled dollar bill in a parking lot. Not much, but now that I'm looking, I find change too. Not often and not much—a dime under a bush, a quarter wedged sideways in a sidewalk crack—but it's there.

I'm bending over to pick up a nickel when I spot an older man watching me from the bus stop. What is that expression he's wearing? Irritation? Sadness?

No. That's pity.

My cheeks instantly burn. I want to explain myself or tell him to mind his own business, but I pocket the change and move on. I'm not here for explanations or doughnuts or lost change. I'm here to get away from the library so I can call my mother.

I don't know how fast Charlie can track my calls, but I'm not taking chances.

My phone takes a second to power on, but once I call, Mom picks up immediately.

Her voice sounds thin on the other end of the line, and she lets out a shuddery breath when I say hello. I brace myself, expecting her to cry. Which isn't even close to what happens.

"I want you to come home."

My stomach drops, terrible scenarios rushing through my mind. "What's wrong?"

"Nothing's wrong."

"It's not nothing. What happened? Did he do something?"

"No, he didn't do anything," she says, sounding tired and irritated at the same time. "This isn't about him. It's about you."

"What's that supposed to mean?"

"You, Mallory! We gave you this time so you could come to your senses and work out your teenage rebellion. I have been patient, but now we've had enough."

"We?" I shake my head. "Not even a month ago, you were ready to leave him. Do you remember, Mom? Tracking our calls. Taking your keys. Telling you what to wear, what to eat. *You* said it was starting to scare you."

"Because you twisted those facts! None of that is a big deal, but you lined these little things up the way you do, knowing how sick I was. You know my condition."

Condition. It's another Charlie word, and it rolls in my stomach like bubbling tar. I hear her fiddling with papers on the other end of the line. A book maybe. Or a magazine.

"Which of those things is so bad?" she goes on. "Is it that he wants me to be safe? That he wants me to eat healthy? He's an old-fashioned man."

"No, Mom, he's an asshole." I clench my fists and force a lower volume. "Please tell me what happened."

She adjusts her grip on the phone, and I try to picture her on the other end of the line. Squaring her shoulders. "I know that you and I have had a unique mother-daughter relationship."

"Unique how? Because we like each other? Because we were partners?"

"See, that's just what Charlie is talking about. You interrupt me. You try to speak for me. That's not how this works. We aren't partners, and I am not your friend."

"So now we're not friends?"

"No, we're not. I'm your mother. And you bullied me into believing my own *husband* was out to hurt me."

"Mom—"

"No, you listen to me." She pauses for a long time, and when she speaks again, her rhythm is strange. Staccato. "You've done damage that might be affecting this pregnancy."

"Now you're blaming me for you being sick?" The voice coming from my mouth is too hollow and small to belong to me. Tears burn my eyes and my throat feels tight.

"I love you, but it is time for you to learn your place. This online school—" She pauses again, awkwardly, and I hear another rustle of paper. What is she doing? "You convinced me in a weak moment, but we are reenrolling you at your old school after the holiday break."

I don't respond. What can I say? She is still the mom who made me Popsicles out of cherry Kool-Aid. The woman who sang into curling irons and hairbrushes to make me laugh.

A part of her is still my mother. But now she is Charlie's wife first. How did I not see this? He will always come first.

"I've had enough of your theatrics and your games, Mallory. You will come home tonight, or I will—" She cuts herself off, a sharp inhale followed by another too-long pause. "I will call the police and report you as an endangered runaway."

The words come out in perfect succession, one right after another. It's like she's practiced. I hear another soft paper rustle on the other end of the line. *Paper?* The truth slams into me like a punch.

Mom hasn't practiced what she's saying to me. She's *reading* it. This whole conversation is scripted.

Cold crawls up the length of my spine as a new picture of her forms in my mind. She isn't there alone, bracing herself for a hard parental talk. *Charlie* is there. Probably leaned over a notebook, jotting down what he wants her to say. He's coaching her.

Rage chases that icy feeling out of my bones. I open my eyes and feel the world tilt back to center. "Is Charlie with you, Mom?"

Her silence is all the answer I need. I shake my head, heart beating fire into my veins. That man is pulling all her strings now. I have no choice but to be strong enough for both of us.

"I'll give you until six to be home," she says, voice trembling.

"I'm not coming home," I say softly.

"I'm not changing my mind on this."

"I'm not asking you to change your mind. You're going to do what you think is right, but I'm going to do what I think is safe. Charlie is dangerous."

She sighs. "He's a good man, Mallory."

"Mom, I love you. And I'm really sorry for what this is putting you through. But in my heart of hearts, I know Charlie is not a good man. I think deep down you know it too."

I disconnect before she can say anything else, and power off my phone.

"Now what?" I whisper.

But I already know what happens next. I'm not going home, and Charlie will force her hand about reporting me to the police. If he can't control the situation by bringing me back, he'll spin it so that he's a victim. A hardworking father worried about his poor, lost stepdaughter.

As I shuffle back toward Fairview, it's as if someone else is pushing me forward. At Main Street, I emerge from my stupor, realizing I'm only ten blocks from the library. My body warms thinking of the stone building with its wide inviting steps, remembering the heat when the door whooshes shut behind me. Remembering the warmth of Spencer's shoulder next to mine.

I don't care that this is the worst time for a relationship. He wants to help, and at this point, I need it.

Six blocks out, the rain starts. Two blocks after that it turns to sleet. I'm soaked through.

I arrive after 5:00 to a deserted lobby, so I stop inside the doors, peeling off my zip-up sweatshirt. It's wetter than I thought—dripping. Even directly under the heater vent, I'm shivering so hard my teeth clack together. I shove my sweatshirt into an umbrella bag by the door and tuck it into my backpack. My hair has come loose in the wind, so I redo my ponytail, pulling back all the soggy strands with frozen, waxy fingers. It's not great, but it's probably good enough that people won't notice.

I walk in farther and someone greets me from the circulation desk. I wave and smile and pretend my shoes aren't squelching and my jeans aren't wet. I don't spot police officers or Spencer, so I head to the browsing room. Might as well get to work.

I settle at the computer with my access code and hands so cold, I can't fathom how I'll type. But today, I won't be doing school work. Not that I have any work due on Thanksgiving break. I have a whole different reason for sitting at these keys today.

I type two words into the search bar: *Charlie Wrightson.*

Sixty-eight thousand matches pop up. Good thing I have nothing but time. I proceed to type in every search combination I can think of.

Charlie Wrightson Ohio

Charlie Wrightson Whitestone

Charlie Wrightson IT

Charlie Wrightson United States Armed Forces

I try other cities. Other versions of Charlie. Charles. Chuck. C Wrightson. I chase his name down a hundred rabbit holes. Each search finds a few uninteresting hits, a long-outdated profile on a career site, a link to his staff picture and email on Whitestone Memorial, and a photo of a young, happier-looking version of Charlie with other young guys, all dressed in fatigues. There's no helpful information. No social media links revealing groups of deviant friends or a carefully chronicled relationship breakdown.

There's got to be a better way to get information on this guy. I'm sixteen years old, and I've never been outside of Ohio, but you can find more crap on me.

I'm missing something.

I try the Ohio search again, scrolling through page after page, scanning for any nugget of promising information. Eleven pages in, I stop. There's a hit with Charlie's name on a blog named Pentel the Pooch. Charlie mentioned a friend with a dog named Pentel once. He said she named all her pets after writing instrument brands. Bic, Dixon, Zebra, and Pentel.

I click the text and an ancient blog appears. Pentel the Pooch is in bad shape. Half the image links don't work, and the last post is three years old. But somehow, it's still up. I scan the site, searching for Charlie's name. It's from a post five years ago, one surrounded by little balloons.

On a final note, I can't end today's post without congratulating my good friend Billie Reeves on her engagement to Charlie Wrightson. It's been a whirlwind of a fairy tale, and Pentel is blowing you both a big poochy smooch. Congrats!

Engagement. Charlie was engaged to someone else five years ago? I scrawl down the name "Billie Reeves" on a piece of paper in my notebook and close down my browser.

"Good evening." The voice over the intercom makes me jump. "The library will be closing in fifteen minutes. Please bring all materials for checkout at this time. Thank you for your assistance and have a wonderful evening."

At the browsing desk, a tall, slim man smiles at me. I try to smile back, but I'm suddenly shaking again. He's checking to see who's here because he needs to make sure we'll leave. This is why I'm always careful to clear the room before these messages.

I stumble to my feet, dragging my backpack over my shoulder. How could I lose track of time like this? I know the library closes at 6:00 on Sunday! I step away from the desk, noticing the spray of rain against the windows. The idea of more cold makes my knees weak.

Not good. None of this is good. I move out into the hallway, between the stairs and the bathrooms. My pulse is thrumming, fast in my neck. I can't stay out in that rain again. I can't even walk to—

Voices and footsteps sound on the stairs, and my focus shifts to the small group heading down from the second floor. There are three of them, but my eyes fix on one familiar head of dark, wavy hair.

Spencer.

He's coming down the stairs with a police officer and a man in a suit I don't recognize. I stumble to an awkward halt, and he meets my eyes briefly. Then he turns to the officer, arm extended for a handshake.

For one terrifying second, I think he's turning me in. I can't quite make out what he's saying, but I don't know if I should run or where to go if I do. Before I can decide, he's down the stairs, coming straight for me. He wraps his arm around my back, all friendly ease.

"I'm sorry I got caught up. You ready?"

I lick my lips to speak, but I'm struck mute by his sudden appearance, by the certainty of his voice, and the heavy warmth of his arm behind me. He leads me quickly to the check-out area, separating from me just long enough to grab his coat from the circulation office.

He is all smiles walking back out, but there's fear lurking in his eyes. He leads me to the lobby, hand on the middle of my back. And then on my elbow. I burn everywhere he touches, my questions and thank yous all dried up in my mouth.

He stops at the door, giving me a genuine look. "Where's your coat?"

"I…"

He doesn't say another word, just peels his off and hands it over. It's a heavy blue thing that feels expensive and still carries his heat. The sleeves hang four inches past my hands. I feel like a kid in an ill-fitting costume, but I'm not about to argue.

We're down the stairs and halfway across the rainy lot when he pulls out a set of keys. A beautiful black car lights up and purrs to life.

"Can I give you a ride?" he asks, ice bits melting in his hair. "Please?"

I nod, and he steers me to the passenger side. The leather seats have warmers, and heat quickly permeates my soaked jeans. It's better than a hot bath, and I can't help but slouch back.

Spencer gets in the driver's seat, knees crammed up around the steering wheel. He swears softly and hits a button and a series of whirs sends the seat into a more reasonable position.

"Mom's car," he says by explanation. "The automatic seat always resets to her."

Right now, I don't care if he's stealing this car. I'm grateful to be inside it.

"Are you okay?" he asks "Did you get caught in the rain?"

"Yes and yes." I exhale. "These heated seats are great."

"Do you have anything dry you can wear?"

"Yeah, in my backpack," I say, but I look around, skeptical. I'm not about to try to wriggle out of wet jeans in a car.

Spencer puts the car in reverse, but he doesn't move. "We weren't crazy last night. Someone was in the library."

"They already painted over the message on the wall," I say. "I thought the police would want to see it."

"They did. And it had nothing on the writing in the supply room. Somebody wrote the same thing over and over in there. And when I mean over and over, I'm talking the whole wall. I've been upstairs for hours with the police."

"Don't your parents have to be there for them to talk to you?"

He nods. "That was part of the delay. Mom stopped by to sign the paper to allow Mr. Brooks to sit with me. She had a critical auction today. Big estate."

My heart squeezes. "What did the police want to know?"

"I told them I thought I heard crying a couple of nights ago. And I told them other little stuff I'd seen. No specifics. They're going to talk to my friends about this little girl Jarvey freaked out, but I don't think it'll get them anywhere."

I swallow hard. "Will they want to talk to me too?"

"The police don't know about you." A muscle in his jaw jumps. "They're not going to know about you."

He pulls out of the spot, and I let out a slow breath, letting that sink in. More messages in the supply room? What is this all about?

"Doesn't the library lock the supply room?"

He waggles his brows. "That's the really creepy part. The police were here for *two* hours checking out the door and tiles in the ceiling. There are strange black smears around the library and tons in that room, but they have no idea how the person got inside."

"Inside the room?"

"They didn't find any evidence of a break-in, nothing that would explain this. It's like someone materialized. They're going to bring in dogs from Columbus to check upstairs, but that has to be scheduled."

"I'm surprised they aren't closing the library until they can figure it out."

"They talked about it, but Mr. Brooks put the brakes on that. Said he wasn't ready to halt library services over some writing on a wall. People need it."

"Need it?"

"Job searches. Homework assistance. Public meeting space. He takes our services seriously."

Spencer pulls up to a red light, and I realize we're right back by the library. He's basically driven us around a giant block.

"Did you forget something?" I ask.

"Yes. I forgot to ask you where you'd like me to take you. And by *forgot*, I mean I didn't want to ask."

"Why not?"

"Because I wanted more time with you, Mallory."

My stomach tumbles end over end. "I don't have anywhere to be."

Spencer smiles, and the light turns green.

I close my eyes and let him drive. It's an incredible relief, having someone else make a couple of choices. A few minutes later, he parks in front of a restaurant called Rubino's.

"What's this?" I ask.

"Home of the best lasagna in Ohio."

"You've eaten *all* the lasagna in Ohio?"

"Don't need to," he says. "It's the best."

My stomach growls, and he laughs. "Well, at least I know you're hungry. That's step one."

"What's step two?"

"Letting the cheesy goodness of Rubino's convince you that my offer to let you stay with me might not be so crazy. Before you start arguing, I'll warn you that I'm picking up the tab. Because, as you know, I'm the Prince of Pillows and—"

"Spencer."

"Yeah?"

"You don't need to convince me. Not tonight."

Tears smear my vision into streaks of parking lot lights and wet pavement. The heat of this car and the sound of Spencer's voice—the smell of him. It's everywhere. Climbing right under my skin until I want…not this car or this life, but an existence closer to it than sleeping on a bathroom floor in a public library.

The first tears spill, and though I'm staring straight ahead, he must see. I feel his fingers against mine, solid and rough. He twines our hands together and squeezes. "This is not your story, Mallory. This is not where it ends, all right?"

"Okay."

"Look at me."

I don't.

"Look at me. Please."

It's the *please* that gets me. This boy has everything I don't. It's easy for him to make promises of golden horizons. And sitting in this warm car with him so close, it's easy for me to hear him. I don't even swipe the tears off my cheeks. I let them be, and I let him see.

"You will find your way out of this," he says.

Something sparks to life in my chest. I think it's the part of me that wants to believe him.

SPENCER

Sunday, November 19, 7:12 p.m.

Mallory is changed and warmer by the time the double slab of lasagna I order arrives. It's on a platter big enough for Mallory to sit on. She eats every bit of her half and two pieces of garlic bread. And she sits on the bench in the booth like I did in preschool, crisscross-applesauce with her legs folded.

"Okay, time for the Rubino's tradition." I point to a sign above the pizza oven.

Make a Wish.

She laughs. "I don't believe in wishes."

"C'mon. Everybody has a wish. I think you should pick three."

"What?"

"Three wishes. That's what the genie always gives people, right?"

Her face screws up, and she takes a drink of her soda. "What are your three wishes?"

"Ah, I see. You're going to cheat. But fine. My three wishes."

I tick them off my fingers. "To climb Cassin Ridge in Denali. To have a lifetime supply of Lemonheads."

"Lemonheads? Gross."

"Are you finished judging my wishes?" She laughs, and I tick off my third finger. "To do something with my life that feels right."

"I'll think on it," she says, but I can tell she won't. She cocks her head, ready to change the subject. "So who do you think is in the library? Personally, I'm hoping like hell all my years of logic are wrong, and it's a ghost."

"Wait. You're *hoping* the library is haunted?"

She shrugs. "Sure. What's a ghost going to do? Rattle some chains? Moan in the attic?"

"Interesting point. Plus, if it's a ghost, you could name it. Casper. Or Scrooge."

She shakes her head. "Scrooge isn't the ghost. He's the crotchety old rich guy."

"Probably a throw pillow tycoon. That's how all the guys get rich."

She sighs. "That's just your bubble of privilege talking, Spencer."

"My bubble of privilege?"

"Yes. Don't you listen to talk radio?"

"Does anyone?"

"Not from inside their bubbles of privilege."

I laugh. "Are you always this fast with the comebacks?"

She chews her bottom lip like it's an important question. "I think so. I used to be anyway. Mom and I used to banter back and forth all the time. Once upon a time."

"What changed?"

Her face frosts over. "Charlie."

I put down my fork, feeling like I took a puck to the gut. "Mallory, does this guy..."

"No." She lets out a harsh laugh. "Whatever you're going to ask, no. I know it's ridiculous, but some days I think it would be easier if he hit us."

"It wouldn't be," I say, and she nods quickly.

"You're right. I know." Then she frowns. "Could we maybe not? Just for now."

"Definitely," I say.

A commotion at the counter catches my eye. My heart sinks when I spot the familiar group. Jarvey and Isaac and Alex's girlfriend, Ava.

"Friends of yours." Mallory nods at them. "Right?"

"Hockey friends," I say. "They were the ones in the library."

She tenses and I wonder if she's thinking the same thing I am. Have the police already talked to them? Shit, is that why Alex isn't here? He doesn't deserve to be mixed up in this, so I hope not.

"They might come over here," I say.

Ava mouths hi and waves. Jarvey bumps his chin at me, and they're on their way.

"Lackluster effort today," Jarvey says instead of hello.

"My luster fields are barren," I say with a shrug.

"Wasn't that bad," says Isaac. "Hell, did you see Joe? Kid needs to stick with lacrosse."

"Renner sucks," Jarvey says, "but you're having a lousy year, Keller."

I turn to Mallory. "Mallory, this is Ava, Isaac, and Jarvey. Ava and Isaac go to school with me. Jarvey is an asshole we know."

Ava and Isaac laugh, and Jarvey puts on a face like he's affronted, but he's not. He likes being the guy who scowls in pictures and takes everything too seriously. Brilliant as he is on the ice, he's been a total drag since the fourth grade.

"Spencer is harsh. Jarvey is a charmer when you get to know him," Isaac says, looking Mallory up and down with a wolfish smile.

"No, he's really not." Ava extends her hand and a genuine grin. I've always liked Ava, and she's not losing any points now. "It's nice to meet you Mallory. Do you go to Hartley?"

Bishop Hartley is a Catholic school nearby. A decent ask.

"No, I'm in a small school."

"So is this what you've been doing with your time?" Jarvey asks, his eyes on the lasagna but pointing the question at Mallory all the same.

"Careful, Jarv, your Neanderthal is showing," Ava says.

"Don't be a bitch, Ava," Jarvey says. "I'm grabbing our pizza."

Isaac follows Jarvey to the counter, calling back to us. "You should come. We're going to Shawn's. Alex is coming later."

"Bring the girl if you must," Jarvey says, not looking back as he pushes the door open.

"Yep," Ava says, winking at Mallory, "total asshole. Shockingly, he hasn't dated anyone seriously in two years."

"Stunner," Mallory says. "It was really nice to meet you."

"You too. And definitely join us if you want. We'll keep our resident jerk in line. Bye, Spence!"

When they head outside, Mallory grabs another piece of garlic bread and gazes at the pinball machine in the back corner.

"Does nothing rattle you?" I ask.

She shrugs. "I live in a library. I'm kind of unflappable."

"Well, you don't live there tonight."

To my utter shock, she doesn't argue.

The unflappable crap goes out the window when we pull up to my house. The foyer lamp is on, which means Mom is home. I can practically feel Mallory tense when she figures it out.

"Someone's home," she says. "Keep driving. You can drop me at the end of the block."

I do keep driving, but I'm not sure why. Coming here was the point. “Mom and Allison are probably zoned out watching TV or asleep.”

“I can’t do this. I can’t sneak around your property like some kind of criminal.”

“Then let’s go inside. We can hang out and watch TV. They probably won’t even notice you’re here.”

“But if they do, they’ll ask me questions. I’m too nervous.”

I doubt it would be an inquisition, but she’s right about the too nervous part. She’s breathing fast and super pale. Mom will pick up on that in a hot second if she is downstairs.

“Okay, then don’t come in. You can wait three minutes and head back to the pool house. There’s a gate on the side fence. If you follow the fence, you can go around the back and let yourself in the door. It’s never locked, and no one will be able to see you.”

“Unless they look out one of the eighty windows across the back of your house.”

“They can look all they want. It’s dark back there. But stay close to the fence and the building. If you get too close to the pool or the main house, the security lights will come on.”

“Comforting.” She lets out a shaky breath. Her fear is palpable.

“Relax. I’ll distract them if they’re down there, and then I’ll come out when it’s safe.”

“What reason could you possibly have to go out to a pool house in November?”

I wave that off. "I've got a couple of old-school game systems out there. It's not unheard of for me to go somewhere in my own house, Mallory."

"House." She scoffs. "It's practically a freaking estate."

"Try to calm down. It's better than trying to break into the library where the police are almost certainly patrolling tonight, right?"

"Right." She squares her shoulders. "Tell me again how to get inside."

MALLORY

Sunday, November 19, 9:48 p.m.

It must be instinct that drives me through the back gate and onto the crisp grass of Spencer's lawn. It certainly isn't *learned* behavior because before all this, I'd never so much as served a detention in school. Now I'm breaking and entering.

Well, entering at least. Nothing is actually locked. He said it wouldn't be, but it's hard to imagine that—doors and gates left open for the whole world. I guess people hanging around a neighborhood like this have their own gates to open and their own houses to indulge in.

Inside the fence, I keep close to the tall decorative grass in the flowerbed lining the fence. It hisses against my clothes so I slow my pace, wincing at the noise. The house is ablaze, wide bright windows revealing the kitchen, where I ate cold pizza, and the beautiful living room.

A flash of pale hair and a woman's face appear at the kitchen window. I stop midstep, my heart dropping through my stomach. In the glass her expression appears startled, as if she's seen me, but then she turns around with a smile. For a second, I don't get it, but then I realize it's Spencer. Her son is home. All his comments about throw pillows aside, this is where he lives, and she is his mother.

It hurts, thinking this, because there's a whisper right behind it, one that asks what it would be like to belong in a home with a mother who… I force my eyes away because there's no reason to go there. I won't ever have these things. Maybe one day I won't even want them.

I remind myself that tonight is about staying safe and getting some sleep. Then tomorrow, I can learn more about Charlie's ex-fiancée, Billie Reeves. Maybe there is some evidence that Charlie is as dangerous as I suspect. If I can prove it, Mom will have to leave.

Time to move. I walk sideways, until I can cross to the back wall of the pool house. I'm grateful for the darkness under the roof's edge. I inch my way around it, staying in the shadows, my hand dragging along the rough brick wall.

At the third corner, I stop. I have to step away to open the door, but the windows feel like spotlights. Spencer wasn't thinking this dark thing through. Getting to the door will leave me completely exposed. Once glance out the window and his mom could see me.

How long has it been? Has Spencer had enough time to get her out of the room? Maybe I've waited too long.

Just do it already.

I chance a quick glance to the windows again. His mom is still facing away from me, and she's not alone. I see the tall blond I met yesterday. Allison. Then I see his mother laugh, and a shadow that might be Spencer moving his hands.

He's distracting them. He's giving me my chance, and I'm wasting it. I run to the door with my heart pounding so hard I can feel it in my teeth. My hand closes over the doorknob. It's like ice under my palms, so cold it burns. I twist, and for a second, it sticks.

Oh my God, he was wrong. It's locked.

I try again, the other direction. The knob clicks. I push hard using both hands, and it jerks open with a scrape that sends every hair on my body standing upright. They heard that. They *had* to hear that.

I imagine the mother frowning in the kitchen. His sister turning for the sliding door. Blood roars behind my ears.

I peek at the house. It's fine. They are still lost in their own world, talking and laughing. My gaze lingers a beat longer than it should before I slip inside and tug the door closed.

There is zero light inside. As a kid I was afraid of the dark, but these days it's sanctuary. I sink down to the tile floor in relief, my breath coming hard and fast in the silence. After my heart slows, I start shivering again. The floor feels like ice.

I test it with my bare hands and recoil. It's freezing. Not just the floor, this whole room. I shift around, moving to my hands and knees. There was a rug or carpet, I think. I work my way around inch by inch looking for it. My memories of this room aren't clear, and I wish they were.

My palms and knees are burning with cold from the tile when I finally find the carpet. Still cold, but *so* much better. I sit in relief for a few moments, then realize it's still not going to be warm enough for sleeping. I'll go hypothermic in here.

Or maybe I just feel like I will. I might not have a pool house, but I'm still a typical American who's rarely forced to deal with the elements. I've also paid enough attention in science and history classes to know my body is capable of much more than my comfort preferences would lead me to believe.

It can't be colder than forty-five degrees in here. Maybe forty. Forty degrees won't kill me. I don't think.

I pull my backpack beside me and unzip it. My sweatshirt is soaked, but I could add another layer. But everything inside my bag feels damp. I find the plastic umbrella bag, and the wet clothes that spilled out of it. Nothing is dry. I swear, pulling my trembling hands out of the backpack.

Think, Mallory.

I try, but my teeth are chattering again, and my brain feels sluggish. When Spencer comes, I'll ask about blankets or towels. Maybe I can lay things out to dry.

Unless he doesn't come.

And he might not. I told him not to come out if his mom was up or if it was weird.

Footsteps sound outside, and I crouch back down. Because I'm not sure until I see him. The door opens.

"Mallory?"

His voice is the barest whisper.

"Yeah?"

"I'm going to turn on the lights. She knows I'm coming out here to play."

The lights flick on and I flinch, despite his warning. The room feels strangely bright. Exposing. I cringe in the corner between the couch and a row of cabinets on the wall.

He shrugs off his coat then grimaces. "Hell, it's freezing in here."

My teeth start chattering as if on cue. He notices, his expression going dark as he comes toward me. I hold up my trembling hands and shake my head. "Turn on the TV. The light is different from a TV. She might..."

I can't quite explain through my chattering teeth, but he complies, searching until he finds the remote. He clicks a button, and I expect the TV, but a fire *whoofs* to life instead. It's in an alcove below the TV, a wide and beckoning ripple of flame. It doesn't feel warm yet, but the glow alone is a welcome sight.

Spencer snaps on the television set, even starting up the gaming console, though I didn't ask for that part. Old school, he said, but I'm pretty sure this is the one Lana's brother plays.

"She's in bed," he says softly. "And the blinds are closed." He doesn't touch the controller. His eyes stay fixed on me, and I resist the urge to squirm.

"They could—"

"Mallory, she went to bed. Her room is on the first floor. Windows face the front of the house."

"What about Allison?"

Spencer puts down the remote, and I know I must look terrified. I hate it. Shame crawls up my spine.

"On her laptop in her room. Before you ask, she never opens her curtains. Claims the sunlight is bad for her sleep. I suspect vampirism."

He wants to make me laugh, but I can't. I'm cold and frightened and completely humiliated. Spencer drops the goofy smile and moves closer.

"Do you want to sit down?" he asks.

I stumble a step or two. And then he's got my hands. His warmth is such a shocking relief it almost drowns out the concern flickering on his face. I know my hands are cold. He wouldn't feel so hot if I wasn't half frozen.

He rubs my hands and sinks onto the couch, taking me with him. I'm fumbling and nervous beside him, but he doesn't scoop me into his arms or make it a thing. He takes off his coat and pulls it around my shoulders, zipping me inside. My skin sucks his leftover body heat up so fast that I'm cold again almost instantly. My nerves and the rain and the cold are all adding up to this moment. I'm cold from the inside out.

Spencer finds a soft, thick throw in one of the cabinets. I command myself to stop shivering. I try to breathe in the smell of chlorine and laundry detergent instead, to distract myself. Just warm up, for God's sake, because this is getting stupid and embarrassing.

The heat from the fire is permeating the room now, and should be making me warmer. It really should. But the shivers won't stop.

Spencer sighs, shifting awkwardly on the couch. "Okay, at the risk of sounding like an absolute tool with a line about shared body heat..."

"No, it's fine," I say. "I'm really cold."

He wraps his arms around me without another word. It isn't exactly a hug. There are thirty layers between us, and I'm possibly hypothermic, but feeling him this close hits me low in the gut.

Even through the throw blanket and his coat and our shirts, his body is hard and strong in all the places mine isn't. When he shifts, my cold nose brushes his hot neck, and every inch of my body feels it. Feels him.

We're both contorted, our bodies lined up at odd angles and my arms mashed to my sides. And despite all of that, I close my eyes and let my forehead rest against his bare neck. Slowly, my shivering slows, and I remember how to breathe.

My eyes flutter open, and my lashes must have tickled his neck because I hear him take a sharp breath. His hands flex on my back. I'm done being cold, but I am not done being close to him.

"Better?" he asks, his voice a soft croak.

"Much," I say. But I don't move, and he doesn't either. I should because I desperately want to touch him and I shouldn't. Kissing a guy is one thing, but this would be more. No matter how right it feels to be near Spencer, I don't trust guys with my feelings. I don't trust them with anything.

Until this moment, I'm not sure I've ever wanted to.

Eventually the stiffness gets to us both. We part, my hair catching on his stubble, and his hand dragging down my hip.

Something changes in that moment, his eyes extra bright in the blue-white glow of the game preview screen. My cheeks burn. Suddenly, I'm way past *not cold*; I'm overheated.

I unzip his coat, and a few seconds later, I pull it off, draping it over the back of the couch. He watches me until I feel squirmy.

"Why are you staring?" I ask.

"Do you really have to ask?"

The warmth flashing over my skin is proof that I'm blushing. He doesn't notice or doesn't mention it. Either way, I'm grateful.

I glance around the pool house because looking at Spencer feels dangerous. I didn't come here for… I didn't come here for any of this, but now the air feels charged. Expectant. I didn't see this coming.

Didn't you?

My body goes cold, a sour taste blooming on the back of my tongue.

Is that what he's expecting? Some sort of payment for his help?

I lurch to my feet, and he tenses. "Are you okay?"

"Yeah. Maybe. I don't know."

It's the truth. I don't know if I'm okay or what I'm doing. Now that I'm standing, I'm second-guessing everything I've done tonight. Spencer's given me every reason to trust him, but who says that's enough.

Life with Charlie made one thing clear: in the beginning, you only see what they want you to see.

"Are you still cold?" Spencer asks.

I cross my arms. "No, I'm not. Why?"

"Because you're shaking."

I swallow, realizing he's right. I'm trembling because I'm afraid.

I glance at my backpack on the floor across from him and the door across from me. He notices.

"Am I missing something?"

"What would you be missing?"

"Whatever has you suddenly freaked out."

"I'm trying to be smart about this." I'm careful to hold his eyes. To make sure he knows that I *will* look him in the eye. "No one knows I'm here. No one even knows I *know* you, and I'm here in your pool house. I don't even think my phone is charged, so if I needed…"

I trail off and Spencer looks shocked and embarrassed in quick succession, but it's something close to hurt that settles on his face. He stands up, and I realize with a start that his advantages don't end with being rich and pretty. He's big, easily six inches taller than me with shoulders and arms I wouldn't stand a chance against.

What do I really know about this guy?

When he looks at me with soft eyes and a hurt expression, I think of Charlie's sweet voice. Charlie buying us ice cream. Holding open doors.

Stop it.

Spencer is not Charlie.

And he's not. Everything in me tells me he is nothing like my stepfather. My heart is screaming it out with every beat. He is different.

But what if I'm wrong? How would I know? Regret pangs through my middle at the mix of hurt and anger on Spencer's face. Whatever secrets he might have, he's lousy at hiding how he feels.

He pulls his phone out of his pocket and places it in my palm. I wince. This is the second time he's paid for Charlie's sins. The second time he's been nice when I've been awful.

"I'm sorry," I say.

"Don't be," he doesn't meet my eyes. "It's smart to be safe. To think about it. But I can tell you I'm not... There isn't any way—"

"I know," I say, because suddenly I do. I just wish believing him was enough to chase the fear out of my head. Is this the way Charlie has his claws in me?

Spencer shakes his head, still clearly hurt. "I'm a lot of screwed up things, Mallory. But I am *not* that."

He goes back to the couch without another word and starts a game. I don't know what to say or do. He's put himself on the line for me. More than once. I don't want him to think that doesn't matter.

I want him to know it's not him I'm afraid of, it's me. I'm afraid to trust my own gut, because it didn't warn me about

Charlie. Ha—look at me now. I would love to believe I'm so much stronger than my mom, but here I am. Frozen in fear, just like her.

I close my eyes, imagining Mom's pale hands wringing together in helplessness, her spirit shrinking day by day. No. I'm not going to live like that. I'm going to fight it, because we can't *both* need rescuing. One of us has to be strong enough to take some chances.

I walk to the couch on steady legs and put the phone on the coffee table. I still don't understand him, but I want to. I want more than the things I can find in his baby book or in whatever police report chronicles his climb up the side of the library. I know the who's, what's, and where's of Spencer. But I want to know the *why*.

"I *am* sorry," I say again.

Before he can feel like he needs to answer, I sit down beside him. I pull my legs up on the couch and lie down, using a throw pillow under my head and stretching the chlorine-scented throw over the rest of me.

I'm sure I won't sleep. How could I, with my heart beating so fast and Spencer right there, his thigh brushing my feet if he moves? He is way too close and way too attractive for me to tune out.

The minutes stretch into a languid rhythm I don't pay

attention to. I don't know I've dozed off until I wake up. He's moving. Standing up. It startles me. His hand brushes my ankle, feather light.

"I should head inside." I can tell he doesn't want to. His hand lingers on my foot, and he doesn't even glance at the door.

He looks mussed and sleepy above me, and I want him to stay.

"I probably shouldn't leave the TV on," he says. "The heater should be working now, but I turned off the fireplace."

"Okay."

"Mom and Allison leave around seven. I'll be over after that."

I lift my hand to my head, like I can rub the sleep fog away. "Don't you have school?"

His smile is quickly becoming my personal kryptonite. "Funny. I feel like I'm coming down with something."

I grin, staying still as he leaves. When the door closes, I scamper across the couch to peer out of a tiny crack in the curtains. He lopes to the house, coat unzipped and his long strides making short work of the distance.

I still don't know why he's so desperate to help me, but tonight I don't care. I curl into the warm spot he left on the couch, smelling chlorine and the couch fabric and Spencer. It's the best sleep I can remember in a long time.

SPENCER

Monday, November 20, 6:19 a.m.

Mom buys the sick business easily enough. She was always a pushover with that sort of thing, but I was always smart enough not to play the card too often.

She brushes a hand over my forehead and pushes a cup of tea across the counter. "You sick enough to miss the tournament tomorrow?"

Shit. Is it Thanksgiving week already? Of course it is, but I forgot all about the tournament. "Not if I kick this headache."

She nods and collects her keys and briefcase. "I've got some showings in the afternoon. Should be home by five, though."

"I can make a can of chicken soup."

"Are you sure? I can bring you lunch."

"Yeah. I just want to go back to bed."

Mom kisses me on the forehead and heads out. When the door closes behind her, Allison puts down her phone. "You're a lousy actor, little brother."

"Who's talking? You tried to get Mom to call you in sick with leprosy in the third grade."

"Well, I learned my lesson early," she says, fussing with her hair.

"Where are you going today?" I ask.

"Internship at the financial advisor firm. I told you about this. Did you sign up for the tours we talked about?"

"Not yet."

"Fine." She turns, annoyed. "I'm not doing this for you. You end up in a school you don't like, and you only have yourself to blame."

"I'm not getting in to some fancy, private school. It's pointless."

"I already told you. Mom and Dad have plenty of—"

"Connections," I finish for her, pushing the tea away. "Yeah, I got that."

"You know, you have *got* to start taking this seriously."

"Yeah, you keep telling me. And telling me."

"I don't get your attitude. We are *so* fortunate to have these opportunities, Spencer. Most people would do anything to have your options. How can you not see that?"

"How can I see anything else?"

She crosses her arms over her chest. "What does that mean?"

"All those people who wish they were us. Just a roll of the dice, Allison. It could have been me."

"But it's not!" she says. "It's not you, and you're wasting your opportunity."

"Fine, I'm wasting it. I'm here, with my golden ticket to the whole freaking universe, but why should I take it?" I stand up, feeling too antsy to sit. "So I can end up here? Why would I want that?"

"Would you rather blow it all off and sabotage your future, screwing yourself and our parents and everything they've worked to give us? Is that what you want?"

"Yes, Allison, all I want in the *world* is to hurt Mom and Dad. You got it in one guess."

I walk away before I go any further. Part of me expects her to throw a parting jab up the stairs, but she doesn't. She walks away, saying we can talk later.

There's nothing to talk about, though. There's no part of this that doesn't result in my disappointing my parents. I don't need any advice. What I should do is crystal clear. I should ride this silver platter for the rest of my life: elite school, big money job, perfect house, shiny car. My parents would be happy; my potential would be met.

And none of it would mean a damn thing.

I take the quickest shower of my life, barely drying off before I put on my jeans and shirt, my whole body drawn to the southwest window in my room. The window that overlooks the pool house. A magnetic pull stretches from the pit of my stomach to the girl in that building, and I'm powerless to resist it.

The cold air feels good when I open the patio door. She's awake when I walk inside, her hair in damp braids. An easy smile rests on her face.

Until she notices my expression, which must be a mix of anxiety and self-loathing. Suddenly, her grin vanishes.

"What's wrong?" she asks.

"Do you want to get out of here?"

"Back to the library?"

"No, not that. I mean, we can go there, but after school hours if that's okay."

"Because you're supposed to be at school," she says softly, remembering.

I nod, and the quiet between us turns heavy.

"Where do you want to go?" she asks.

She looks up at me with bright eyes, and I feel a buzzing under my skin. A thousand what-ifs are crowding my mouth in languages I don't even know. What if this was her house? What if I was the runaway, sleeping in the pool house?

The tumble of possible answers is suffocating, so I offer another question. "Have you ever been climbing?"

She shrugs. "I mean, trees and fences, but other than that? No."

"Are you afraid of heights? Or not into that kind of thing? No, don't answer that. Do you want to? Go climbing, I mean. Would you want to try it? Yeah, answer that one."

"Which one? There were like fifteen questions there."

I laugh. "Do you want to go climbing with me?"

Her smile is a flash fire, bright, but brief.

"I don't really have anything to wear for that."

I bite my lip. "I might have an idea. But I'm going to need you to deal with one of my *weird* friends for like ten minutes."

"Okay."

"Just like that?"

"Yeah," she says, taking my hand. "Just like that."

I check around before we walk next door. This time when Mallory hesitates at the property edge, I get it. Though it doesn't have the instant curb pizzazz our house has, even around here, the house next to ours is imposing. Three stories, a four-car garage, and—I kid you not—a garden complete with a hedge maze and fountain out back.

Mallory is tense, but true to her word, she doesn't bolt when I ring the doorbell. After my second ring, I hear footsteps thunder down the inside stairs.

The door swings open to reveal Ava, wearing a pair of her brother Tate's Carnegie Mellon sweatpants and a giant T-shirt. Her hair is piled in a heap on top of her head, and she stares daggers at me, until she notices Mallory behind my shoulder. Her whole face softens, but I don't miss the interest in her eyes.

"Hey," she says to me, and then to Mallory. "Hey, again."

Mallory takes a breath, so I think she's recognized her, but she looks at me, not Ava when she speaks. "Does no one in Fairview go to school?"

I shrug. "Ava's an art prodigy who doesn't need our little mortal school full-time."

Ava waves that away and leans in, closer to Mallory. "Some clarification here. First, I'm not a prodigy; second, I do go to school; and third, Spencer doesn't know what mortal means."

Mallory's laugh makes Ava smile. "I go down to the art college twice a week," she explains, "which means I get to sleep in those days. *Usually*."

"What would you do if I wasn't here to wake you in time to enjoy this beautiful morning?" I gesture at the flat gray sky and naked trees.

"I'd sleep. Come in. It's cold out here."

Mallory follows me inside. Ava's house is different than mine, and not only because it has an entire extra story. It's enormous and old, and unlike most Fairview houses, this one hasn't been renovated from the ground up. Ava's house doesn't boast modern walls of windows and open living spaces. It feels more like an undiscovered tomb. Dozens of paintings crowd the narrow halls. Inside the rooms, china cabinets stand shoulder to shoulder, cluttered with trinkets and dishes and crystal goblets, most more dusty than pretty.

We've been neighbors our entire lives, so I don't think about it much anymore. Having Mallory here makes it hard not to imagine how it appears to her.

Ava leads us down a long, dark hallway, past a stuffy office, and into the family room in the back. Even with the generous number of windows overlooking the lawn, the room is murky. Sagging leather couches offer seats beneath shelves lined with probably priceless vases. Ava flops onto the nearest couch and gestures at the coffee table. I spot a scattering of nail polish bottles and a white box of pastries.

"Want a cannoli? Dad just got back from Sicily."

I can see that Mallory is too uncomfortable to willingly reach for a cannoli in here, but we didn't have breakfast, so I take one and tear it in half, handing her the larger portion.

"It's good," I say around a bite.

Ava shrugs. "So what's up? I doubt you smelled the cannoli from your house."

"I was hoping I could borrow Tate's extra climbing harness. And maybe some pants?"

She laughs. "You having a pants shortage next door?"

Mallory tenses and I realize I didn't think this through. One instant after that, her cheeks go red, and my neck burns. Terrific. Now Ava is thinking the same thing Allison was yesterday. I've got my foot so far in my mouth, I'm digesting shoelaces, but maybe if I explain—

"Oh," Ava says softly, because she's sharper than she looks. And sweeter. "Shit, guys, I'm sorry. I wasn't trying to pry."

"It's not like..." Mallory's voice is small, and she stops herself. Naturally. She can't say what it *is* like, so where is she going to go?

Ava shakes her head. "No worries. Really. I should've figured it out. Or kept my mouth shut."

Mallory is still flushed, and I'm not helping. My mouth is opening and closing without a single helpful thing coming out. Ava stands and shoves between us with a laugh, taking Mallory's arm and glaring at me.

"God, Spencer, of all the times for you to lose your ability to bring the funny." Then to Mallory. "Come on. I'm pretty sure my stuff will fit you."

Mallory hesitates, but Ava tugs her gently along. "Eh, the awkward is already out there. Let's get those pants. But promise not to judge me because my room is out of control."

They disappear, leaving me surrounded by crowded walls and a giant box of pastries. I take another cannoli and follow them up the wide stairs, heading right at the top toward Tate's room, which is every bit as spartan and immaculate as the rest of this house is cluttered.

Tate was in Allison's year. He hung around one summer due to a short-lived crush on my sister. Our friendship, however, lasted. We never played the same sports, and since we weren't in the same grade, there was zero competition. But we walked to the pool in the summer, held snowball fights in the winter, and both learned to climb after my freshman year.

Well, technically, I learned in Utah, and after Mom found out I was practicing without equipment on the forty-foot outdoor climbing wall downtown, she enrolled me in classes. Tate tagged along. He picked it up even faster than me and was always up for a climbing adventure. Until he headed off to college, met Maggie, and promptly fell ass over elbows for her.

Tate's baseball trophies line the south wall, but I head for the closet, hoping to God he kept Maggie's harness. I never got the impression that she was too serious about climbing. It seemed like she did it to make him smile.

I find her harness next to his, carefully stored with extra rope and carabiners. No women's climbing shoes, but climbing barefoot is fine for your first time.

I follow the sound of Ava's voice to her bedroom. Mallory is perched on the edge of her bed like she's been directed to sit there—and is miserable about it. Ava's oblivious, standing in a heap of clothes by her closet. Four of five pairs of stretchy pants lay over her left arm. A stack of bags from Saks and Nordstrom are crumpled between the door and the dresser.

"Most of these are black or gray, but I've got this pink pair if I can find them."

"It doesn't matter," Mallory says. "Really."

"Oh, wait, I might have a white pair."

"Black is fine," Mallory says. She catches my eye in the doorway. Her expression conveys both terror and amusement.

"Maybe you should try them all," Ava says, frowning as she peers into a Nordstrom bag on the floor.

"No, no, it's fine," Mallory says. "I'll take a black pair. Your least favorite."

Ava scoffs and throws her some pants. "You are terrible at borrowing clothes. And by borrowing, I mean taking, because I clearly have a black pants surplus."

"This is Ava's end of the world plan." I gesture at the stuffed closet. "If she dies in a zombie plague or gets hit by a meteor, she'll be well-dressed doing it."

"And you'll be giving a stand-up routine," Ava says.

I laugh, but Mallory doesn't. She watches me until I feel like a puzzle she's piecing together. More power to her. I have no idea what's up with me, but maybe she can figure it out.

Ava flops onto her mattress with a *whump*, and Mallory bounces at the foot of the bed.

"So, what the hell is up at the library?" Ava asks.

Mallory stands so abruptly I clear my throat and kick at the edge of Ava's door to cover her sudden burst of motion.

"What do you mean?" I ask.

"Mom's on the board," she says with a shrug. "They've had like a thousand meetings since that lady overdosed. So sad."

I nod. "I barely saw her, but she seemed young."

"Shut up." Ava sits up. "You were there when the lady died?"

"I was there when they found her."

"Sorry, Mallory," Ava says. "Do you know about this?"

"A little," she says, voice surprisingly steady. "Just what Spencer's told me. But I thought it was a little while ago."

"Well, the weird keeps coming. Mom told Dad they found all this writing on the walls inside the library."

"*Where are you?*" I say, nodding. "I saw it."

"They tried to run fingerprints, but so far, no matches."

"What do they think it's about?" Mallory asks.

"I mean, Dad was going on and on about how they need to do something about security there. Because you know, the lady was a Jane Doe. They think she was homeless. They think she might have been trying to stay there. In the library."

I scoff because I don't know what else to do, but Mallory is pale. Shaking. I need to get us out of here.

Ava puts up her hands. "Dad's paranoid. He thinks maybe it's some druggie friend of hers, coming back to the library. Like there's a whole colony of squatters."

"Most of the writing was written on the inside of a locked supply room." I pluck a glittery hat off a peg on Ava's wall and prop it on my head. She laughs, and I use a cartoon duck voice. "I don't think squatters are generally experts at picking locks without a trace."

Mallory is pale, her eyes glassy. I stay in duck voice, to cover her sudden change. "What does your mom think?"

Ava bites her lip, and her eyes gleam. "Mom likes the little girl's ghost theory. You know, old building. All that history. And now a dead woman? What if she wasn't ready to leave this world?"

I pull the hat off my head and toss it at her, Frisbee style. "Maybe she should suggest a séance at the next board meeting."

Ava's still laughing about that when we leave. The door closes behind us, and Mallory's hand curls over my arm. Her fingers are cold and damp. Clammy.

I don't chance saying anything until we're back in my yard, almost to the driveway.

"You ready to get out of here?"

She lets out a shaky laugh. "Beyond ready."

MALLORY

Monday, November 20, 9:08 a.m.

I have never seen anything like this room. It didn't look like much from the outside, a boxy gray building nestled in an industrial area on the northwest side of Columbus. I halfway suspected Spencer had taken a wrong turn until he pulled into a parking spot. A small sign on the door read:

Ascension

Bringing You to New Heights

Now I'm standing in a small carpeted waiting room with large picture windows overlooking the climbing area. It's taller than I expected. I was thinking of the climbing walls you see at playgrounds or the sporting goods store, but this is a whole other animal. Blue padded walls run from floor to ceiling, angling this way and that, covered in irregular colorful knobs. A few climbers are in various states of ascent, each latched to a rope, each clinging to the wall in awkward poses, feet arched or flexed, knees bent and arms splayed. They all look up, eyes fixed on the goal.

"Mallory?" Spencer nudges me gently with the clipboard. I spot the form and open my mouth to protest, but he lifts a hand. "Just a signature and a date. I told him we've been climbing before."

"Then what is this?"

"A release form."

I spot the two signature sections, one for an adult, one for parental signature for anyone under eighteen. Alarm plucks at the base of my skull, but the guy behind the counter isn't paying attention. He's on his phone, headphones in, and lost in his own world. I sign my name on the adult line. It doesn't even feel like a lie.

Inside, Spencer explains all the basics while he steps into a strappy contraption and puts on a pair of special shoes. The harness is the main thing, he tells me. It appears to be an ugly belt with miniature belts for each thigh. After his is adjusted, he holds up a slightly smaller version.

"So you might need to adjust it, but it's a woman's harness."

"Okay."

"This one's for you to wear."

"Right. I got that," I say, still not touching anything.

Finally, I take it and try to put it on, following his instructions.

Ridiculous is the only word that fits. It's like putting on a diaper made out of furniture straps. We're both laughing by the time I get the straps adjusted, but then Spencer frowns at me. "Check the waist. It needs to be above your hips. Cinch it in."

"What?"

"The belt part. That's what keeps you from falling to your death if you flip upside down."

"Super comforting." I fiddle with the plastic adjuster, but somehow make it looser. "Which part do I push through?"

"The top one."

The black strap wraps in and out, and it shouldn't be this hard, but I'm lost. "Help?"

Spencer grabs the belt, and I suck in a breath while he loops straps quickly and efficiently. He hooks his thumbs in two loops in front of each of my hip bones, tugging them hard enough to make me stumble.

And of course, I stumble closer.

He pauses. It's not really a *moment,* but he could use it if he wanted. I think he knows it too. Even with his dark complexion I can see the flush in his cheeks. I want to—I don't know. Run. Kick him. Pull him closer. We spring apart awkwardly.

The gym is incredibly quiet. Part of that is the padded floor, but part of it is silent embarrassment that makes me painfully aware of the few sounds surrounding me. Two climbers are softly conversing at the far end of our wall. The auto-belay, I think that's what Spencer said it was, whirs softly as a climber on the opposite wall drops to the ground. But we are quiet. We stand, fidgeting, looking at everything and anything but each other. Finally, he laughs.

"Should we talk about—"

My face turns hot in a rush. "Uh, can we please, *please* not?"

"Of course. Do you want to start?"

The wall stretches above me, a blue behemoth with misshapen knobs. Spencer said forty feet, but there's no way—it's more like a hundred feet. Maybe a thousand.

"You should go first," I say.

First, he starts in about the belay system and ropes and how certain loops and knots work, and I'm lost by the time he's on the second sentence. Thankfully, when he explains the auto-belay system, I nod in enough of the right places for him to move on.

"Okay," he says. "Climbing. The super basics." He dips his hand into a small black pouch at his back. His hand comes out chalky, but he ignores it, staring up at the wall, head tilted and eyes shifting.

He's like a different person. His smile fades, and his shoulders roll back. It's the way I'd imagine a surgeon steps into the operating room. Or a pilot takes off. He stares at the wall, and his hands twitch at his sides, pinching and turning. I think he's rehearsing.

In his mind, he's already climbing.

When he begins, he doesn't say a word. I've never really seen anyone do this, and it's not what I initially believed. It's slow and quiet. When he's not moving, his back isn't to me the whole time like I thought it would be. His body swings to the left or the right, like a door on a hinge.

He isn't all bent knees and elbows either. His arms stay straight, stretched high above him, and his body is low into his knees, one hip always snug against the wall. When he moves, he swings his body to the opposite side, arms flexing and feet and hands repositioning. Sometimes it's wicked fast, like a jump. Other times it's a steady push. The whole thing is an intricate dance, and I'm mesmerized.

When he reaches the top, he taps his forehead once against the wall. Then he pushes out from the wall, his limbs loose as he descends on the auto-belay. He smiles at me on his way down, and it's like no other smile I've ever seen. It hits me square in the chest and leaves me half sick with a feeling I haven't had since sixth grade.

It's a crush. Maybe more than a crush. A feeling so big I can't fit it in my chest, so it spills out everywhere, filling all the spaces in me.

"I guess I didn't teach you much," he says softly.

"It's okay. That was cool."

He shrugs, the familiar Spencer grin returning. “It’s an easy route. I was just showing off my muscles.”

He’s not wrong, but he’s not being honest either. He wasn’t thinking of me when he was climbing that wall. I don’t think he was thinking of anyone at all. I wonder how often he gets to let go like that or if he’s ever realized that’s probably why he likes it so much.

When he approaches the wall again, he dips a hand into his bag and then shows his fingers.

“For better grip,” he explains. “I need it when my hands get sweaty. Now everybody approaches climbing a little differently, so don’t worry about doing things right. Besides, once I clip you in, you’ll probably forget everything I’m going to say.”

“Not reassuring.”

“It won’t matter. I’ll tell you again if it’s important. I forgot everything my first time too.”

“And what happened?”

He laughs. “Uh, I fell.”

“What?”

He tugs the rope at his waist. “That’s what this is for, remember? Do you have any questions about the belay system?”

“God, no.”

He laughs and tells me about holds as he climbs again, slower this time. They have interesting names: jugs and pinches and crimps. He talks about straight arms and the swinging that he does. It's all about center of gravity. I nod like I'm listening, and I am. But my focus drifts. I'm watching his body, the way his feet flex and point, his arms stretched up, nothing but sinew and muscle. He's good at this.

He's only halfway up the wall, then drops down. When he hits the ground, I'm startled.

"Okay, you're up," he says as he hooks my harness to the belay.

I bite my lip. "I really don't know if I can."

"Don't think about it. Find your starting point. Focus on the purples and blues. Those are mostly jugs and mini-jugs. Easy to hold. Take a look and pick your path."

I do as he says, trying to find a plan. Looking for a place to start. I shift closer to the wall, reaching for a bright blue knob. A mini-jug.

I'm painfully aware of my body, of the inescapable fact that it will be *my* arms and legs pushing and flexing when I begin to climb. I wonder if I'll do it wrong. Then I wonder what I'll look like while I'm doing it and immediately hate my brain for going there.

"Hey."

He touches my shoulders from behind with warm light fingers. They leave smears of chalk on the shirt Ava insisted I take along with the pants.

"You're too tense," Spencer says, hands still on me. He pulls back, pointing at the wall. "Get over there and pretend you're eight years old again."

I take a step closer but wince. "I don't know what to do."

"Yes, you do." He laughs. "You, of all people, *always* know what to do."

I force myself to grab the jug and then another with my left hand. I find two good perches, one blue and one red thing I think he called a slope, and my bare feet grip and grip hard. Okay. It's different, but it's okay.

"Let yourself sink into your knees. You're aiming for straight arms," he says.

I nod and look up, a maze of holds spreading to the ceiling. A trail of giant jelly beans, and suddenly that's what does it. I don't think about appearances or whether or not I can do it. I focus on the burn in my legs and learn the reach of my arms. I marvel over the strength in my hands, and how quickly it fades.

Spencer calls out a few encouraging thoughts here and there—*swing your hip to the wall, that's it, there's a crimp to your left if you can use it*—but mostly it's me and the wall. My hands ache, and my feet cramp on the perches, but I make it halfway up before my hand slips, my knee jabbing into a tiny hold I didn't notice. For one second, my breath catches hard in my chest, bracing for the fall.

But I don't fall. The auto-belay kicks in, and I sink back to the soft padded earth, where Spencer is waiting for me, beaming. I feel amazing, like sugar and fire are burning under my skin. I'm breathing hard when he checks the double-eight knot holding me to the auto-belay.

"See? You know what you're doing," he says.

I want to kiss him.

The impulse is so sudden and strong I have to take a step back. Because it isn't like that in here for him. That's not what climbing is about, and I don't want to ruin it. I want to learn.

"Want to go again?" he asks.

I nod and he laughs. His laugh is bigger and brighter in here, like his smile. I'll never get enough of it.

We climb until we're both gross and sweaty. I hurt in places I didn't know existed. My hands are the worst, chafed and throbbing. Spencer buys two bottles of water and we sit side by side, my shoulders on fire and my feet bruised from pushing against countless holds.

When he points out how high I climbed, I'm disappointed. It seemed higher.

He smiles at me, eyes luminous. "I think you did great."

"Not like you. How long have you been climbing?"

"Four years. A little less maybe."

"You seem…different here."

"You mean disgusting and sweat-drenched?"

"No, happier. Like you belong here. Like you were born to do this. Is it this way when you climb outside?"

"It's better."

I grin. "You should teach people how to do this. You love it enough to make everyone love it."

Spencer's smile pinches tighter. "Not much money in professional climbing instruction."

"Maybe not, but is money what you're after?" I grin. "I mean, you've already conquered pillows. Maybe you're not meant for a cushion kingdom."

I intend it as a joke, but his face shutters like a window. It happens so quickly that I follow his gaze, sure he must have seen a disturbing commotion in the waiting room outside. There's nothing out there, though, so it must have been me.

"Spencer?"

The flash of agony in his eyes is so clear it steals my breath. Before either of us can speak, a service door opens nearby and someone emerges.

"Mallory?"

My head turns toward the voice. I can't place it, until I see the man standing at the wall near the back door with a patchy graying beard and a tool belt around his hips. My stomach constricts like I've been zipped into a too-tight dress.

"Mr. Andrews," I say, voice breathy. "What are you doing here?"

"Shoot, I'm only at the high school Wednesday through Friday these days. Budget cuts, you know, and a man's got to make a living. Why are you here? I didn't think Whitestone was out today."

"It's not. I..."

Mr. Andrews looks at Spencer and then me, and my alarm spikes every time his gaze shifts back and forth between us.

"I'm actually in an alternative school now." My voice is chirpy and strange.

Mr. Andrews's brows lift, the creases at the corners of his eyes deepening. "Well, I'll be. *Alternative*. Charlie didn't mention it to me."

"He must not have had a chance to tell you," I say. The world is swaying dangerously, going dark at the edges. I have to get out of here.

"Well, we sure had time for it to come up." His laugh is warm and genuine, but it makes my stomach curdle like milk in the sun. "Friday was a long one. Some kid spilled a mop bucket on the second floor. Soaked right through the tile and dripped through the ceiling! We had to rewire the whole media center, and boy-o, Charlie was in a state by the end of it."

"I bet," I say.

"Didn't you see him?"

"What? Oh, yeah. Of course."

His eyes narrow. "So your new school isn't in today?"

"Holiday. No school all week because of Thanksgiving." My voice catches. Cracks. I can't be here. I can't talk to this man for one more second.

"Uh-huh. And this is one of your new classmates?"

"I'm Spencer Keller," he says, and I shoot to my feet, panic firing through my veins.

"I'm so sorry. We have to go," I say. Before Spencer can push to his feet, I edge away, moving for the door. I flash Mr. Andrews what I hope is an apologetic smile. "Lots to do for the holiday. You know how it is."

"Well, all right then."

"It was great seeing you!"

"I'll tell Charlie we bumped into each other. He'll get a kick out of that, won't he?"

I force myself to utter a cheery response. To fake it. But I can't. The name conjures my stepfather's image outside the bathroom door, his cold, cold eyes promising terrible things.

I don't stop to see if Spencer is following me. I don't stop until I'm outside, under a sky the color of skim milk and a wind so cold it cuts right through my clothes.

I turn around at the car, panting, in time to see Spencer push the door open. The stony expression I saw earlier is replaced with concern. He's carrying both of our harnesses and jackets. I bolted out and didn't even think about grabbing my stuff.

"Did he watch me leave?" I ask.

"Not really. He told me it was nice to meet me and went back to work. Who is he?"

"No one. A guy that works at my old high school."

"I got that. But who is he? Why are you so freaked out?"

"He works at my school. He knows Charlie. We have to go. Please, Spencer."

He hesitates for a second before he nods. We get into the car. I'm shaking so hard my knees knock together. He pulls my coat around me and cranks up the heated seats, a furrow forming between his brows as he watches me.

"Please drive?"

Spencer pulls out of the lot, and I watch the building in the rearview window until it disappears.

SPENCER

Monday, November 20, 12:08 p.m.

Mallory goes silent while I drive. Which is good, because I'm not sure I could hear her over the sudden barrage of chirps from my phone. My phone blows up with seemingly a million messages at once. I finally check it at a red light. A stupid group text about the team we're playing tonight.

Jarvey: They've got that goon Smiths on the roster.

Alex: Number 14?

Shawn: Thought he was disqualified.

Jarvey: No, 24. No, not disqualified.

Isaac: He's probably 24 years old. It's bullshit.

Alex: Truth.

Shawn: Need to rethink the lines?

Jarvey: No. But defense better be ready to put this bitch on his knees. You hear me?

Alex: I'm down.

"Everything all right?" Mallory asks.

"Yeah. Just..." Just what? Am I really going to tell her my hockey problems when she's scared shitless her stepdad is going to come after her. "It's not important."

Jarvey: Spencer? Where the hell are you, man? Don't you dare tell me you're sick and bailing.

Me: I'll be there, and I'll pound him plenty.

"Sorry about that." I shove my phone back into my pocket, and the light turns green.

"He's going to tell him," she says, sounding breathless. "Mr. Andrews will tell Charlie where he saw me, and then he'll snap. What if he hurts my mom? Oh my God, if he remembers your name—"

"He won't remember my name. Breathe, Mallory."

"He might remember. He might. Oh my God, Mom told me they would call the police because I'm a runaway, so they'll never believe anything I say."

"Wait, she hasn't already reported this?"

She shakes her head. "She agreed to let me go for a bit to let things cool off. Charlie thought I'd come back, but I didn't, so now he's changing the rules. He's forcing her hand. And I don't know what to do. If I don't go home, he could take it out on her."

"You said he doesn't get physical."

"He's crazy. I don't know what he might do."

My phone buzzes. Two more times. I pull it out and throw it in the back and then change lanes. "Try to breathe."

"I can't sit here and breathe and pretend this isn't happening."

"Okay, then come up with a plan. You're good at that."

"I don't know." She sniffs, swiping at her cheeks. "What kind of plan can I have for a scenario like this? I have to go home. If he hears this at school, he could go home and blow a fuse." She gasps. "He could hurt the baby. I have to get her."

"No. No chance are you going back there if this guy is dangerous."

"That's not your decision."

"I know that." And I hate it. But I keep my mouth shut.

"I have to get her away from him."

I take the ramp off the freeway and head left, into Fairview.

"You said you couldn't make her leave before," I say, trying to reason with her.

It gets through a little because I see her squeeze her eyes shut. "I know."

"Maybe you need something more serious. Did you find anything on him?"

"I found a name. He was engaged before."

"Okay, that's something. Maybe one of the librarians can

help us. They have access to databases we don't. They know how to search court records."

"Really?"

"Yeah, really."

She nods, and I can see her settle. Her hands go still at the sides of her thighs, and her jaw unclenches. She stares straight ahead, but I'm pretty sure she's focused on the plan she's forming, the steps she'll take to make it all happen. It's fascinating watching her think.

I wish to hell that ability would rub off on me.

Then again, maybe she comes at life like this because she doesn't have a choice. No one's got a safety net under this girl, so she doesn't require one. Mallory's the kind of person who figures everything out.

And what kind of person am I?

My mind reels back to that moment at the gym. Her eyes drinking me in as she asked me if money is what I was after.

What the hell else is there after high school? Am I going to go home and tell Dad I want to be like Connor, my Colorado climbing instructor? Sure, they'll love that plan. The guy keeps everything he owns in three duffel bags, following the climbing season around the world.

If I told my parents that my grand plan for the future was to climb rocks, they'd both stroke out on the floor. Who could blame them? They give me a winning ticket to the adoption lottery, and I chuck it all so I can be a free spirit? I owe them more than that.

Truth is, I want more than that too. I don't crave freedom like Connor or money like my parents. I crave *purpose.*

"Wow, you really are a hundred miles away," she says softly, bringing me back to my senses.

"Sorry. I got lost in my head. I've been—" I cut myself off because I'm not doing this. Mallory is running from a lunatic and currently homeless. I am not going to whine about my non-problems. "Hey, I was thinking. When does this guy work with Charlie again?"

"He said Wednesday through Friday, right?"

"The Wednesday before Thanksgiving? Most schools are closed, right?"

"Oh. Yeah, I didn't think about that."

"So you can let this go until after the holiday."

"I guess so. He might work Friday. Sometimes they do updates and maintenance work on days like that."

"But you have at least until Friday. So a little time for this research."

"You don't want to go to the library now?"

"I just..."

I don't know how to answer, but there's something about my jangling nerves that won't settle in that building. I can feel that much. Looking at the window I broke and the wall I climbed is a pretty pointed reminder that this little life crisis I'm having is going to have to be dealt with soon. And I can't face that right now.

"I think I need a minute," I say. "Maybe we can grab lunch and I can get a shower. Would that be okay?"

"I could use a shower. If you don't mind."

I nod, swallowing hard against the lump in my throat. I'm sitting in a car with a girl who asks permission to take a shower, and *I need a minute?* My stomach squeezes so hard I feel sick.

Back at my house, the quiet isn't comfortable anymore; it's swollen and tense. Mallory is jumpy moving through the kitchen, her eyes darting as we eat turkey sandwiches at the counter.

When we're done, I take the dishes and put them both in the dishwasher. I close it tight and glance at a photo of my family next to the sink. They are a sea of pale skin and blue eyes. And me. I wasn't born to any of this. I'm a motley mix of who-knows-what from who-knows-where. It must be some seriously cosmic shit show that landed me in this house while a girl like Mallory lands in the street outside.

"What's going on, Spencer?" she asks. She's blocking my path, and her expression tells me she's done taking my brush-offs. I can't smile. I feel queasy and shaky.

"What's wrong?" she asks, still insistent.

"I'm sorry. I hate that all this is happening to you." It's true, but not the truth of the moment. And she knows it.

She frowns. "Maybe I should go. I didn't want to drag you into any of this."

"It's not that." I shake my head because it terrifies me, the idea that my badly timed freak-out would send her out into the cold. "You're not leaving."

Fire lights her eyes, and her chin comes up. "I already told you that's *not* your decision."

Panic flutters behind my ribs. "I know it's not. I know that. But—"

"But what? I'm not here so you can save me," she says. "This is my life. My problem."

"You're absolutely right. I know it's your choice, but please make a good one here."

"You don't want me to make a good one, you want me to agree with your choice."

"I'm not saying any of this right."

I close my eyes, trying to sort out an explanation. Why *am* I freaked out about her leaving? Because I'm such a good guy? Because I like her so much? Or because I know it could have been me? I could be sitting right where she is. Anybody could. I don't know how I'm supposed to walk around and ignore that in another life, this situation could have been me.

And I wouldn't handle it nearly so well.

"I don't want you to go because of this," I say. "It's the last thing I want."

"Okay."

"You'll stay?"

She nods.

I tell her where the towels are in the pool house. Her clothes are still damp in the dryer, so I find her my hockey jersey from freshman year and a pair of my old sweats. Our fingers brush when she takes them, and even that tiny touch tethers me back to the here and now.

After my shower, I walk to the window that frames our pretty, gated lawn. My whole life is the view out this window: comfort, security, and the quiet certainty that I will always have enough. And that it will never *be* enough.

I'm going to have to tell my parents I want something else.

I get dressed and head across to the pool house. Inside, I can still hear the shower running. I sink down onto the couch and drop my head into my hands. I don't open my eyes until I hear the bathroom door crack. The smell of soap and shampoo fills the air, and I turn when she emerges.

She's surprised, shower fresh, and only wearing my hockey jersey, which hangs almost to her knees. The sweatpants must not have fit because she's got them draped over her arm.

A feeling between heat and desperation runs through me at the sight of her. I have no business feeling this way with everything she's going through. But I don't have a clue how to stop myself.

MALLORY

Monday, November 20, 1:41 p.m.

He looks like he's on the verge of flipping a table or breaking down in tears. I can't tell which, but this broken look in his eyes has been growing since the gym. My heart clenches at the red around his pretty eyes.

I move around the couch to stand in front of him. "Something's wrong."

"No. I'm fine. Everything's fine."

"No, it's clearly not."

He laughs. "You're too good at this. But no. There's nothing going on that gives me a valid reason to be upset."

"I'm sure there's a reason."

"Not a good one."

It's like he's cracking apart in front of me, his face crying out all the pain he won't speak. A muscle in his jaw jumps, and my hands lift a little. I want to touch him. But I don't know what he needs yet. I don't understand what has him behaving like this.

"Will you talk to me?" I ask.

"Talk to you?" He shakes his head. "You don't need to hear this. You're dealing with *real* things, Mallory. Things that could hurt you. I'm being a whiny asshole. Please let's drop it."

"But if we talk about you, I can *not* think about my real things for a minute," I reason. "Tell me."

"Tell you what? That you're right about me not being happy here? That I don't want a future that ends with a life like this?"

I shrug. "Then don't take that future."

"You're right. It's the opposite of a problem." He stands, looking embarrassed. "I'm bored with my own voice. Let's talk about something else. Movies. Food. Throw pillows."

He's trying to deflect by being funny. But I don't want him to be funny. I want him to own whatever this is. So I stay quiet and watchful, knowing he'll fill the silence.

"We could talk about the creepiest things in china cabinets over at Ava's house," he says, taking the bait. "There's a human skull. True story."

"Stop it, Spencer."

"I can't!" His eyes are too bright, and his voice is frayed at the edges. "This is who I'm supposed to be, Mallory. I'm supposed to make people laugh and go to a private college and get a cushy job so I can buy a giant shiny house like this one."

"But you know this isn't what you want."

"It doesn't matter! My parents are decent people giving me a good future. How do I tell them that none of it feels right to me? That I feel like I live in a gold cage and all I can think about is getting out?"

I throw up my hands. "Then get out! Go travel or teach climbing."

"That's not what I mean. I don't want to teach climbing, I need to get away from this world." He gestures around vaguely. "I have to get out of here so I can see what else there is."

"If your parents are decent people, they'll hear that and support you."

"Yeah, they'll hear me. And they are good people, so they'll relent because they love me. But it will hurt them. I'll have to live with letting them down every day."

"Wouldn't it hurt them to not give you a shot at a future you really want? Can't they tell this isn't it?"

"No one has ever been able to tell. Hell, I didn't figure it out completely myself," he says. "Not until you."

His words are soft, but they push past this frantic moment, into all my quiet spaces. I don't know what to say, so I press my hand to his chest gently to feel that fast, hard pace of his heart beneath my fingers.

"Maybe they can see more than you think," I say.

"Most people see what they expect."

"Maybe people will surprise you."

"*You* surprised me," he says.

He lifts his hand to cover mine, surrounding my fingers with the heat of his chest and his palm. His gaze drops to my mouth, and my stomach flips. When he traces the side of my thumb to the underside of my wrist, my breath catches.

He laughs softly, his gaze cloudy. "And you thought I wanted to be your hero."

"Don't you?"

"Sometimes. Sometimes I want to rescue you. Sometimes I want to be more like you. Mostly, I just want to be *with* you."

Every part of me is tingling. Expectant. I know what comes next. I know when his thumb feathers a circle over the pulse point on my wrist. I know when he steps closer, trapping both of our hands against his chest.

"What is it about climbing?" I ask because the world is slipping sideways, and I'm desperate for something to tie me to steady ground. He makes it hard to think. Hard to breathe.

"You can't sleepwalk through climbing. You can't deny the power of gravity when you're clinging to the side of a rock eighty feet up. You can't go through the motions when you're on the verge of getting frostbite. You have to be present, you know? Totally one hundred percent aware."

"So when you climb, the future doesn't feel stressful?" I say, guessing.

"When I climb, it doesn't even exist. All that matters is the next hold. The next second. The next breath. Everything else falls away."

My chuckle is a soft rush of fire up my throat, and his answering smile is uncertain.

"What's so funny?"

"The way you describe climbing," I say. "It's how I'd describe being with you."

He makes a sound in the back of his throat, and now I'm sure he'll kiss me. It's inevitable. But he pulls back instead.

"Do you *not* want to kiss me?" I ask him.

"You have no idea how badly I want to kiss you. I just don't want to mess this up."

"Can you get over that already?"

He clears his throat, and I can tell he's going to smirk and say some smart-ass thing. I don't want this to start with the guy who wears his jokes like armor. I want the real Spencer. So I lean in fast, pressing my lips against his neck, beneath his jaw.

His breath catches, and I feel his hands twitch at the sides of my too big shirt, his fingers grazing my hips. I close my eyes before I can chicken out, before I can remember all the reasons I should stay away and focus on what matters. In this moment, I don't want to think at all. So I don't think when I press my lips to his jaw. His cheek. The side of his mouth.

For one frozen moment, he doesn't move. Doesn't even breathe. And I try not to think about that either. The way he hesitates. Did he change his mind?

His kiss answers my unspoken question.

It isn't sweet or tentative; it's hungry like he's been holding himself back for a long time. His mouth opens mine with a sigh, and I don't have the slightest thought of pushing him away. Despite all that's happening in my life, this moment matters to me. *He* matters.

He parts long enough to breathe my name against my mouth, to press his forehead against mine. I feel a rush of something bigger than affection. Something I'm too afraid to name.

We kiss again, this time like we're half starved for it, his hands in my hair and mine tracing the lines of his arms, learning the angles of his neck. Everywhere he touches me ignites, and I crave the burn.

My mind slides into a buzzy web of heat and hunger. There's no past, no future, nothing at all beyond the press of his body against mine. I cross my arms behind his neck and feel his grasp on my hips tighten. He's half lifting me off the ground when the door opens.

The door?

Shocking light and cold pour in, and we spring apart, blinking in the sudden appearance of a woman in the doorway. My lips are swollen and tingling, but a rush of adrenaline chases the fire in my veins with ice. I know this woman. I saw her at the window.

Spencer steps in front of me, but I can see her silhouette. Her carefully upswept hair and crisp collar. Even if I hadn't seen her in Spencer's kitchen yesterday, I would know by her expression who she is.

"Mom," Spencer says, confirming it.

"What the hell is going on here?" Her voice is low, but it isn't calm like Charlie's. It sounds like her temper is about to blow.

"It's a long story," Spencer says, still panting. "And probably very different than the story you're thinking."

"I'm sure it is. Because the story I bought is that you were sick."

"I'm sorry about that. I am."

"Sorry for skipping school? Or for staying home to hook up in the pool house?" Then her gaze and her hand sweep my way. "Who *is* this, Spencer?"

"I'm Mallory, and we weren't hooking up."

I'm surprised that there's more hurt than anger in her eyes when she speaks. "You'll pardon me if I have a hard time believing that."

"Mom!" Spencer steps fully in front of me now. "If you want

to be pissed, be pissed with me. But leave her out of it. I'm telling you this isn't what you think."

"She's standing in my pool house half-dressed with wet hair!"

The dryer buzzes, startling me out of my momentary shock. I jolt back, face so hot I'm sure my hair, wet or not, will catch fire. Tears smear my vision into a watery blur, but I do my best to hold her gaze.

"I'm very sorry," I croak. "I'll leave."

"Mallory, don't!" Then to his mom: "Just stop and listen because this isn't what you think. She's not a stranger. I met her at the library. She's having serious issues at home, and I'm trying to—"

My stomach bottoms out, hands rolling to fists. "Spencer, stop!"

"You met her at the *library*?" His mother's voice is close to a shriek now, her lips gone white. "You've been working at the library for a month! How long have you known this girl? You've said nothing about her."

"Maybe I would have talked to you if I didn't know you'd act like this!"

I take advantage of the fury, turning and collecting my backpack off the ground, then I go to the dryer and drag out my clothes.

"She's doing laundry? How long has this been going on? Do I need to call her parents?"

Out of the corner of my eye, I see Spencer move around the couch. "No! You can't! That's not safe for her."

"I'm fairly sure her parents would want to know what's happening here."

I'm shaking so hard it's a miracle I can get the dryer door open, but I do it. Heat and the scent of fabric softener fill my senses. For one second, I think of my mother with the crossword puzzle, my legs swinging over the side of a Laundromat folding table. Tears sting my eyes, but I blink them back. I inhale sharply until a strange hum of calm settles over me.

It's like being underwater.

Their arguing continues behind me, but I'm floating above it. On autopilot. I pull the clothes into my bag as fast as I can, burning my arm on a zipper, dropping a sock and a pair of undies on the floor. I snag them fast and shove them down, jerking on the zipper until it closes halfway. Good enough.

My toothbrush and comb are in the bathroom so I march in and close the door. Collect my things and rip off Spencer's jersey. I pull on a still-hot wrinkled T-shirt and a pair of jeans as fast as my hands will move. My shoes are on the opposite wall of the sink—thank you, God—so I push my feet into them and catch a glimpse of my reflection.

I'm a horror. Mouth red from kissing and face so pale I look near death. Too late to fix any of that, so I turn and pull open the door.

His mother is waiting on the other side.

"What is your last name, young lady?"

"Leave her alone." Spencer is trying to edge between us, but she stands her ground.

My chest burns, and my stomach rolls. I'm like a cornered dog. They're both there, blocking my way out. It's like a hand gripping my throat. And squeezing.

His mom pales. "This secrecy is scaring me. I'm beginning to wonder if it's the police and not a set of parents I should be calling."

Spencer lurches between us, fists clenched. "Go ahead, Mom. Call the police. But if you do, you'd better tell them to arrest me too. I brought her here! I could say I forced her to come."

"What is this?" she asks him. "I have *never* seen you so angry."

"Because you're not listening to me! Stop blaming her and blame me. I brought her here!" Spencer screams, and I can hear the tears in his voice.

She must too, because her face changes. It's like she catches herself, realizing what she's said and done. Her shoulders drop and her expression softens. She reaches toward him, but he moves closer to me, shaking his head.

"Spencer." I touch his arm, and a strange calm comes over me. His eyes are red again, and he's breathing *so* hard. "Thank you for helping me."

I look past him to his mother. "I'm Mallory Halston. And I'm very sorry for upsetting you and for not asking for your permission to be here, but Spencer is right. He was trying to help. He wanted to do the right thing."

I move past her, bumping Spencer with my hip, so I can avoid touching her. He takes my hand. "Mallory, please don't—"

"It's okay. I should go."

He lets out a sound that breaks me.

"Spencer, please. Tell me what's happening." His mom's voice is gentle, her hands lifting and then dropping slowly. All the rage has burned out and she's simply a worried mom.

He won't answer, so she turns to me, her expression tentative. "Are you in trouble? Do you need help?"

"I am," I admit. "But it's not the kind of trouble you need to worry about, and I promise it has nothing to do with your son."

She takes a step back and smooths her hands down the sides of her skirt. And then she goes to the door, turning to me as she passes.

"I'll give you a moment."

To my surprise, she steps outside, but she leaves the door open. I search the area fast, finding a hair tie on the back of the couch and throwing away a water bottle I left on the table. Spencer grabs me as I pass back from the trash can, pulling me into an embrace so hard I can barely breathe.

"I'm so sorry," he breathes against my neck.

Tears come immediately, coursing swift and hot down my cheeks. I press my face against his neck and tell him it's okay. That I'm okay. We both know I'm lying.

We both know a lot of things we didn't know ten minutes ago. We don't come from different worlds—we come from different galaxies. Nothing is ever going to change that, and maybe we could have been okay with that if we hadn't kissed. But we did.

Spencer shoves a hand in his pocket and fishes around. "I have hockey," he says softly. "A tournament out of town. But I'll be back Wednesday night."

It won't matter, but I don't tell him that. I force a smile through my tears and nod.

He shoves a wad of bills into my hand, and I immediately shake my head, trying to give the money back. He pushes me away.

"Don't," he says, voice breaking. "Don't you dare. I can't do *anything* else."

I check, but his mother isn't watching. She's true to her word, giving us the promised minute. The chance for a goodbye. So I put the money in my pocket and pull him in for a soft kiss, one salty with tears—his or mine, I don't know.

"I hope you find the place that feels right," I whisper.

"I did," he says. And he's looking at me.

Outside, the air is cold and bracing. I square my shoulders, but his mother stops me by clearing her throat.

"Don't worry. I won't go through the house," I tell her.

"I wasn't—" She stops herself. "I'm not a hateful monster. I'm a frightened mother."

"One who's raised a great son."

She hesitates, and Spencer appears in the doorway, more composed, but still clearly upset. Her face is soft and broken like his. She's not good at hiding her emotions either.

"I don't want you to be out there wandering the streets," she says. "Let me call someone for you."

"It's not like that. I'm not in that kind of danger."

"I doubt you can be sure of that, Mallory," she says, my name stilted and clearly unfamiliar on her lips. "If you'd like, I could put you in touch with an agency that might..."

"No. But thank you. I appreciate the offer. I really am sorry for this."

I head for the gate, and I don't dare a single backward glance. I don't think I can bear to see Spencer watching me go.

I cry for the first eight blocks. Then I wander in a daze, too numb to think, and too upset to be still. I'm not sure if Spencer's mom will send someone to the library that night, so I avoid it. Instead, I sit at Starbucks, nursing a cup of tea and a cookie until they close.

I shift to a Steak-n-Shake after that, where I pick at a small order of fries, and then to Walmart, where I wander for almost two hours before buying a pair of gloves and a bottle of water. It's almost one in the morning when I leave.

I'd hoped it was later. There are still way too many hours between now and daylight. Where am I going to spend them?

I'm searching for the least expensive item I can buy in the all-night drugstore when it hits me. Suds and Fluff is open twenty-four hours a day too. I remember the cheery 24/7 sticker on the door. It's not the greatest area of town, but this clerk is already eyeing me and I'm running out of all-night stores to visit.

I arrive after 2:00 a.m. To my surprise, there's a woman in scrubs finishing her folding. Everything I own is freshly laundered, but I dump it all into a dryer and deposit my quarters, setting the timer as long as it will go. This is how I spend my Monday night, dozing in a plastic chair in sixty-minute shifts. The dryer buzzes or the bell over the door jangles, and I jerk myself awake. In comparison, the library is an Embassy Suites.

I give up at 7:30 when a whole family arrives. Four little kids carrying a basket each, followed by bickering parents with trash bags full of clothes. I fold my clothes and wash up in the bathroom. Outside, the sunrise is promising a bright and sunny morning. Any other time, it's the kind of crisp November day that would put me in a good mood.

Today the sun in the sky doesn't do a damn thing to brighten the world I'm living in. I pick up coffee so I can stick to my not-too-early routine at the library. Still, I end up arriving by 11:30, and I'm too tired and crabby to delay going in.

I'm ready to find the skeletons in Charlie's closet. There's something to his story with Billie, and I'm going to find it and cram it down my mother's throat so she will snap out of this delusion and leave him once and for all.

The building is quiet and warm, and Gretchen smiles and waves the moment I'm inside. Good. Hopefully that means Mrs. Keller didn't call the library.

I pad quietly to the browsing room, taking a guest pass I won't use to the computer. All the stuff about Charlie isn't going to find itself. But I sit there for long, long minutes, staring at the compartment in the desk. Wondering if I should have said something else to Spencer. Wondering if I'll ever see him again.

"Hey."

I'm startled by the soft voice, and more startled by the curvy blond standing over me. It's Ava. She's wearing ratty sweats again, this time with a frayed Carnegie Mellon sweatshirt layered on top with a coat.

I swipe my hands over my hair and try to smile.

She waves off the effort. "Spencer texted me. He filled me in."

Dread pools in my chest. "Filled you in?"

"He wouldn't say much but begged me to check here for you. I'm guessing from your puffy eyes and his lack of shitty jokes that you got caught together."

"He told you I'd be here?"

She looks down. "He told me a little."

I feel a strange and unwelcome rush of anger. "I'm not some kind of Fairview group project, so you can go."

She half rolls her eyes. "Calm down, nobody's thinking project here. Why the library, though?" She wrinkles her nose. "It always smells weird in here."

"You mean, like books?"

"Yeah, books. And…I don't know. Library soap?"

I laugh, relaxing marginally.

"So why are you here?" she asks. "I mean, why are you not home?"

Honestly, I can't imagine a good reason to bother lying. "I have a creepy stepfather."

I expect outrage or shock. Maybe revulsion. But Ava doesn't deliver. She sits down with a soft sigh, nothing but quiet acceptance in her expression. It makes it easier to keep talking.

"I'm here because I'm avoiding him. And because I want to find something on him from the past so I can convince my mom to get the hell away from him."

"Like old relationship dirt?"

"I'm hoping for criminal records."

"Well." She perks up, and she yanks out the chair beside mine. "I'm always up for a little independent woman action."

She throws her keys on the desk between us and taps something. I look past the silver Mercedes key chain to the plastic Fairview Library key chain she's touching.

"Put this number in."

"I'm on a guest pass. But thank you."

She laughs. "Put it in. I have a staff card so I have access to the librarian databases and such. The stuff that can get expensive." Off the question in her eyes, she shrugs. "My mom's on the board, remember?"

"They give you a staff pass for that?"

"She donates like five thousand a year. And we both volunteer sometimes. They'd probably give me random paintings off the wall if I asked. Put it in. My password is three-four-three-seven."

I do and navigate to a search engine. "I don't even know where to start, honestly."

Ava shrugs off her coat and pulls the keyboard closer. "Okay, let's start with legal records. Has he always lived in Franklin County? We'll start there either way, but if you have others you know about, you should write them down. The counties have different websites."

"How do you know this? I thought you were an artist."

"My mom is an attorney. I learned this when most kids learned to ride a bike. Well, come on. What's the name?"

I spell out Charlie's name, and Ava's fingers fly over the keys. It's magic watching her work. She opens so many windows I have zero idea how she doesn't get lost. Her phone buzzes constantly, but she ignores it, asking me questions, jotting down notes.

We don't find much, but it's not for lack of trying. Two unpaid parking tickets from the nineties that might or might not be him. Nothing with Billie. No marriage ever took place.

"Spell her name for me again," Ava says.

I pull out the crumpled paper, and she taps in the letters. She searches while I roll my neck and try to ignore my grumbling stomach.

"You could call him, you know," Ava says, without a single pause in her typing.

"Spencer?"

"Obviously. They've got hockey tonight so he's probably on the bus moping. Alex said he's been a mess the whole trip."

Hope flickers in my chest, but I push it down hard. "It's probably better that I don't."

"Stubborn, but okay." She clicks something with a frown and makes a sound.

"What is it?"

"Um…you didn't know this person, right? Billie."

"No, why?"

"Because she died. Four and a half years ago."

Cold runs up the back of my neck. "She got engaged to Charlie *five* years ago. What happened to her?"

She tenses and looks over at me, her face pinched. "Blunt force trauma."

I jerk the monitor toward me and lean in, sure she must be wrong. That it's the wrong girl. Wrong date. But there it is, listed out in black and white. It's Billie Reeves, age thirty-one, died of blunt force trauma, death ruled accidental.

A bitterness surfaces in the back of my throat.

"I should go," I say.

"Sure."

"I'm sorry. This is really helpful. I should call someone, so I can look into it."

"You can call me if you need me, you know," she says. Then she fishes a green Sharpie out of a gorgeous leather messenger bag I hadn't noticed because she slung it down like a sack lunch. She scrawls her number on the inside of my wrist and puts a smiley face next to it.

I stare at her with surprise. "Why are you doing this?"

"Because Spencer never cares about anything," she says, "but he cares about you. I think it probably means something."

Everything I could say in response feels stupid, so I keep quiet. I do take a sheet of notebook paper, borrow her green marker, and write a quick, four-line note.

I reach past Ava to put the note in the compartment, and then I press my finger to my lips when I close it and make a *shh*ing face that makes her chuckle.

“A little library espionage?” she asks.

“A little throwback to how it all started. Don’t tell him I put it there. If he needs it, he’ll check.”

“And if he doesn’t check?”

“Then he doesn’t need it. And that’s probably for the best.”

Ava doesn’t look convinced, but Gretchen comes up and taps her on the shoulder gently.

“Hey, Gretchen,” Ava says.

“Hi, you! I have a weird question for you. Did you get a wild itch and make an elaborate book display in the art cabinet?”

Ava laughs. “Not my idea of wild, and no. I haven’t been in here in months.”

I don’t know Gretchen well, but I can spot a fake smile as well as anyone. Something’s wrong, and I’ll bet a million dollars it’s attached to the footsteps and the crying. To the writing on the wall.

Haven’t the police found this person?

Gretchen makes a few excuses and heads back to circulation, but I see her glance at the back of the browsing room on her way out. Ava notices too.

“Come on,” she says.

She doesn’t have to ask me twice for me to follow her. I know

I should leave. I need to talk to Ruth at the women's shelter to see if she thinks this information about Billie could help me. But I'm curious too. Why would a book display make Gretchen nervous? What would it have to do with all the rest of the stuff going on?

It's in a display case at the back of the browsing room, not directly visible from the service desks, so I could see how they'd miss it. I don't know what I was expecting, but this is over the top.

Towers of books, probably hundreds—some thin and long and some chubby paperbacks—are arranged in the shape of two seated people. Some are splayed open, balanced facedown on the tops of spiraling stacks of closed books. It doesn't look like an advertisement for a reading topic. It looks like art.

"I'm flattered they thought I could do this," Ava says, mirroring my sentiment.

"I've never seen a book display like this."

"I've never seen anything like this." Ava shakes her head. "It's not a display. It's a sculpture. This would have taken hours. There's even a theme."

"What theme?"

"Sisters."

She's right. The two book people could be female—they're huddled side by side. But upon further inspection, the books confirm it. Every title involves sisters.

My Sister and Me

Sisters Like Us

Lost and Found Sisters

The Almost Sisters

The Sisterhood of the Traveling Pants

Bringing Home Sister

My eyes freeze on that title, my stomach shrinking. My mother is having a girl, so technically I'm a sister. Or I will be soon. It feels like an awful coincidence, and then Ava moves right up to the glass, her messy bun flopping behind her.

"What are you doing?"

"There's something on that book," she says. "The one they're holding."

I move up too. The book they are holding is angled, and right across whatever words are written, there is another message. One written in slanting black marker, words that choke the breath out of me.

Sister, Where Are You?

SPENCER

Tuesday, November 21, 2:18 p.m.

Mom insisted on driving me to Michigan because "*we need more time together.*" Even if it's partly true, it's partly not. The main reason she did it is because she's afraid I'd somehow sneak away from the bus to stay home and look for Mallory. She wouldn't have been wrong for thinking it.

Still, I'm not in the mood for together time, so I was an asshole all the way here, refusing to engage in any conversation. After several efforts to talk, Mom listened to talk radio, and I watched the foliage on the side of the road turn from bare brown to snow-dusted brown. We had practice and another game last night and a game in the morning, so giving her the silent treatment has been easy.

Not that it's fair. She had every right to be pissed about Mallory. I know how the situation looked to her, and I can't sit here and pretend my mind was in an entirely innocent place at the point when she caught us. Still. I wonder if it would have been different if she'd caught me with my ex or any other Fairview girl.

Girls from Fairview would fall inside the lines of the future she wants for me. Mallory is a complete unknown. What Mom doesn't realize is that I'm an unknown too. The idea of it hums just under my skin, an ugly energy I can't seem to shake.

It's been a crap tournament so far—one loss, one win—and this game is going to be a grind. Still, I all but leap out of the car to get inside the rink. We've got warm-up time on the ice with another team—typical for the limited rink space—and usually I drag my feet for warm-ups. Today, though, I'm the first one out there. I'm the first of everything, probably because I'm desperate to get the whole thing over with.

My skates hit the ice and I fly, tearing around our half of the rink as fast as possible. Everyone's stretching and shooting, practicing passes. I skate circles until the coaches start bitching for me to grab a stick. Until Shawn checks me lightly.

"Knock it the hell off."

I'm breathing hard and already sweaty inside my gear. And all the adrenaline is still pumping. It's 0 percent better. I line up for a passing drill. A puck bobbles wild, and Jarvey passes the centerline to pick it up.

Twenty-four gives him a little jab on his way out. Not much, but it catches my eye.

"You see that?" I ask Alex.

"Yeah."

"That's not going to go well."

Especially since Jarvey's jawing at him from the centerline. We loop around, rotating back through the drill. Jarvey drifts too high again, and twenty-four throws an elbow. It catches Jarvey in the side of the helmet, and he goes down hard. Twenty-four has his hands up in a second, all total-accident-nothing-to-see-here. But there *was* something to see, and I'm watching.

I feel a delicious thrill of rage blaze through my chest as I charge across the ice full tilt. I'm on him before I can think, before the trainers get to Jarvey to check him out. I'm dropping gloves and throwing a fist into his side. Right in that sweet spot between his shoulder pads and hockey pants, the one there's no pad to protect.

"Get your hands off my center!" I scream.

I can't count the number of obscenities he swears back at me, his hand on my cage, mashing my helmet into my brow and ear so hard I'm sure I'm bleeding. Whistles scream, but I punch him again, and he's throwing it right back. Good. I hope he never stops hitting me. I hope we tear each other apart for the rest of the day, because when my adrenaline roars like this, I can't hear *anything* else. All the voices in my head are blissfully quiet.

We separate before they can really make a thing of it. If you play hockey long enough you'll figure out exactly what you can get away with before the refs and coaches get serious about a punishment. Games are different, but you can pull a lot in a practice. An out and out fight is serious punishment. A little scuffle on the ice? Hell, that's just good hockey.

Twenty-four rips off his helmet, and I skate backward, grinning.

"You want another dance?" I ask.

"Keep your boyfriend on a leash!"

I flip him double birds before scooping up my gloves. Coach Tieger catches me halfway to the bench. The look in his eyes tells me I didn't judge the scuffle-fight line well enough.

"You think you're real cute, don't you?" he asks.

Probably not. I can feel my eyebrow swelling. But I force my smart-ass grin all the same. "You think so? I always feel like these pads make me look fat."

This time Tieger isn't amused. "You'll have plenty of time to feel whatever you want. I'm benching you for the first period."

Six months ago, I might have talked him out of it. I'd come up with something funny enough, some apology that would get him reliving his hockey glory days, and he'd probably cut it to the first half of the period. But now I've got nothing. My hand aches, my head pounds, and there's a hollow in the center of my chest I imagine is shaped like Mallory's face.

I take my helmet and skates off in the locker room, figuring I've got plenty of time. I have a desperate need to move. I need to get out of this rink and out of my damn head. Maybe check in with Ava to see if she found Mallory.

I throw open the locker room door and stop cold.

Mom is waiting for me, face placid, her cell phone in her hand.

"Time to talk, Spencer."

"I already told you. I don't have anything to say."

"You can explain that to your father."

She hands me the phone and walks away, and I know there's no getting out of this. It's not like my dad to get involved. Mom handles our household issues just fine when he's out of town, so when she does call for reinforcements, he's like a dog with a bone.

I cringe as I put the phone to my ear. "Hey."

"I've got a funny story," he says. It won't be funny, and it won't be a story. It'll be a recap of everything that happened in the pool house.

"I can't wait."

"Your mom calls me. Tells me she finds you half-naked in the pool house with a girl." He waits a beat for effect, before continuing. "The real kicker here? Apparently, this girl is in some kind of mysterious, serious trouble, but you won't talk to her about it."

"Because it's not her business."

"Our son half-naked with a girl in the pool house isn't her business?"

"No one was half-naked! I was fully dressed, and Mallory was wearing a hockey jersey that came down to her knees. Whatever you've got in your head is wrong."

"Good, because for a minute I was thinking you were skipping school to make out with a half-dressed girl in the pool house."

His pause is significant because he knows he's got me. And I know it too.

"I don't know what you want me to say."

"Well, you generally start with a joke, but I'm considering grounding you until you're thirty-five right now, so I'd consider going with the truth."

"You really need me to go into all the gory details of getting physical with a girl?"

Dad lets out a sigh, and his tone softens. "No, Spencer. I need you to tell me why you're failing half your classes, and why you're refusing to get serious about college applications, and why you intentionally waited on that library roof, not even making an iota of an effort to run for it when the police came."

He knows. My skin prickles with the shock of it. I always figured he wasn't paying attention, but I should have known better. Dad's like me. A funny guy. It doesn't mean there's nothing else to him.

"Would you have wanted me to run from the police?"

"I think getting in a position where you have to make that choice tells me something is wrong. This isn't you, kid."

I close my eyes. "I don't know what to say, Dad. I have a bad feeling you aren't going to like my answers."

"Spencer, when we picked you up at the hospital, and the nurse handed you over, you wouldn't stop crying. I mean you were two days old, and you were *wailing* like you had the lungs of an opera singer. Did you know that?"

"No. Mom said I was perfect."

"Well, you were a handful. The nurse couldn't settle you. Your mom couldn't settle you. We were all a wreck, me included. You were bound up in one of those blanket bundles. Those baby burritos the nurses create for all newborns."

"Dad—"

"There's a point, so just listen. For one second, I had this terrifying thought. Maybe we didn't deserve you. Maybe you were crying because you knew some other family would love you better or give you a better life."

My throat goes thick with tears. "I've *never*—"

"And then Mom handed you to me, because she was feeling so terrible that she couldn't fix your sadness. She thought she'd lost her mom-touch. So, I reached down and tugged on your blankets. The nurse was hollering, but I wanted to see you, so I ignored her. Everybody was griping at me, but the second I got you unwrapped, you stopped crying. Just like that."

I let out a short laugh. "This somehow leads to me making out with a girl in the pool house?"

"No. But it reminds me that when you looked up at me in that hospital, I knew two things. One: that you'd be better looking than me. You should have seen the nurses fawn over your curls."

I laugh again. "And the other?"

"That you and I would figure it out."

I breathe hard, a lump swelling in my throat. I don't want to do this here. I don't want to feel any of this, and I sure the hell can't talk about it.

"It wasn't a random hookup in the pool house, okay? It wasn't cheap or gross."

"That's not the issue, and you know it. As far as I know, this girl didn't do a single thing anybody has a problem with. Frankly, I'm a little pissed with you for putting her in such a bad position with your mom."

"Mom was pissed with her."

"No. Mom was freaked. And she was mad because you lied to her. She's worried because you're not acting like yourself and you're keeping secrets."

"What if I am acting like myself? What if I'm just changing?"

"Change, we can handle. But you need to help us out. Tanking your grades and getting in trouble with the police isn't how you do this. You talk to us."

I let out a slow breath. "Okay."

"Okay," he repeats. "I'm going to give you a little time. Let you get through the holiday."

"And then what happens?"

"And then you're going to give me some answers."

MALLORY

Tuesday, November 21, 7:19 p.m.

It's colder outside than I expected, and dark enough that it feels like midnight. I pull up my hood, and I'm surrounded by the smell of dryer sheets. It takes me back to Spencer's pool house, and I can't be there. I can't think about him.

I must focus on the things I can control. I have to be grateful that I had one nice day with him. That I'm wearing clean clothes, and I'm on a good night's sleep.

I tell myself this as I leave the library. As I turn around to view my temporary home, a curtain moves in the upstairs window. The same upstairs window where I saw a face before. My mind recalls the writing on the wall. The message on the book inside the display.

Sister where are you?

Is the person in the window behind all this? Is that possible? Is there some way it could be Charlie in there? Messing with me?

"Crazy," I say, because no matter how much it feels directed at me, it can't be.

Unless what happened to Billie Reeves was Charlie's fault. If he's capable of killing a woman he promised to marry and hiding it as an accident, then I'm pretty sure he could manage an elaborate display in a library.

But would he be insane enough to stalk me here? To leave these elaborate clues for me to find? And why would he wait if he did? He had every opportunity to attack me the nights I've stayed here.

It's not him. My every instinct tells me that's not the answer.

So, what if I'm reading this all wrong. Maybe this is someone trying to help me.

Or warn me.

At the window, there's no one by the curtain, no evidence this library is different than any other.

I turn away. I need to talk to Ruth about Billie. She might know how to find more information. And I need to call my mother because if she doesn't know about Billie and he's planning something—no. I can't go there yet. One step at a time.

Main Street is busy, and I don't want to be walking too late, so I move fast. My backpack slams again and again into my shoulders, and the wind is so cold it cuts tracks of tears down my face. Sends icy knives into my lungs.

I turn on Grayson and head north, eyeing the darkening sky with a frown. A car passes me, going slower than the others. I shove my hands into my pockets and put my head down. The wind is painful and relentless. Brake lights flare red in my vision. I walk less quickly as I see the car that passed me has stopped in the middle of the road.

It's idling twenty feet ahead of me. I look left and right, wondering why it would stop, but there aren't any houses. No open businesses or even driveways. There's *nothing* around here.

Nothing but me.

I'm here.

My heart loses a beat, but I take a steadying breath to force down the panic. Is it car trouble? Is it someone I know? *Please let it be someone I know.* But nothing about the sloped bumper or metal grill is familiar. The taillights are red slits—narrowed eyes watching me.

This could be nothing. A stranger checking the address of a party. A friend in a car I don't recognize. A lost pizza guy.

The car makes a soft mechanical clunk. White lights appear between the red. Reverse lights.

It's like a brick dropping through my middle, seeing those lights. The car rolls backward, so slowly I can hear the crisp friction of rubber tires against cold pavement. Random images around me take on new, important meaning.

There is a bridge behind me. There are dark houses across the street. An alley.

Not good. *None* of this is good.

A frantic energy seizes my mind, and I flip through my options. Fight. Hide. Run. The last is the only feasible option. The closest public building is a corner store one block up. But I have to get past the car.

I clench my jaw and set my eyes. Start walking with my eyes straight ahead and my chin up. The bumper comes into view in my peripheral vision, but I don't look. I act like that car rolling backward doesn't exist. The car stops beside me—a motorized whir sends goose bumps up on my skin. They are rolling down the window.

There are rules to this sort of thing. Like hikers encountering a bear in the wild, women have a reliable set of if-this-than-that responses for handling unknown men. And I'm way past the be-aware-but-not-paranoid phase. Now I need to look like more trouble than I'm worth.

"Cold out here, isn't it, girly?"

Cold sweat is trickling down my back, but I snap my head toward the driver, locking eyes with him. "No."

He laughs, breathy and slow, but I'm already facing ahead again, cataloging the quick snapshot of his image.

I walk faster, going over the image forming in my head.

White man, maybe in his thirties. Bad teeth. Sparse beard and red-rimmed eyes that confirm there's probably more than a Camel Light behind the smoky, sweet smell rolling out of the car.

The engine shifts gears, from reverse to drive, I'd bet. The tires crunch-pop on the pavement, rolling forward now. Following me. Keeping pace. My heart is moving as fast as my feet, and my throat feels tight. Swollen.

"Hey, don't worry. I'm a nice guy. I'm not trying to hurt you."

I say nothing.

"I'm a concerned citizen," he says, and I hear a laugh. It isn't the driver.

I gaze back at the car. A figure moves in the interior, the dark vague impression of a person in the passenger seat, at least as large as the driver. There are two men in that car. Two of them and one of me.

My heart is at full gallop now, but I do everything in my power to keep my expression stony. I speed up, moving to the farthest right edge of the sidewalk, away from the road. *Just get to the store. Just—*

"Where you going in such a hurry in this weather?"

"Tell her we'll keep her warm," the other faceless voice adds.

The rasp of his voice sends an electric shock of terror into my limbs. I bolt, hearing their laughter trailing behind me, the slow crunching roll of the tires. My backpack slides off one shoulder, taking my jacket off my shoulder. I think I hear them laughing. One of them comments on my sweet little ass.

A car horn blares, and I turn back—a large white minivan pulls up right behind the car harassing me.

"Hold your damn horses!" the bearded guy screams, and then he punches the gas and blares by me, one hand extended out the window, middle finger raised. He screams at me too, after he's passed me. It's short and obscene. I don't know if it's the encounter or the running or simply everything, but I'm suddenly sure I'll throw up. Right here and now.

The van passes too, but I stop, bracing my hands on my knees, my breath a panicked steam in front of me. In and out. In and out. A month ago, I was a normal girl. I had good grades and people to sit with at lunch and, yes, an asshole stepfather who scared me.

But I had a home. A life.

Now I'm on the side of the road, cold and hungry and terrified.

I glance at the numbers on my arm and tears spring to my eyes. I liked Ava, but how can I go back there? How could I sit in a house next to Spencer's and think about how much I loved being with him and know I'll never have those feelings with him again? It's better this way. He can be the one guy in the world who never hurt me. If I go back, that could change.

Given his mother's reaction, it would definitely change.

I suck in a shuddery breath and remember what I need to do. I try to power on my phone, but the battery's dead. I don't get so much as a flicker. So I head to that corner store, slipping inside the heat and warmth with a sigh of relief. It's claustrophobic inside, with crowded, narrow aisles and weak lights. I hear music, but have a hard time seeing the clerk behind the cigarette racks and displays of lighters and key chains and other hodgepodge by the cash register.

A small girl with dark hair emerges from the clutter. She has a beautiful tattoo of lilies behind her ear. She isn't smiling. "Can I help you?"

Absently, I pick up a candy bar and a black beanie cap and put them on the counter. As she's ringing me up, I decide to ask.

"Is there a pay phone anywhere around?"

She gives me an odd look, glancing at the cheap phone chargers in a plastic tub beside a display of bumper stickers. A charger isn't the problem. Finding a safe place to plug it in...

I sigh. "My phone got stolen."

She gives me the total, and I hand over my cash. "Is there a phone anywhere nearby? I need to make a two-minute call."

She looks reluctant, before pulling an ancient black cordless phone from behind the counter. "It won't call long distance, so don't bother."

"It's local," I say, and then I dial the number to the women's shelter, the one that's easy to memorize, because I guess you want a number that's easy to memorize when battered women are running for their lives when they need to use it.

Ruth answers on the fourth ring. "Hello?"

"Is this Ruth?"

"Yes, who is this?"

"It's Mallory."

She pauses, which tells me she knows I'm not at home. I don't know if she called my mom or if my mom called looking for me. I'm not sure it matters either way.

"Mallory, it's good to hear from you. Where are you?"

"Can you talk to me without having to make a call?" I ask.

She is breathing on the other end of the line. I can almost see the frown on her face. "Your mother is very worried about you. Are you at home with her?"

"Did she call you?"

"She did. Yesterday. She's concerned."

I clench my fists. "If you're going to call her, I need to go. I don't want him to know where I am."

"All right, then talk to me. Where are you?" Ruth asks.

I ignore the question because there's no way that information wouldn't trickle back to my mom. "It's not important. Listen, I looked up some things on Charlie."

"What kind of things?"

"Information on the internet, from his past. He was engaged." My eyes flick to the store clerk, who's definitely close enough to hear me. She's engrossed in her phone, but she could be listening. "The girl he was engaged to died of blunt force trauma."

"I'm…sorry to hear that."

"Uh, yeah, so am I because he's in a house *with my mother*."

"And you feel like this is proof that he might hurt her?" When I'm quiet, she adds, "Was the death ruled a homicide or suspicious in any way?"

"I'm…I'm not sure."

"It would have been on the death certificate," she says.

She's probably right, and I feel like it's not a detail I would have missed. I wince and check the girl at the register again. She looks at me but shrugs one shoulder. A universal I'm-not-judging gesture.

"Do you have reason to believe he did something or is it wishful thinking?" she asks.

"I'm not wishing for people to be hurt!"

"But you're looking for some kind of proof, aren't you?"

My shoulders slump, but I don't answer. Ruth fills in the blanks.

"I know you want proof for your mother, but often there isn't proof."

"I don't expect to prove anything. I just want her to have a good reason to leave."

"I've been doing this job for thirteen years, and one of the things I've learned is that there is no magic line that makes women leave."

"I remember. You told me before."

"Then listen this time. I've seen women cleaning the stitches in their eyebrow while they tell me he isn't so bad. I've seen women read police reports and swear they had it all wrong."

"Yeah? Well, what about women who find out their husbands have a dead ex-fiancé? What then?"

I hear a soft thump and imagine her putting down a mug of coffee. "Mallory, blunt force trauma is most often the result of a car accident or a fall. If it was suspicious in any way, the death certificate would indicate as much."

I press my forehead to the cold metal shelf nearby. My breath drains out of me because she's right. I know this is a Hail Mary, and I'm about to lose the game.

"Mind you, I'm not saying he's innocent," Ruth says.

"Just that my mom would probably ignore this too." I stand up straight, glancing out the window at the dark street. "So it's not worth going to the police?"

"I think you should talk to the police. You can talk about this and your situation."

"What do you mean?"

"I mean *you*, Mallory. What are *you* going to do? Not your mother or the baby. I'm asking about you. You can't stay on the streets. You're way too smart for that."

"What can I do? I can't abandon her. She's having a baby. Once the baby is here…"

"You're a bright girl," she says, ignoring my talk about the baby. "Good grades and a solid head on your shoulders. Have you thought about emancipation?"

"That's when you separate from your parents, right? You're like an adult, early. I thought there had to be awful abuse to get approved for that?"

"At your age and in your situation, it wouldn't be an unreasonable request. If your mother agrees to the move, it's mostly a matter of paperwork."

"But emancipation only helps me. I'd leave her. And the baby."

She lets the line stay quiet, giving me space to let my words sink in.

I shake my head hard, to push them away. "I can't. She's my mother. I love her."

"I know that. But I hope that there's still room to love yourself too."

"I have to go," I say.

"What if you came here? I'll drive you over to the Mulberry Manor myself."

"I'm not ready."

"It's almost Thanksgiving," she says. There's a softness to her voice now. A warmth I don't remember from before. "I don't like the idea of you out there alone."

I laugh. "That makes two of us."

"Will you at least think about it?"

I promise I will before I hang up, but I'm not sure it's the truth. Before I knew my mother had called there, I thought maybe I could convince her to let me stay at the shelter. Just for the night. I could call my mother and check in. Maybe come up with a plan.

But if Mom called Ruth, then they definitely called the police. I don't even know what that means. Could I get in trouble for leaving home? Am I breaking some kind of law?

I tap the phone against my shoulder while I think. It's been too long since I checked in with my mom. She'll be worried about me, and I don't want that.

"Can I make one more call?"

"You make as many as you need."

In that instant, she is more than a girl with a tattoo behind her ear. She is a girl who heard enough of that conversation to snap her out of her haze. There's a hardness to her face that makes me think she's angry, but not at me. Maybe *for* me.

I dial my mother's number with shaking fingers. Charlie won't like the unknown number, but Charlie can bite me. I have to try to tell her about Billie. I have to try one last time. To keep the baby safe, if nothing else.

Her number rings seven times. I'm sure it's going to voice mail when the line clicks.

"Hello?"

It is not my mother.

Charlie's voice is a cold shock, stiffening my spine. My grip tightens on the phone, the blood draining out of my face. I open my mouth, but nothing comes. My voice is trapped inside of my throat.

I have to hang up. I should have hung up already.

"Hello?" he says again, his voice different. It sounds like he's working on a problem, but I don't want him to solve our problem.

I move my thumb to the button to end the call, the speaker away from my ear. But his voice scrapes through the speaker again, tinny and distant.

"Mallory, is that—"

I end the call before he finishes. I hand the phone back with shaking hands and thank the girl, who barely acknowledges me. Whatever fleeting connection we shared is gone.

The door shuts behind me with a soft whump, and the darkness stretches out. It's 8:17 p.m. so I need to hurry. I already know where I'm going, and I'm not afraid of repeating the walk.

The dark street and the bridge stretch before me, but I don't care. I'm not thinking about strange cars and scary men when I set out. I guess there's not much that scares me more than the man on the other end of that phone call.

It's twenty minutes till closing when I get back to the library. This time, I take every possible precaution to avoid winding up on camera. I walk in right behind a large man and slip behind the front displays so the circulation staff won't see me.

Before, staying in the library didn't feel scary. But now my mother is looking for me. Mrs. Keller knows my name. And there's someone else here—someone the police are looking for. Spencer said they'd bring in dogs after the holiday, but maybe something changed.

This could be a bigger risk than I know.

As risky as turning myself in to Mulberry Manor, where they'll call and try to twist my mom's arm into letting me stay, regardless of what Charlie would do? I don't know anymore. Maybe Ruth is right about thinking about myself.

But if I let go of my mother, does that mean Charlie wins?

Nothing but hard choices are around me, and maybe that's why this one was easy. It's better than the Suds and Fluff. Especially since being here makes me feel close to Spencer.

I use the bathroom trick again, but weirdly, the lights don't go out after the closing announcements. With my phone still dead I don't know the time, but the soft murmur of voices outside goes on and on. God, I wish they would stop talking and go home.

My legs cramp from being folded up so long, my feet going numb on the toilet seat. I crouch as long as I can, finally propping my legs on one of the stall walls. It's an improvement, but it's not a solution. I need to get up and move.

I can't stay in here forever.

What on earth is taking them so long? A meeting before they close for the holiday?

Sweat beads drip down the back of my neck, and my shoulders ache from my backpack straps. I listen with my eyes closed and my senses on high alert. I'm almost certain the voices are coming from the lobby area, and that doesn't make sense. No one would hang out in the lobby this close to a holiday, would they?

Unless it's a radio. Or—*God*—it's the cleaning crew! They might be here early because of the holiday week. I know this pattern because I've listened to it before from the basement, but I'm a long way from the safety of the puppet theater.

Okay, stop. Think it through. What's the pattern? They clean the front, then they'll work their way to the back and lock up when they leave through the loading dock doors.

Which means… They'll be in the bathroom any minute.

My body coils like a spring. If I stay, the crew will come, and I will get caught. If I run? I don't know. My chances aren't good either way. My thoughts are trapped hummingbirds that flutter with my thumping heart. Eventually, the stress pulls me to my feet. Better a small chance than no chance at all.

I slip to the door as quietly as I can, and push it open an inch to listen. Nothing changes. The radio goes on, newscasters are talking about the weather over the Midwest. I hear a slosh in the other room, then a heavy wet slap. A mop.

A chill moves down my body from my cheeks to my toes. The mopping starts at the front and will move right down the center aisle. I need to get to the carpet. The stairs? No, they'll see me. The browsing room? I think it's carpeted everywhere.

I creep out of the door, my stomach clenched and my limbs clumsy as I keep myself close to the wall.

Just go. Move.

I don't think or breathe. I dash into the browsing room, slipping between two tall shelves holding old sheet music. Everything smells of paper and ink, faded by time. I thank God for the ugly carpet that muffles my steps. Then, a vacuum roars to life at the opposite end of the room.

Trembling, I shift my body around the back of the tall shelf and crouch down. How did I not think of this? I've heard the vacuum before. I should have known better.

My breath shakes. I press my hand to my chest, forcing calmness. It doesn't work. Not yet. If I can figure out where the sweeping will end, tracking its path, I might know how to get out of here without getting caught.

And then what? I still have to take the stairs, and whoever is mopping will definitely see me. I try to visualize the stairwell. The steps leading to the second floor are closer. I'll be hidden by the wall after the first three or four and will have a better shot at concealing myself, but what if I can't find a place to hide? I have no idea what's up there.

One problem at a time. The vacuum, first. I can't tell if it's coming from the windows at the north end of the room or by the south entrance, which is my only way out. I peek around the edge of the shelf at the middle aisle, scanning the room.

Nothing.

Nothing.

There.

I whip my head back, swallowing hard. My throat is painfully dry. It hurts to breathe. I only caught a glimpse of the man with the vacuum in the corner, broad-shouldered and stout.

Was he facing away from me?

I check again. He's facing away from me, backing out of one of the aisles along the west half of the room. When he finishes that, he'll cross the middle aisle to my side. Okay, new plan. I'll take the far east wall all the way to the southeast corner of the room, then I'll follow the south wall back to the entrance. It'll take longer, but I want to spend as little time as possible in that wide-open middle aisle. The second I'm out of the browsing room, I'll take the stairs to the second floor.

And hope to God I can find a place to hide.

I walk fast toward the far east wall, where another set of bookshelves, perpendicular to this one, leads south. Okay. I follow this and—

The shelves abruptly stop, opening into a reading area I had forgotten. I drop to all fours and hold my breath, checking the area. It's meant to be a quiet space, but there's a wide rectangular cut-in along the wall. They probably couldn't find standard shelves back here due to wiring. So voilà—a reading nook. Also known as the place where I probably get caught because nothing but armchairs and round tables live in this whole area.

Still. The vacuum is in the other half of the room. I could make it. Maybe. I hope.

I make myself as small as possible. Crawling on public carpet isn't particularly appetizing, and this section has *never* seen the business end of a dust mop or cleaning rag, in my opinion. It's *filthy* back here. Gray-black smears cover the wall and the backs of chairs, and there's a vaguely charred smell to the air. Even the carpet feels gritty.

The next rows of tall shelves are in sight. I push aside my distaste and crawl into their shadows. I've never been so grateful in my life to see old audiobook CDs. I turn right two aisles from the southeast corner to glimpse the entrance before I bolt for the stairs.

The angle is awkward. I can see the entrance, but I have no idea where the mopping situation stands. I lean in, ducking my head between two shelves so I can get a clear view. I just need to—

"Hey, Dillon!"

I leap up and crack my head *hard* on the edge of the shelf above me. White seizes my vision, turning the room smeary and bright. Pain explodes across the back of my skull, and I stumble back on one knee.

A man walks right past me in the middle aisle—not four feet away. I hold my breath, my heart in my throat, because he must have heard me.

But he doesn't glance my way. He heads straight for Dillon and his trusty vacuum. I wobble when I try to stand, catching myself on a shelf. The palms of my hands are black with grime.

What the hell is this?

I can't think about it. I try to run. The world tilts like a boat rolling over a wave. The vacuum switches off, and the sudden quiet reveals the stutter in my breath, amplified by my plodding steps that sound like drumbeats.

The men are muttering across the room. Still on the western half? My vision swims. I'll have to run for it. The stairs are right there. Ten feet from the entrance, maybe.

Just do it.

Pain drives me forward in a hapless stumble. I don't know much about head wounds, but this feels bad. Beats of lightning burst behind my eyes in time with my pulse. Each breath comes harder than the last. I'm sure they'll hear, but I fumble onward. I have to try.

I brace myself, sure they'll spot me and shout out. Somehow, they don't. I stumble out of the room, too bleary and off-balance to care when I fall down on all fours. Something wet slides down my cheek. Drips on my hand.

Blood.

Don't think about it. Keep going.

I drag myself up the steps one after another, my blackened fingers digging at the carpet. At the top, I'm sweating and sick. I heave once without warning, but nothing comes up. I'm still dizzy and spinning. I'm going to be sick again. I reach at the back of my head where my hair is wet and the pain screams. My fingers come away red.

Not good.

I stumble to my feet, hand smearing streaks of black and red along the pale paint. It gets darker as I move down the hall, so I feel my way from one locked door to another. Finally, one door opens into a wide carpeted space with a gleaming table and leather chairs. No—I don't know how often they clean up here, but I've had enough vacuum dodging for one night.

Saliva pools in my mouth, and my stomach clenches. I pause to steady myself. The world feels muddled, full of strange cottony sounds. I keep moving, finding another door at the back of the hall. It pushes easily under my fingers, so I slip inside.

Shelves rise up on either side of me, cardboard boxes and rows of unused binders. A closet, and it will do nicely. I pull the door closed and slide down the wall, my shoulder resting against a tower of heavy boxes. Cases of paper maybe.

I feel awful. Even sitting, I feel wobbly. I might throw up, and I'm sure I'm still bleeding. It occurs to me distantly that if they clean up here, they'll see that mess on the wall. I'll have to clean it up when they leave. I need to check the stairs too. I was dripping. But now I can only wait. The pain blooms brighter, and the topsy-turvy world begins to spin. I open my eyes, but my vision has gone gray. I'm passing out.

Thin, cold fingers touch my arm.

The world goes black.

SPENCER

Wednesday, November 22, 7:18 a.m.

After our final match last night—a nightmare of a game that we lose over some ugly ref calls—we're done with the tourney. It had been a wreck of a performance, but none of the parents cared. They were all smiles, bumping fists with us as we trailed off the ice. I get it. With Thanksgiving this week, there's plenty to do.

Mom wasn't in the line of parents greeting us. She was the one giving the silent treatment.

After a quick practice this morning, I undress quickly in the locker room, ignoring the symphony of resentment and bruised egos. I try to slip out without being spotted, but Alex corners me in the hall outside.

"What's going on with the at-the-elbow escort?" he asks, bumping his chin toward the lobby where my mom is likely waiting to pick me up. She hasn't let me out of her sight, hovering in the background, eyes firmly on her wayward son.

"Mom's pissed."

"Because of the Mallory thing?"

I tense, and he holds up a hand. "Blame Ava."

I nod. I can't be mad at Ava. She was nice enough to check in on Mallory yesterday and to text me with details.

"How much did Ava tell you about all this?"

Alex shakes his head. "Not all that much. Ava gave her cell number to Mallory in case she needed somewhere to crash. Not that anyone would want to crash at the mausoleum."

"It's not that bad," I say.

Alex grimaces. "They probably keep a mummy in the attic." Then he drops his voice. "Spence, is she—is Mallory pregnant?"

I give him a hard stare. "What the hell, man?"

He shrugs. "Hey, I don't know, all right? You've been distant since school started, and there's this girl. I figure maybe there's something to it. Then there's some showdown at your house with your mom, and you show up in Michigan looking like someone shot your dog."

"I don't have a dog."

"You know what I'm getting at. What was I supposed to think?"

He has a point. It wouldn't kill me to extend a little trust. "She's not pregnant. That's not even close. Things are bad for her at home. She was staying with me. *Just* staying there."

"Then your mom finds out about it," he says, putting the pieces together.

"Yeah, the timing wasn't great. She didn't catch us knitting scarves for orphans."

Alex laughs. "What are you going to do?"

"What can I do?"

"I don't know. Talk to them." Alex tugs off his jersey, his hair sticking up in a hundred directions. "Maybe when you do, you'll tell them you're freaking out."

"I'm not freaking out."

"Like hell you're not. Dude, Ava had this showdown with her folks years ago, and it was fine. Maybe you need to calm down."

"Ava's already in college! She's not letting anyone down."

"Yeah, she's in art school. In a family of lawyers that goes back five generations. Believe me, no one in that house was praying for Ava to want a bachelor's in fine arts."

"At least she knows what she wants."

"Whatever, just talk to them. Because you're getting to be a worse drag than Jarvey."

We both laugh. Shawn calls for Alex from the locker room, and he shakes his helmet. "I've got to get in there. Let me know how this all shakes out."

"Thanks," I say.

When he leaves, I feel his words pressing on me. I have no idea what to say to my parents about me or about Mallory. But my guess is there are a hell of a lot of ways for me to screw it up. Then again, after the pool house incident, how far do I have to fall?

Not that far, if I'm honest.

The worst is quiet disappointment and a few super tense family dinners. But Mallory? If I don't explain that part right, she might end up in real trouble. Back at home. Or maybe even blamed for all the things going wrong at the library. I'm already worried that a review of the camera footage will be a quick hop, skip, and jump to the one patron who went in, but did not come out.

The locker room door bangs open, and Isaac sticks his head out. "Spencer!"

"Isaac."

"Don't forget old-school game night. We're starting early. Get there at two. Bring extra controllers."

"I'm probably grounded."

"Sneak out."

"I'll do my best," I say, though I probably won't. Annual tradition or not, game night isn't enough to tempt me tonight. I've already got plans for sneaking out.

MALLORY

Wednesday, November 22, 7:31 a.m.

I wake to the taste of vomit in my mouth and the worst headache I can ever remember. I take a deep breath that smells of cardboard and Clorox wipes and maybe blood. It's painfully dark, and I have zero sense of time.

Where am I and how long have I been here?

I blink slowly, trying to put together pieces of my scattered memory. I remember the library. Hiding in the bathroom. Hitting my head. A vacuum cleaner. Vomiting on the floor. I don't know how these things fit together. It's like trying to catch fog in my hands. Everything I try to grab disappears.

Eventually, my head clears, and my vision adjusts. There is a crack of light coming from the door. From that meager light, I see a metal shelf beside me. White linoleum underneath me. The floor and my arms are stained with black smears.

The night before returns in rightful order. I wince, as I

remember slamming my head into the shelf, dripping blood on my way up the stairs. I found this room, and then someone touched my arm.

The last memory jolts me fully awake. I try to sit up. It's too fast, and the world droops like a sagging balloon. I lean heavily against the shelves to wait it out.

I don't know what time it is. Or how bad the gash on the back of my head is. And who the hell was touching my arm. I look for a clock on the storage room walls.

I find a manifesto instead. Line after line of beautiful black writing stretches across the back wall. *Where are you?* Over and over. Spencer told me about this. This is the supply room where they think someone hid.

Panic flutters in my throat, but I swallow it back. I am in no shape to jump up and run. I read word after word, my head throbbing in endless, nauseating waves. How bad *is* my head, anyway?

I reach gingerly for the source of the pain. My hair is stiff and sticky, and that's enough to tell me it's not good.

I search the floor, finding wads of cleaning wipes and paper towels. They're all covered in blood and other things I don't want to think about. The thing is, I didn't know there were cleaning supplies in here last night. I don't remember cleaning up after myself.

Because you didn't do it.

Cold washes over me again, but other than the mess on the floor and the creepy writing, it's a pretty standard supply room. Old book carts and some rolling shelves clutter the back wall. The rest of the room is office stuff. Paper and pens and binders aplenty, but no boogeymen crouching in the shelves.

My gaze lingers on the black finger-shaped smears on my arm. So where is the boogeyman who left these marks?

I stand up slowly, more memories rushing back. I definitely wasn't alone in here. I remember someone who helped me get my backpack off. It's in the corner by the door. That same person touched my forehead. Patted my arm. Did they speak?

No.

So this person cleaned up my vomit and tended to my head wound without ever speaking? Or even turning on the light?

It doesn't make sense, but it's definitely an effort to *help* not harm. I was in a god-awful state last night, and this person came out of hiding for me. I want to know why. And I also want to know how on *earth* the police haven't caught them. They've searched every single inch of this library! People cannot *disappear* to avoid being seen.

A prickle runs up the back of my neck as I remember Spencer's haunted theory. The scratching and tapping in the walls. I don't think I believe in ghosts. But after all this? Maybe I'm not so sure.

I struggle to take a few steps and then pause at the door, my eyes on that black writing again. Those words—*where are you?*—catch me like a lump in the throat.

Does Mom wonder this about me? Does she lie awake pacing her floors asking this same question? Given the wall in front of me, the thought is too creepy to linger on. This room itself is too creepy. I've had enough.

I turn the doorknob slowly and wait a beat, listening. Silence greets my ears, so I crack the door. The upstairs is quiet, the doors all shut tight. Maybe it's too early for the library to be open.

I spot a clock inside the boardroom. It's 7:57 a.m. The library isn't open until 9:00. I'm alone in here. Except I don't think I'm alone at all.

I slip from the room, feeling exposed in the shocking brightness of the hall. My head is still a muddled, pounding mess, but when I see the smears of my fingerprints on the wall, I return to the closet, taking a can of cleaning wipes. I work my way down my night in reverse, wiping blood and black from the walls. Inch by inch, I erase my presence.

When I'm done, I push everything—my soiled wipes and the paper towels and cleaning wipes in the closet—into a plastic bag. There are dozens of them, grocery bag leftovers, so I bag the trash again and again, until the blood doesn't show.

It's 8:15 when I'm finished, and I'm so winded you'd think I ran a mile. Holding my eyes open hurts, and I know I have to rest.

But I can't spend one more minute in that cramped closet, and the thought of being downstairs with loud voices and banging… I can't.

Not yet.

I slip into the conference room instead, checking the schedule on the wall. There are no meetings listed, and the early closing—1:00—gives me a deadline. I can rest and try my mom again. With any luck, the stuff about Billie will freak her out enough to leave. Then she can come get me, and we can go see if I need to get stitches and—

Maybe all of this can be a bad memory.

A small voice in my head tells me this can't be a memory. Whatever is happening here isn't over.

SPENCER

Wednesday, November 22, 11:01 a.m.

We hit traffic in Michigan, so it takes longer to get home. Mom pulls into our driveway, parking behind a Volvo with Minnesota plates. My aunt's here, and Mom's already muttering about how many things they need to do.

"So what are your plans?"

"I figured you'd ground me until the end of time."

She turns to me then, looking more tired and less angry. "No, I don't think we're going to ground you. But when this holiday is over, we're going to talk. Sound fair?"

"More than fair."

She touches my forehead, and her brow wrinkles. I think of that story my dad told me and try to remember this cool, collected woman panicking over a crying baby. It's hard to imagine.

"I would like to know your plans tonight," she says.

I'm not the kind of guy that lies to his parents often, and

doing it now feels especially low. But she won't like it if I admit I'm going to look for Mallory, and I won't be able to breathe if I don't find her. I don't know what's the greater wrong, lying to my mother or ignoring a girl who might have no other place to turn.

"Isaac has that old-school game thing," I blurt. "Tradition and all."

"You going to stay all night?"

"Probably. They'll twist my arm."

She nods, and I can tell she's holding back what she really wants to ask. Which is just as well, because she won't get a truthful answer.

"Spencer, you'll tell me if your plans change, right?"

"Of course."

Mom's worry caves to the chaos in the kitchen. By the time I've hugged my cousins and said hello to my aunt and uncle, Mom's wrapped up in an intense conversation about where they can get replacement cranberries because these are awful, and oh, let's call Dan since he'll have to drive home from the airport anyway.

I shower in record time, flinging on clothes. When I wrench my bedroom door back open, Allison is waiting for me in the hall.

Neither of us speaks. We stare at each other for a long minute. Laughter rings up from the kitchen. Aunt Jan is in there, working on the pies, and *Oh, would you look at that crust?*

It will be like this until tomorrow, when the talk of food will give way to chatter on stock prices and business opportunities and whatever house project or overseas vacation they're planning next.

Before now, I always played along. But, before now, I could be inside this house and ignore the fact that my future is destined to look like this.

"I'm not going to apply to any private colleges," I say. I let the words hang there for a minute, allowing myself to feel the weight of it lift off my shoulders. "I'm not interested. The clubs and the fraternities and the drive to impress—it's not my thing, Allison. It's pointless to me."

"You think those things are pointless?" she asks. "I'm at Amherst, so I guess the last two years have been pointless for me."

"I'm late. I have to go. I'm going to talk to Mom and Dad about it after the holiday."

"Spencer." Her hand is on my arm, warm and light. And in her eyes, I see that big sister who carried me home when I busted my knees. The same sister who checked my closet for monsters and gave me her balloon when I popped mine at a fair. "Please talk to me. I know you don't want a life like Mom and Dad's, but you refusing to do *anything* is not a solution."

"What are you talking about?"

"It's like you're paralyzed. You don't want what Mom and

Dad want? Fine. But you need to figure out what you *do* want. Maybe you're wrong about school."

"I'm not. I don't want Mom and Dad to spend seventy thousand dollars a year so I can live in an even smaller version of this town for four years. I need to see what the world looks like without the Fairview lens. I need some time to figure it out."

"Okay."

"Okay?"

She nods. "I don't agree, but I get it. I do."

"Yeah, for now you do." I sigh. "When I tell Mom and she starts frothing at the mouth, you'll knuckle under and try to convert me again."

"I'm your sister, Spencer. If you want me to give you time, then do me a favor."

"What's that?"

"Give me some credit."

Ava has no idea where Mallory is, so I check the only place I can think of. It's a short walk to the library, but that's the easy part. Staying after closing and getting back out without getting caught will be trickier.

Even as I pull open the doors, I know this might be a bust.

According to Ava, Mallory left the library, and she hasn't been in touch since. For all I know she is staying with a friend. Or maybe she even went home. Still, I've got to try.

It's mostly part-timers at the desk, staff members I barely know who probably agreed to take the pre-holiday shift. I'm surprised when I see Mr. Brooks at the information desk. Before I can dodge him, he calls out my name and waves me over.

"Hey, Mr. Brooks."

"It's Ben," he says. "Just Ben. Did you not get my message about the shift today? I hate to think you came in for nothing."

"No, I did. I wanted to get away from the house for a bit." I smile, forcing the nerves out of my voice. "You're on desk all day?"

"All day? We close at one. Tell me your holiday plans."

I wonder how he'd respond if I told him the truth. That the entirety of my holiday plan is to find Mallory.

I force a grin instead. "My plans involve elastic pants and four servings of sweet potatoes." Then, choking on my fear, I ask, "Any luck finding our library vandal?"

"We talked to the police again. We're ordering interior cameras. Plus the dogs from Columbus will be in on Friday."

"Dogs?"

"I don't like it, but I suppose we need answers."

I nod, feeling like my head is a pendulum on a string. Then I plaster my smile in place and head to the DVDs with a claim of needing something to watch.

It's all a song and dance, and I'm grateful when a family crowds around his desk, so he doesn't pay attention. While he's distracted, I double back for the lobby and wish everyone a good holiday, like I'm ready to leave. In truth, I'm not leaving this library until I'm 100 percent sure Mallory isn't here. What else can I do?

After the Mr. Brooks run-in, I'm careful to stay in the stacks. I browse poetry and history, checking the study tables now and again. Ava texts me at 12:30.

Ava: Okay, I can't do it. She left you something. In a desk. She didn't want me to tell you.

My head goes fizzy and light with hope as I text her a thank-you. The desk in the browsing room isn't manned—skeleton crew is on duty—so it's easy to slip in and check the compartment. A single folded sheet of paper sits inside the cubby. I don't unfold it until I'm back across the room, tucked into a corner of stacks near the sitting area no one ever uses. Mallory's note isn't long, but it's enough.

Wish One: Two weeks in Prague.

Wish Two: Another slice of that lasagna we had.

Wish Three: I'd spend this one on you. For you to find a future you can love.

I fold the note back in half and close my eyes. The heaviness of my next breath sinks like a weight through my chest. I don't think she's coming back. This letter feels like a goodbye.

There probably isn't much point to staying any longer. I know I'm well past a shot in the dark and into desperate territory here.

I'm going to have to accept that she's gone. Is she? Because she could be hiding out until close. I wasn't watching the bathrooms every second.

If I don't wait—if I'm not *absolutely* sure she's not here—I think I'll wonder for the rest of my life.

I've still got thirty minutes until close, so I slip up the stairs to the break room.

There are four tubs of homemade cookies in the break room. I take a few and move on. I head back to the hallway. Mr. Brooks' door is closed, like most of the other doors, but the conference room is open. No one's having a meeting a half an hour before holiday close, so it's as good a place as any to wait.

I'm biting into my second cookie when I settle into a leather chair at the end of the table in the conference room. Something rustles in the room. The hair on the back of my neck stands up. I freeze, cookie halfway to my lips.

Everything is still and quiet. I can hear the whisper-soft *tick-tick-tick* of the wall clock. The rhythm of my breathing. But I'm not stupid. Noises in this library are rarely nothing, and I definitely heard something.

I stand up and search under the table, beside the large credenza. There's a desk, too, on the other side of the table, but—

I stop midstep. There's something curled up under the desk, in the alcove where the chair rests. I spot a tangle of hair and a single pale arm. A flash of the dead woman comes back, but this time it's real. This is another body.

And then the body moves.

My throat closes around a scream, but then the head turns, and that pale arm extends, pushing the chair until I see frightened eyes.

Mallory.

MALLORY

Wednesday, November 22, 12:45 p.m.

The first closing announcement begins the second Spencer sees me. The intercom is too soft and distant to understand the words up here, but I know these messages by heart. Spencer moves toward me, but I shake my head and hold my finger to my lips.

I'm still rattled by the terror that struck me when I heard footsteps in the hallway, coming fast. There was no time to leave, and I knew the desk was terrible cover. When I heard him rise, I was sure it was over. A part of me was relieved.

But it isn't over. I'm still here—with Spencer. He is an answered prayer, his eyes dark with concern. The second I nod my permission, he hauls the chair out of the way and reaches to help me.

"Mallory—"

I shake my head fiercely. I know no one is close enough to

hear us. Still, using normal voices feels like a dare, and I can't afford it. Everything about my day proves my luck has run out.

His worry seems to grow as he examines me. I can only imagine what he sees. Spencer touches my shoulders, trying to turn me so he can check my head. I avoid that, because I know what he'll think. I'm almost positive I should be in a hospital getting stitches and treatment for a concussion. But someone here helped me last night. I can't leave them.

"What happened to you?" he asks softly.

"I'm okay," I whisper, then I hold my finger to my lips again and point at the clock.

I don't want to talk again until we're alone. Well, mostly alone, anyway. I doubt my secret helper is going anywhere. Spencer watches me, body tense and his hand gripped tightly around mine. But to his credit, he doesn't force the issue.

His patience is definitely tested too. It's 1:30 before distant voices trickle up from the parking lot outside the window. Spencer checks, but he's careful to stay out of sight. Through the window I see thick clouds covering the sky, leaving the room flat and gray. It's going to rain.

"Okay, they're gone. It's just us," he says.

I take a breath. "No…it's definitely not."

I spill the details of the story as quickly as possible, pausing so I can make sure he's listening before I start in about the person who helped me. And the more I think about it, this isn't a person. It's a girl. The fingers on my arm and the person we heard crying—definitely female. Even the two girls in that book sculpture indicate this is not a man.

I tell Spencer about hitting my head and crawling up the stairs. I tell him about the closet, where I was patted and cleaned and helped. Saying it again convinces me that the writing and the crying and the pacing, even the lipstick message I found on the mirror—it's all the same girl.

People have been looking for her all this time. But instead of someone finding her, she found me.

"Spencer, I think she's been in here a long time."

"Why? Why stay hidden even in the middle of the night? You don't."

"That's the thing. I've never been more alone or more scared in my life than I am now, but I'm not totally alone. I have Ruth and my friend Lana and..."

"Me," he says. "You have me."

I nod, feeling the solid heat of his hand in mine again. "Yeah, I do. And she doesn't. I think something terrible happened to this girl. Something that scared her so much she'll do anything to stay hidden. But she is not evil. Evil people do not administer first aid."

"No offense, but that's some of the shoddiest first aid I've ever seen. You need to see a doctor. You said you were dizzy and sick—both signs of a concussion."

"It's not that bad," I say, though I really don't know. The world still feels a little slanted, and my head hurts so much, it's like my skull is trying to come apart. "But I'll make you a deal. I will go to a hospital. I promise. As soon as we help this girl."

"Mallory..."

"Spencer, I can't leave her. I have to try to get her out."

After a beat, he runs a gentle hand down my arm. "I get it. I get wanting to help, but is it really the time for you to be the hero?"

I feel the weight of his question. And the equal weight of the answer.

I press my lips together. "When I left home, I did it because I was afraid Charlie would hurt my mom."

"I know."

"You don't know the rest. I thought that if I left she would follow. She's my mom, you know? I get that she's sick and Charlie is so messed up that he can make you feel crazy." I shake my head. "But she's my *mom*."

Spencer nods. No pushing. Just waiting.

"I figured if she realized how scared I was, how far I'd go to stay away from him..."

"You thought she'd come for you," he says.

I nod, unable to do a thing about the tears coursing down

my cheeks. Spencer steps closer, puts his hands on my face. And I love that he doesn't wipe my tears away or offer me a tissue. He lets me cry.

"She *should* have come for you," he says, and he sounds angry. Not with me, but *for* me.

"Yeah, she should have. And that's why I have to stay. Because someone should help this girl. And that someone is me."

Spencer relents with a sigh. "Okay."

"Okay?"

He nods. "Let's go find out where she's hiding."

SPENCER

Wednesday, November 22, 2:03 p.m.

The supply closet is a dead end. Literally. There are about ten thousand black smears, a ton, strangely, on the carts in front of the back wall, but no helpful notes or maps that explain why the supply closet is the central hub of activity. Or how she gets in and out.

She must have found a master key. We have a few of them, and the building is old. Maybe the library lost track of one years ago and she found it.

It still doesn't explain what the hell is all over her hands.

I glance up at the dark, dropped ceiling tiles. They could maybe hide her prints. Could she be hiding in the ceiling? How would she get up there? Neither of us has a likely answer for that, so we head downstairs.

Mallory wants to start in the lowest level, which feels smart. The clouds outside aren't leaving much light in the lower level. We search every possible nook and cranny using the meager light from the windows and the help of my cell phone flashlight, but we don't find anything. Trained police officers didn't find anything, so this isn't a shock.

We climb back to the first floor and Mallory slumps against the wall at the top of the stairs. "Maybe I should call out. Offer help."

"This girl found you last night. If she is here, it makes sense that she'll find us, right?"

"She never came out until last night though. And I was injured and in her hidey hole. I think she's afraid."

I'm a little afraid too, mostly because Mallory is glassy-eyed and breathing hard. "How's your head?"

"Awful. I want to find this girl and get this checked—" She gasps, cutting herself off. "Spencer, look."

There, in the low emergency light, I see what she's talking about. Four black smears on the wall outside the browsing room, stark against the white paint, like someone did one of those messy charcoal drawings and then dragged their hand down the wall.

"Was that there before?" I ask.

"No."

It's possible we missed it on our way down, but I'm almost sure we would have noticed that print. The cleaning crew *definitely* would have noticed last night, so it hasn't been there long.

A chill rolls up my spine, and I have to remind myself that this person helped Mallory. Or *tried* anyway. Real help would include calling an ambulance.

"My hands," Mallory says softly, peering into the browsing room.

"What?"

She turns to me, face lit with discovery. "I hit my head in the browsing room trying to get out. At one point I had to crawl behind these weird random chairs."

"The reading nook. Yeah, I know it."

"Well, I got filthy. My hands and knees were covered in black from the carpet."

"Are those your prints then?"

"No. I stumbled straight for the stairs. I didn't touch the wall."

I let out a slow breath. "That's the black we've seen around. Footprints and smears on books."

"I saw footprints too, in the cookbook aisle. Honestly, I've seen this black stuff all over, but there's tons of it against that wall." She inhales. "She's got to be hiding in there."

We enter quietly, searching the shelves and desks and study tables. Any dark smudges would be easy to miss in here from the charcoal carpet to the dark wood shelves. It's eerily quiet, and darker than usual. Still, I know this room. There are long rows of shelves, a couple of study areas, and a reading nook.

This is not a place where someone could live without people knowing.

What are we missing?

"Is there any storage beneath this room?" Mallory asks. She steadies herself with a hand on the shelf, and I feel a prickle of worry in my throat. The back of her hair is matted and dark.

"I think we need to get you to a doctor," I say. "I don't think anyone's in here."

"She's in here, Spencer. She's searching for someone, and she's alone. Just...please help me try a little longer."

"I think we have to be missing something. A way in and out. There's nowhere to hide in here, Mallory. You can't just disappear—"

A picture on the back wall catches my eye, and I pause, stepping closer.

Fairview Public Library:

A Center For Higher Knowledge, 1929

The sepia-toned photograph shows the long-ago browsing room. The same windows rise behind a different librarian desk, but most of the shelves are missing. The room is filled with long wooden tables surrounded by high-backed wooden chairs. The bookshelves line the walls of the room, except for on the east side, where a large fireplace crackles.

There was a fireplace in this room.

I turn and look at the strange rectangular jut along the east wall where the reading nook sits. I've always thought it was the weirdest place to cluster a bunch of chairs, smack-dab in the middle of the stacks, with no good light from the windows at the back. But that awkward jut in the wall isn't a design mistake. It covers an old fireplace mantel.

I point at the photograph on the wall. "Mallory, I think I know where she's hiding."

She swears softly. "The backs of the chairs—they were covered in that black stuff. It's soot, isn't it?"

"Only one way to find out."

I head toward the reading area and hear Mallory behind me. I pull two of the heavy chairs out of the way and shine my flashlight along the wall. I press my fingers to the carpet, and they come back black.

Mallory gasps softly. "There."

She's pointing at a seam in the wall. Halfway down, strategically hidden by the chairs, I spot small brass hinges. It's not tall enough to be a door, so I'm guessing an access panel. I train the flashlight beam along the edges of the panel to confirm it. I could walk past this a hundred times a day and not notice.

Mallory points at smudges along the right side of the panel.

They're familiar. Finger shaped. Ice slides up my spine as I imagine real fingers sliding across that panel. Curling in to pull it open.

I crouch, wedging my hand into the seam until I can get a grip.

Mallory grabs my arm. "Be careful."

I don't need to be careful because it isn't difficult. There's a wooden scrape as I pull the door open far enough to reveal the black-stained brick of an old fireplace.

This panel could have been opened without moving the chairs, and there'd be plenty of space for someone small to slip through. The possibility moves through me like a shock wave. The girl could have been in this fireplace, but as I push the door wider, it's clear she's not here now.

"She's gone."

I push the panel far enough open to step inside, crouching so I won't hit my head. I brace my arm to hold it wide, unnerved by the idea of being closed into the darkness.

It's a big fireplace, but I can see every inch. Plastic crinkles under my shoe. I move my cell phone light to my feet, spotting the red-and-white wrapper of a pack of crackers. The brand from the vending area. There's a cap too. A marker? No, a tube of lipstick.

"Do you see anything?" Mallory asks, trying to peer around me.

"Yeah, someone was definitely here," I say. "But she's gone. Maybe the thing with your head scared her off. Maybe she thought she'd get in trouble."

"I don't get why we keep hearing her upstairs, though. If she's hiding down here, wouldn't the crying be from here?"

"No clue," I say.

Mallory sighs outside, and I step closer to the back of the fireplace, feeling a faint draft from the chimney. Which is weird. The flue would've been closed a long time ago. I crane my head and glance up, wondering if that's how someone got in without anyone knowing. Hell, if she could climb this chimney, I'd be impressed.

It's pitch-black so I worm my arm inside and flip my phone so the light shines straight up the wide chimney. Four brick walls form a narrow passage all the way up. I can't tell if there's grating at the top, but it's likely. You'd get bats and other pests without some kind of protection. Of course, a human would be strong enough to move it.

"This chimney is huge," I say, staring up in wonder. "Santa's dream fireplace."

"Do you think she climbed out?"

I check the walls with my light, scanning the black-coated brick. Sure enough, I see smears here and there where the bricks are cleaner. Always on the ridges that stick out. If I squint, I can almost see the path.

I give a little laugh, feeling a bizarre rush of admiration. "Actually, yeah, I think she has." I use my light to follow her path upward. "I think that's why the food is down—"

Something pops into my line of vision. Long hair and the dark impression of a face.

There's a person. A person staring down at me.

I jerk back, swearing. I bump my head and scrape my shoulder on my rush to get out of the chimney.

"What's wrong?" Mallory asks, alarmed. "Spencer?"

"She's still here. She's up on the second floor."

I squirm out of the fireplace, closing the panel tight. Mallory has her hand at her throat. I'm sure it's the shock of what I've told her.

But it isn't. Mallory is staring at the ceiling. Footsteps thunder across the floor above, so fast and loud, I flinch.

Whoever I saw, she's running.

MALLORY

Wednesday, November 22, 2:39 p.m.

"We need to call the police," he says. "Right now."

And he's right. We do. But there are puzzle pieces filtering through the haze of my fear, and I want to put them together. The footsteps thunder left and right. I hear a panicky cry, and my heart squeezes. She doesn't know where to go.

"Was she still climbing?" I ask.

"No, she popped her head out. She must have been in some kind of alcove."

"Another fireplace," I say. "That's common, right? They stack fireplaces in the same spot on different floors so they can use one chimney."

He shakes his head. "There isn't one. There's nothing up there."

"There could have been before. Where are we? What would be above us?"

"I don't know—the hallway?" Then his face goes soft with the realization. "It's the supply room. It has to be."

"They had a fireplace in the supply room?"

"It's been remodeled. The whole building has, but especially the second floor. Closing off the fireplace probably made the space awkward."

"Which could be why they turned it into a closet," I say.

"There were fingerprints all over the carts on the back wall," he says. "There's probably an access panel back there. That's why she was in there."

The footsteps stop and that cry comes again. Fear still picks at the back of my neck, but I am not my mother. This girl is desperate. She scrawled things on walls. Crawled around in the filthy darkness of a fireplace. No one should have to live like that.

It doesn't matter that it scares me. What matters is what I choose to do.

"I'm going up there."

Spencer grabs my arm. His phone screen is lit. He's already calling. "Wait for the police. I'm calling now."

"Tell them no sirens," I say, and he does. He tells them there's a girl in the library, and she's scared and maybe sick. He tells them to send an ambulance for me too, and I don't argue. I head for the stairs, my heart pounding so hard I feel each beat in my ears.

The girl's ragged sobs are easier to hear now. And there's no mistaking this for a ghost or my imagination. I can hear the rasp of her clothing against the wall. Staccato breathing and shaky whimpers. She's up there. Somewhere in that hallway.

"It's me," I say softly. "The girl you helped last night."

"Mallory, don't do this," Spencer whispers, but he's on my heels too.

The cries stop. I don't hear anything, but she's not moving, so I keep climbing. "I won't hurt you."

Another sob and it hits me right in the chest. I don't know how old I expected this girl to be, but I thought my age. I thought wrong. She sounds *young*. A girl younger than me is terrified and crying out in the darkness. As lonely as I've been, I haven't known that kind of isolation.

"Mallory," Spencer whispers when I'm at the top.

I lift my chin to him. "I'm not leaving her up there. I don't want her to be alone when the police come. She's scared enough."

Spencer's expression clears. He laces his fingers through mine, and we finish our climb to the top. The hallway is dark, the only light filtered from the boardroom at the end of the hall.

But I can see her, a shadow in the corner, small and still. She tenses, inching away from the wall. A frisson of panic runs through me. Seeing her in the flesh is different than knowing she was here. It changes everything.

"It's okay," I say softly, but she bolts for the boardroom. She is a wisp of pale hair and thin legs, but she is real. And she is too young to be alone.

Footsteps rush around inside the room. Her cries turn quiet and panicky.

"I saw your message," I try. The footsteps stop, so I keep going. "I saw your message, and I know you're trying to find someone. I want to help."

The hall stays silent for one beat. And another. Spencer squeezes my hand tighter, and I know what I need to do. This time I don't have to wait for her to come to me. I can go to her.

"Okay, I'm coming in. Just me. You remember me from last night."

She whimpers, the fear obvious in her voice as I approach the doorway, holding my hand up to keep Spencer back. I move like I'm underwater, all slow, fluid moments. Nothing jarring. Nothing that might break this spell of calm that's fallen.

I step inside, and for the first time, I see her clearly.

She is huddled at the wall under the windows. She is crying softly, and her bare feet are stained black with soot from the chimney. It's on her clothes, too, long streaks of it up the sides of her pants and shirt. Her clothing looks small, like she's in that awful phase where you grow four inches in two months and your pants never fit right.

When she turns, revealing her profile, I see that's exactly

what it is. She's almost as tall as me, but her face still holds the round cheeks and soft chin of a child. She's thirteen, maybe not even that. She's just a kid, and she's been in here by herself.

But she's not alone anymore.

"My name is Mallory," I say. The girl doesn't respond. Tear tracks streak through the dirt in her cheeks, old and new. There are layers to her tears. A map of her pain.

"This is Spencer," I say, and he steps in, but stays at the back of the room. "He won't come too close. I promise."

She still says nothing, but she drinks me in with large, hungry eyes. I can hear her breathing, shaky and fast. But she is not running. She is coiled like she could sprint in a moment, but she stays still. And quiet.

There's something in her clenched fist. A marker.

I frown, tilting my head, thinking about the messages on the wall. The display in the case. Even the crying we heard. All this time and not once have I heard her speak a word. Maybe she can't.

"Are you able to talk?" I ask.

No response. Wide eyes and more fear. I crouch down, and then half fall to my butt, my head thumping hard in protest. She flinches, and I smile.

"Sorry. I'm still a little wobbly."

She swallows, and I can see her neck is rail thin and milk pale.

"Can you tell me your name?" I ask.

She rocks, fingers tight on her marker. And then she turns to the wall, but she doesn't move.

"Can you tell me who you're looking for?" I try.

She moves her head upright and uncoils one of her arms. She doesn't meet my eyes, but she lifts her hand and I see a marker in her grip. She's only half watching when she presses the tip at the wall. It's like someone else is holding her hand when she writes.

where is she?

It's the same writing we saw on the wall. The same black smears left behind by her fingers. I swallow against my rising tears.

"Where is who?" I ask softly.

She begins to rock slowly, finally lifting her marker to the drywall again.

sister.

I open my mouth to ask questions, but then the pieces fall into place. The woman who died in the library. Was that her sister? How long ago was that? She couldn't have been alone in the dark all this time.

But a sickening knot in my gut whispers that she has. She has been waiting in the dark, staying hidden like she was told.

Night after night, she searched for a sister who would never return. My chest aches.

Why didn't she come out? Or call for help?

Car doors open and close, and she whimpers in a strange rhythm, her hands twisting back and forth. Twitching. She didn't come out or call for help because she can't. She can't speak. The beautiful writing. The book display. That was her only way.

"It's okay," I say softly. "They're loud, but they're here to help. They won't hurt you. You aren't going to be alone anymore."

She slaps her hand at the wall, gray-black smudges left around the word she's emphasizing.

Sister.

She bangs it again and again, and I close my eyes. I want to tell her that's okay, too, but I can't, because her sister is gone. She rocks faster and faster, but I can't think of a single thing to offer her. The truth is terrible, and a lie would be worse, so I stay silent. I pray for help to come faster because I'm powerless against this kind of pain.

SPENCER

Wednesday, November 22, 2:48 p.m.

It feels like the police take forty-five minutes to get here. In reality, it's four and a half minutes. Funny how time works when the world turns inside out. Sometimes it goes so fast, you're afraid to blink. Other times, the seconds tick by like hours.

Mallory stops them at the door, both hands raised. "Please don't scare her. I think she's… I don't think she can talk. She's very upset."

"Do you know this girl?"

Mallory shakes her head, then winces. "I think she's been in here for a while. I think she came here with her sister."

"Cooper," the female officer says. The male officer checks Mallory's head and calls for additional paramedics.

Officers hover outside the door, but only Cooper and his partner go in. They are patient. Gentle. They ask the girl to sit down and other officers lead Mallory and I down the hall. Maybe so we can keep things calm.

"Where is the girl's sister now?"

My chest goes tight. "I think you were here for her almost two weeks ago."

"She's the woman we found in the stacks," Mallory says softly.

Their faces cycle through awful emotions as they piece the story together. Yes, this little girl has been hiding in this library. Yes, her sister died of a heroin overdose, and she's been waiting for her. And yes, there are reasons she didn't come out like most girls would. She needed help desperately, but she's clearly not capable of asking for it. Her messages were all she had.

I follow them to the top of the stairs, where several more officers and paramedics are waiting. In contrast to the quiet in the boardroom, there is a flurry of activity here. Flashlights blare and radios chirp.

The paramedics arrive, surrounding me with supplies and plenty of questions. They take my information and start an IV for Mallory, and I do not float away in a bubble. Here with the chaos and the fear and the smell of blood and ash around me, I feel the edges of something important forming. A purpose.

The world didn't leave me dehydrated and mute in a chimney. And it didn't leave me homeless with a shit stepdad and a mom who chose to let me go. If I walk out of this room, I'll be in my cozy Fairview bed in ten minutes. I could pretend this was nothing more than a bad dream because for me it doesn't have to be anything else.

But it is *everything* else. And it is changing me.

All of the shitty worries I had feel like fog under a hot sun. Just wisps of something that used to slow me down. A hand that doesn't have the power to strangle me anymore.

I look at Mallory, my heart swelling. I slide down the wall next to her while the paramedics ask her to count fingers and tell them dates and times. A paramedic slips into the boardroom. He comes out for more supplies, holding a blue backpack.

"Is this yours?" he asks.

"It's mine," Mallory says.

The paramedics are looking at Mallory's head, using gauze and cleaners to assess the situation. One sits back, shaking her head. "I think we need to get you in for some scans. We'll need to contact a parent or guardian. Who should we call?"

"My mom. I'll call," Mallory says, digging through her bag for her phone. "I charged it. Sorry. It takes a minute to power on."

"We've got time. Kya has to walk all the way down for the stretcher. I'm Gail, by the way. You said your name is Melanie?"

"Mallory," she says, but she looks at her phone and frowns. "I'm having trouble with this. My eyes aren't quite working."

"That's why we need to get you checked out," Gail says. "I can call if you like."

"I don't know why I don't remember her number. Spencer,"

Mallory says, handing me her phone. "Can you read it? It's on speed dial."

I take the phone and cringe at the message on the home screen. That can't be right. She can't have missed that many calls.

I look over at her. "It says you missed thirty-two calls. And you have fourteen text messages."

"What? Who? No one calls me." She tenses visibly.

I open the screen and see the list.

26 missed calls—Mom

5 missed calls—Lana

1 missed call—Charlie Wrightson

"Mostly your mom. A few from Lana." And then I decide to tell her the rest of it because she'll find out anyway. "One from Charlie."

She flinches and asks me to dial her mother's number for her. When it goes straight to voice mail, she presses the button to try again. The second time, worry flits over her features. I read her the text messages, which are nothing but a bunch of variations of "call me" from her mom. Except for one.

I don't want to tell her about that one, but I do. "There's one more message from your friend Lana."

"Tell me."

"It says you have to call her right away. Your mom had the baby."

MALLORY

Wednesday, November 22, 6:02 p.m.

After the scan confirms a concussion, they wheel me to a room to wait for an on-call neurologist and a treatment plan. The swelling is mostly minimal, whatever that means. And they aren't inducing a coma or anything crazy, so it must not be too bad.

I don't know much about my mom or the baby. At first, I knew nothing, but when I started having a full-scale meltdown on the way to the ambulance, Gail took pity on me. Once we were on the road, she called the hospital where Mom had the baby and talked to a nurse she knows.

She told me as she dialed that she absolutely couldn't tell me anything and that doing so would be a violation of some privacy law. But then as the ambulance bumped and jostled through the library's parking lot, she held a loud, slow conversation that filled in the critical pieces.

So she delivered the baby without any incident?

Wonderful! A girl?

Okay, so she's in NICU, but doing all right?

Well, they're sending us to Mercy East with her daughter. They'll need consent of course.

I think Gail threw that last bit in hoping it would get my mom released for a visit. No such luck. She had an emergency cesarean and is still recovering. It was a mess at first, my hospital calling Mom's hospital. They needed consent to treat me. I thought that flurry of calls might result in me talking to her at least, but it didn't. The staff here won't even discuss letting me have a phone until the scans are done, though I have no idea why. I also don't know what happened to my backpack.

The doctors want me to rest. They assure me everything is fine and my mom knows I'm safe. I guess that's all they feel I need to know. So, I'm alone in this hospital room, miles away from my mom and the baby. My sister.

I close my eyes and the threat of tears heats my eyes. I am clean and dry and medicated with all kinds of painkillers. But the terrible screaming pain in my head isn't gone. It's moved, migrated south to the center of my chest.

I am a sister now.

It should feel better than this.

I hear a knock on the door. I'm expecting Ruth because I asked the hospital to call her when I found out Mom couldn't be released. Still, expectation or not, some part of me is hoping that it's Spencer's dark head peeking around my bedside curtain.

It's not Ruth, and it's definitely not Spencer. It's his mother. Her eyes are red-rimmed, and her hair is limp.

"Mrs. Keller?"

"May I come in?"

I nod, completely confused by her presence.

"I admit I had to lie and say we are old family friends," she says softly, approaching my bed. She places my bag gently on the chair and offers my cell phone. "Spencer wanted to come. He's still at the library answering questions."

I didn't even tell him goodbye. Things got hazy after the message from Lana. My blood pressure went up. There was an oxygen mask. An IV. I got dizzy enough that I forgot about my phone. Where I was. Really, everything.

"Is he okay?" I ask.

"He's fine. Concerned about you."

"What about the girl? Did you see her?"

"They got her calmed down and brought her here too, I believe. Her name is Lily," she says softly.

I sit up straighter, surprised. "She spoke?"

"No. I believe she's nonverbal. She wrote her name down, but the police already suspected. There's an endangered missing child report for a girl of her description and age. Lily receives art and music therapy through a government program, but she's missed the last several weeks."

Art therapy. I think of the book display.

"Can't they find her parents?" I ask.

"The parents abandoned the apartment. Drugs were involved, I believe. Her sister took her to her appointments."

Tears burn at my eyes again. I swallow hard. "And no one was looking for her? They were looking for Lily, but her sister *died*. Doesn't anyone care about..."

"Keira. Her name was Keira, and she had just turned twenty," Mrs. Keller says. Her voice catches on the last half of the word, and her eyes mist over. I bet Allison is twenty, so that can't feel good. "She wasn't a minor. She didn't receive services. No one knew to look for her."

Mrs. Keller doesn't say anything more, and I don't ask. The truth in the silence is awful enough. Keira wasn't chased or called or written up on a milk carton. She disappeared, and the world rolled on.

"The chief is a friend, so I know a bit, but all of this is confidential, of course." Mrs. Keller clears her throat before speaking again. "The working theory is that Keira tried to leave with Lily to get her away from their parents and the drugs."

"But Keira died from an overdose."

"Breaking addiction is hard. I think she tried. I think she certainly wanted better for her little sister."

"But she failed," I say, swallowing. "I can't believe he told you all that."

"Oh, officially he was quite discreet," she says, adding in a whisper, "but the police chief lives on our street. Since my son was involved, I was…insistent."

"What do you think will happen to Lily?"

"Foster care. Good services. Probably a real shot at a good life."

"Does anything good happen in that system?" I ask.

"Yes." Her shoulders go back and her face cracks open. There is no more polished smile and studied poise. There is only love. "Spencer happened."

I bite my lip, ashamed I didn't think of it. I suppress the thought that Lily's story might not turn out so well.

Maybe Mrs. Keller believes all surrendered children wind up in a world like Spencer's. And maybe I'm too jaded, believing happily ever after is only for fairy tales. The truth is probably somewhere in the middle.

"I should go and let you rest." Mrs. Keller smiles and shoulders her purse. "If you don't have plans, you're welcome to join us for Thanksgiving dinner tomorrow. We eat at four, but you can come any time."

It's a sweet and surprising offer after our first run-in, and my shock must be written all over my face. She lets out a slow breath at the door and turns back.

"I was harsh the night we met. I didn't know—" She cuts herself off with a sigh. "Well, I suppose I didn't know a lot of things, including how much my son cares about you."

"Is he in a lot of trouble?"

"For doing everything in his power to help a girl he cares about and rescuing a troubled child in a terrible situation along the way?" We share a warm smile before she shakes her head. "No. He's not in trouble."

"Good." She's at the door when I call out to her. "Mrs. Keller? Thanks for the invitation tomorrow, but I don't think I can make it. I'm hoping I'll be meeting my little sister."

Twenty minutes after Mrs. Keller leaves, Ruth arrives. She sits in the plastic chair, and we exchange all the little pleasantries about feeling well and getting rest. And then she takes my hand and just like that, I start to cry.

"I'm glad you called. I admit was surprised," she says.

"I know. I know this isn't your specialty or area or whatever."

"It's all right. Better to reach out to someone than no one at all."

I blow my nose on a scratchy hospital tissue and pull myself together. I don't want to say any of this while I'm blubbering away, so I don't. When I'm calm, I clear my throat.

"I'm afraid of this because I know I might lose my mother and my baby sister forever. I'm afraid of a lot of things, honestly, but I know now I need help."

Ruth nods. "Fear makes sense. Even help itself is scary. It changes things. Forces us to make hard choices. It opens our eyes to the truth."

I roll to face her in my scratchy hospital gown and think on that. After so much wishful thinking, a life with choices and changes terrifies me. But what kind of life could I have without those things?

One where I never move forward.

I close my eyes, thinking of my mother and the baby. *My* little sister. It hurts to think that she might grow up without the mom I knew before. The mom who folded laundry and hummed in the kitchen. The mom who would have chosen me over everything.

Mothers are like the rest of us, I guess. Our choices change us.

"I should tell you that I looked into Billie Reeves," Ruth says. "She died in an automobile accident. She wasn't wearing her seat belt. It was not ruled suspicious. I shouldn't tell you more, but I want you to know there were no reports on file for your stepfather."

So that's that. All that hard work, all that suspicion. It could really turn out to be nothing.

"Did you know that only thirty-four percent of domestic

abuse victims receive medical treatment?" she says. It seems out of the blue until she holds my gaze, willing me to make a connection.

"It isn't always reported," I say softly.

"No," Ruth says. "It'd be more accurate to say it isn't *usually* reported. Calling us was a big step. A sign of strength."

And now it's time for my next step. Time to stop living on blind hope for someone else's epiphany. The only rescue mission I should plan for is the one that sets me free.

"Ruth? Can you still call your friend at Mulberry Manor? You talked about early emancipation and a place to stay where I can be safe. I think I want those things."

"I'll get in touch with them now," she says. "Do you have any questions before I call?"

A million, I'm sure, but they can all wait. I lie back, woozy from the painkillers and exhausted from all that's happened. I don't know where we go from here, but I'm not afraid.

SPENCER

Thursday, November 23, 4:32 p.m.

"Library or social work?" Dad asks, putting down the bowl of stuffing with a thump.

"Public service. I'm pretty sure about that, but I want to leave my options open." I turn to Allison. "Can you please pass the sweet potatoes?"

Allison bites back a smile and hands me the dish. Most of the table is staring like I've announced plans to lop off a couple of my fingers with the turkey knife. Dad stays strangely quiet, and Mom starts in with nervous laughter.

"It's common to change majors," she says. "But this list of schools. Are they really..."

She trails off because they're not bad schools. But they aren't special either. I chose them because they have strong libraries and good services for students struggling with homelessness or financial issues. Oh, and climbing options nearby.

"They have all the amenities that are important to me."

Not that I knew how to find any of that. Mr. Brooks helped me compile the list at the library. He came in after the questioning and sat with me until Mom got back from the hospital. Before landing on librarian, he'd been a coffee shop manager, a vocalist in a jazz band, and a pastry chef. I figure given his path, I should be fine taking some time to figure it out.

"A librarian," Dad repeats with a laugh. "Do you even read?"

"I read plenty. I'm just not interested in financial reports."

"Point taken," Dad says.

"Point taken?" Mom's face tightens. "Don't tell me you're fine with this?"

"What do you want me to do, force him into investment banking?"

"I want you to press for an appropriate college."

Dad points his fork at me. "Are you going to a four-year college?"

Aunt Jan clears her throat. "I hate to add a bee to this bonnet, but I've done quite well on my two-year degree."

I bite back a grin. Jan is an executive chef and *quite well* is an understatement. Dad once said between cookbook sales, restaurant consultations, and celebrity guest judge appearances, Jan could probably rival his take-home pay, and that's before you add in her restaurant salary.

"Jan, you're not helping," Mom says.

Dad reaches for another roll. "She does have a point. Did you see her pies?"

Mom grips her silverware harder, so I reach over Allison to touch her hand. "I'm still planning on college."

Dad claps loudly. "Good enough. We'll figure out the rest after I have pie."

I grin, feeling lighter than I have in months. Conversation and forks pick back up, and the snooze button is officially hit on this subject. I'm half sure I'll float out of my chair, but then Mom quietly excuses herself from the table. The balloons in my chest fill with lead.

I find her in the kitchen, faucet on but ignored as she stares out the window.

"Mom?"

I can only see her profile, and she's not crying, but she's close. When she turns, the faucet is still running, so I turn it off for her.

"Is it a bad life?" she asks.

"What? No."

She sighs. "Your dad says we should have seen the writing on the wall, but I think I missed something."

"You didn't miss anything."

"But I did." Her eyes are thick with tears. "If I did it right, you wouldn't hate it here. Your *home* should feel right."

I put my hand over hers and feel certain for the first time in months about what I'll say next. Because I get it now. Why this town feels strange. Why Mallory got to me in the first place. Why I'm so desperate to do something that matters more than moving stocks around. And maybe I understand why my mom is so desperate to give me everything too.

"I've always felt right with you and Dad," I say. "That's part of it, Mom. Some part of me knows I could have ended up with *any* family. It's a *miracle* I ended up with you."

"You are my son. Mine. I knew it the instant I looked in your eyes, Spencer. I can't imagine any version of my life where you are not with us."

I squeeze her hand, chuckling. "I believe you. But other kids don't get this. I could have landed anywhere, Mom. You gave me an incredible life. I want to live it in a way that matters. But I'm afraid of what you'll think when I pick a life you wouldn't choose."

"If it matters to you, it will matter to me."

"Well, you say that now."

"Try me. I'll argue, because I'm your mom. But I usually come around," she says.

"Usually? You mean after years of begging and convincing. Flowcharts and slideshows."

"Always the joker," she says. "Spencer, you do have one thing dead wrong in all of this."

"What's that?"

"We didn't do anything for you. We aren't heroes." She reaches for me, brushing my hair off my forehead like she did when I was little. "*You* were the miracle."

My phone rings two minutes before halftime on the football game we're watching. I pull it out of my pocket, but don't recognize the number on my screen.

"Hello?"

"Spencer Keller? I'm calling from the National Knitting Association."

I feel my smile bloom from the center of my chest. "I'm sorry, I only accept calls from the Crochet Cadets."

It's been a handful of words, but I already love Mallory's voice on the other end of a phone line. And her voice has nothing on her laugh.

"I'm glad you called," I tell her. "How's the concussion?"

"We're friends. I named him Vincent."

"Ha ha. Are you in the hospital?"

"Released earlier today and…there's a lot that's happened. Things are getting better."

"Good. Tell me everything."

"I can't. Not yet. But…I wanted you to have my new number. For yarn emergencies."

I can't stop smiling. "When can I see you? How about now? Or maybe now? Does now work for you?"

She laughs again and I close my eyes, imagining her pretty green eyes and the mischief in her smile. Then she sighs, and it's like the first time I touched her fingers. Electric.

"Not now, but maybe later? I still don't know how it's all going to work."

"Later is good," I say, and I don't ask for the specifics.

Specifics can come later. Right now, the sound of her voice in my ear is enough.

MALLORY

Thursday, November 23, 6:04 p.m.

Lana holds my hand, but I still feel shaky in the elevator. I watch the numbers on the lighted panel glow floor by floor. One. Two. Three. Four.

Ding!

The doors whoosh open, and my knees turn to water. Lana's grip tightens as I sag, and then another hand—small, rough, and warm—squeezes my free fingers. Lana's mother, Maria.

"I am going to be right here," she says.

"Okay."

"This is hard, and you've done many hard things. But in my family, women stick together, and that's what you are now. You hear me, *mija*?"

"Yes." My voice is shriveled, and my next breath tastes like disinfectant and…baby lotion?

Lana's mom gives my hand another shake. "I am going to

keep calling that worker. We will figure out some visits. Some dinners. You need good food."

I blink back tears and wonder why I didn't tell her the truth sooner, why I couldn't see she was a person I could trust.

"Thank you," I say.

I hear a distant high-pitched cry and take a steadying breath. I approach the nurses' station, where they take my name and call my mother's room. I tense. For all I know, he could be back there. He could come out here.

And you'll deal with it if he does.

"You want to go in alone?" Lana asks. "Or should I come with?"

"They'll only let me in. It's a NICU thing."

Lana's untangles her hand, and we exchange a hug. Maria is in the waiting chair closest to the nurses' station and the door back to the unit. She looks up at me above a *People* magazine, her eyes dark and knowing. "If that man gives you any trouble, I will be *right* here."

"Okay."

Charlie is nowhere in sight; it is my mother who comes to the door. She's in a bathrobe and moving slow. I hug her gently in the hallway, letting my embrace linger. I missed her. Her hair smells like hospital soap, and she's crying into my neck, and in that moment, I feel a million emotions all at once: anger, sadness, relief, even hope. The way I feel about my mother is a tangled, messy knot. Maybe it always will be.

"Your head? Are you okay?" Her fingers feather over my bandage, barely a graze against the gauze, but enough to make me wince.

"I'm okay. It's better. Will they let me see her? The baby?"

"Of course. I just need to go in first."

She links her thin arm with mine, and we start down the hall in the same rhythm. In this moment, it is like before. I remember Sundays at the Suds and Fluff and singing into hairbrushes. Even now, even after everything, there is still good mixed into the bad.

Mom stops at the NICU door, rubbing her hands with the sanitizer outside the door. "They say she's very strong. They might release her to the regular nursery tonight."

"That's great."

"I'll go give them your information and then they'll wave you in. It shouldn't be more than a few minutes."

"Take your time."

She slips inside, and I'm left in the hallway with the soft burble of conversation from the nurses' station and the muted sounds of a television in a patient's room. I relax my shoulders, staring through the sliver of window in the doorway. I can see my mom near a plastic incubator. There are rows of them, but I can only see the tops. The window in the door is too high to reveal the babies inside.

I squeeze my hands together at my fluttering stomach, my nerves giving way to excitement. Something close to giddiness.

All the way here I worried about seeing Charlie. I didn't think she'd convince him to give us time, so I went over it a million times in my head. What I would say, how I would act. I almost forgot about the baby, but now she's all I can think about. I wonder if she has brown hair like me or long fingers like my mom. Maybe she'll—

"Mallory."

I whirl at the sound of his voice, the hair on the back of my neck rising. *Charlie*. I don't say his name. I'm not sure I could get the word out.

"I knew you'd come back." His voice is poisoned candy. The flutter in my stomach tightens into a breath-stealing clench of muscle. "I told you, didn't I?"

"I'm not back." I hate how panicky I sound, how I can feel the sweat prickle at the palms of my hands. The way I shrink under his look.

He steps closer. I back up, my shoulder blades hitting the hospital wall. "Don't think you're going in there until I say so."

There's nothing sugary about his voice anymore. It's a honey-dipped scorpion. And there's something new too. His fists. They're clenched at his sides, his knuckles tight and white.

I think of Billie in the car. Is this how the end started for her? Did his control slip into clenched fists? What comes after that? A car accident for Billie. Was he there? Was he driving?

It doesn't matter because I can't prove it.

And I know it wouldn't matter if I could.

"Who sees her is up to my mom," I say, surrendering to it. It's always her choice. And she might choose to be with this man forever.

"*Nothing* is up to your Mom. This newest stunt of yours. Living in a group home. Emancipation." He says it like it's a filthy word. "You think I'll let that happen?"

"I don't think you get to decide."

"Who do you think decides for this family? Her?" He jerks his head toward the door with a hard laugh. His control is slipping. He's red. Mottled. Stepping too close. "She doesn't have the stomach for it. She leaves me to make the hard choices."

My heart pounds. I look through the glass where Mom still has her back turned. Down the hall, nurses chatter. I could get help if I need it. I could scream and run. Or I could stand here and take it until my mother lets me through that door so I can meet my sister.

What I can't do is argue with him, because he's right. She does leave him to make the decisions, and it will always make this harder.

Charlie leans in until I can smell his aftershave, until I am trapped between his dark threats and the wall against my back. "You remember, I'll always be here. I'll always be watching you."

"Excuse me." The voice that interrupts us is unfamiliar and female. And impatient.

A flash of white sleeve catches my eye, and I step back automatically. Because it's a hospital, and white means doctor. Charlie does not respond so quickly.

"Sir! Excuse me." The doctor is slim and tall and not in the mood to be ignored.

Charlie finally stumbles back, looking uncertain and annoyed in equal parts as she brushes past, marching fast toward a room.

"Miss!" he barks after her. "Hey, miss!"

Neither the doctor or the two nurses trailing her spare him a backward glance. Charlie's jaw twitches in distress, hands clenching and releasing. Clenching and releasing. A strange feeling comes over me, seeing him like this. Helpless and forgotten, just another faceless, annoying jerk standing in their way.

It is the first time he has ever looked small to me.

And once is enough.

Charlie takes a breath, all the distressed pieces of his face returning to his careful mask of control. But it's too late to fool me. The game has changed. It's his turn to catch up.

The door to the NICU swings open before he can speak, and a nurse with dark eyes and a tired smile looks at us.

"Mallory, are you ready to meet your sister?"

"I'll be coming in too," Charlie says.

"Sorry, only two at a time," she says brightly. "You can come in next. Just use some of that antibacterial gel, Mallory. You don't have a cough or a fever?"

"No, ma'am."

"Okay, great."

The nurse holds the door open and I pause, watching the quiet fury roll over Charlie's face.

"Hey Charlie," I say, my voice honey dipped like his. "I'll always be here too. Always."

To anyone standing nearby, this would be endearing. A sweet, loving sister promising devotion to her family. Which is exactly why I lean in a little closer, dropping my voice so no one can hear when I tell him, "And I will always be watching you."

Inside the NICU, I follow the nurse to my mother who tells me to sit, sit, sit. I stare into the plexiglass box, but there's nothing but tubes and monitors and tiny pink feet in the one closest to the rocking chair I'm in.

"They take such good care of her," Mom says. "They tell her she's beautiful all the time."

"Because she is beautiful," one nurse says as she opens the plastic incubator. She swaddles the baby, tucking and wrapping and moving cords like it's muscle memory.

The nurse turns to me, and then I realize she's offering the baby to me. Some part of me freezes, a thousand terrified objections crowding into my mouth. But before I can put voice to them, she puts that bundle of baby into my arms. She weighs next to nothing.

I peer at her, finding a pink face with round cheeks and a button nose, one small tube disappearing into her left nostril. My nervousness vanishes, and a mix of awe and affection takes its place. Beautiful *is* the right word. It might be the only word.

I curl my arms around her and take her in. This is my sister, a brand-new human, warm and breathing in my arms.

"She's perfect," I say.

"She really is." Mom sighs and then bites her lip. "Charlie thinks she looks like you."

I look up, not surprised she would bring him up, but surprised it would not shake me. But it doesn't. The power has been stripped from his name, and I am free.

Mom looks at me, like she knows the spell is broken. "He asked me how long you would be at Mulberry Manor."

"I'm seeking early emancipation," I say, still rocking, my gaze latched onto the baby's perfect skin, the soft rise and fall of her tiny chest. "I think they already talked to you about this. You can sign it or we can go to court and do it all there."

"I'm going to sign it," Mom says. "I already told him."

I stop rocking and look at her.

Mom's fingers graze the baby's cheek, and then they touch

the back of my hand. "I know you wanted me to leave with you. Maybe someday I will, but I'm not ready."

"It's okay." I'm surprised that I actually mean it. Being in a house with a man like Charlie isn't okay for me, but I don't get to decide what's right for her.

Maybe that's best. It's hard enough figuring it out what's right for one person.

"Thank you for agreeing to sign the papers," I say.

"Thank you for coming to meet your sister," she says.

I curl the baby a little closer to my body, a twinge of regret cramping my chest. I wish so many things for this baby. A better father. A better life. Things I can't provide. But I can give her a sister who is strong and independent. I can give her love and the encouragement to find her own way.

I touch the edge of the baby's blanket, trace a small yellow duck, and feel a surge of love that's bigger than all that I've lost.

Love for my mother and my perfect new sister. Love for Ruth who showed me the way, and for Lana and Maria who are pulling me into their family. Love for Spencer who reminded me that risk can be rewarding. And love for Lily, who at this very moment is probably tiptoeing toward her new life too.

"What's her name?" I ask my mother, only now realizing I hadn't asked before.

"Abigail."

"Abigail," I repeat. "You've got a lot of choices ahead." I touch her cheek softly, feel the newness of her skin. "Be brave enough to make them count."

ACKNOWLEDGMENTS

Every book is its own miracle, and each one changes me. I'm grateful for that ever-renewing miracle and for God's grace to allow me to be part of it.

To the teens who are experiencing homelessness or fear at home: You matter. Your life is important and there are people who want to help. You can reach the National Domestic Violence Hotline at thehotline.org or 1-800-799-SAFE (7233).

This book wouldn't be possible without the incredible Sourcebooks Fire team, especially my brilliant editor Annette Pollert-Morgan, who helps me find my way through even through the muddiest manuscripts. And to my wise and supportive agent, Suzie Townsend, who has a knack for knowing when to lend a hand and how to keep me on course. I am a better writer because of both of you.

I'm blessed to work with some of the greatest library folks

I've ever had the pleasure of meeting. To Jen, for understanding my Bowie feels and for always shooting straight; to Heather, for bringing me smiles, hugs, and forty-two million cups of coffee; and of course, to Ben, who deals with an abundance of sass and squawk, and who really is both a treasure and a delight.

The construction of my books is an ugly process that wouldn't be possible without daily phone calls and frantic last-minute edits with Jody Casella, who still tells me to calm down and to go take a walk. And to Romily Bernard, who can reach in to pull me out of even my darkest places. Thank you. There are so many writers that support me in countless ways. Thank you Margaret Peterson Haddix, Linda Gerber, Julia Devilers, Lisa Klein, Erin McCahan, Edith Pattou, and Mindee Arnett.

There are lots of other folks who help along the way too. Thanks to Leigh Anne for always cheering me on and Sharon for being my angel with sage advice and coconut cake. And of course, to my incredible, supportive readers. Thank you for your lovely reviews, your kind emails, and for having a knack for reaching out on days when it's just too hard.

I always thank my family at the end, because none of this begins without love and support at home. Dad, thank you for leaving your voice in my heart and your stubbornness in my soul. I miss you. David, thank you for your endless patience with often ridiculous writing hours. We've certainly been through the trenches, you and me. And to Ian, Adrienne, Lydia: All the books in the world wouldn't hold enough words for how grateful I am for you. I love you.

ABOUT THE AUTHOR

A lifelong Ohioan, Natalie D. Richards works at a small library by day and writes creepy stories by night. A champion of literacy and aspiring authors, Richards is a frequent speaker at schools, libraries, and writing groups. She lives in Ohio with a Yeti and a Wookiee (her dogs) and her wonderful husband and children. *What You Hide* is her sixth novel.

#getbooklit

Your hub for the hottest young adult books!

Visit us online and sign up for our
newsletter at FIREreads.com

 @sourcebooksfire

 sourcebooksfire

 firereads.tumblr.com